Final Truth

Final Truth

A Novel of Suspense

MARIAH STEWART

BALLANTINE BOOKS • NEW YORK

Copyright © 2006 by Marti Robb

All rights reserved.

Published in the United States by Ballantine, an imprint of The Random House Publishing Group, a division of Random House, Inc., New York.

BALLANTINE and colophon are registered trademarks of Random House, Inc.

ISBN: 0-345-48383-9

Printed in the United States of America on acid-free paper

www.ballantinebooks.com

9 8 7 6 5 4 3 2 1

First Edition

Book design by Caron Harris

To Becca, my darling girl,
with endless love and enormous pride.

Your dad and I will be here for you—always.

Acknowledgments

Huge thanks to Mary Kennedy, Psy.D., for her ever-helpful insights into my villians, and her widely entertaining stories;

and

Hon. Christopher R. Mattox, District Justice, for once again providing the legalese to make my judge more . . . judicial—and, as always, for having the right answers—and as often, the right questions.

Final Truth

Prologue

Lester Ray Barnes was a man of many addictions.

Nicotine, alcohol. Sex, drugs, rock and roll. Underage girls. Gambling. There were others, acquired over the years, but right now, it was the last that was sending that old familiar hum of excitement buzzing through his brain to remind him just how good he'd once been at playing the odds.

It had started when he'd overheard Dan, the night shift guard, chatting up Armas, the guy in the cell next to his.

"So, Armas," Lester Ray had heard Dan say, "guess you're gonna be looking to have your DNA retested, huh?"

"Whachu talking about?" Armas had mumbled in his lazy, off-hand way.

"Heard Cappy—the lifer down on D?—had his done over, month or so ago. Tests came back different this time."

Lester Ray could picture the smirk on Dan's face.

"What different?" Armas's voice moved closer to Lester Ray's cell now as he got off his cot to approach the guard. "Whachu mean different? What Cappy done?"

"What Cappy *done* is find himself a get-out-of-jail-free card." Dan paused—for effect, Lester Ray figured—then dropped the bomb. "This new test said it couldn't tell for sure if he did rape that woman."

"How come it couldn't tell?" Armas asked.

"They're saying the guy who owned the lab, he was messing up the samples. Like, maybe he tested the wrong stuff or something, and didn't testify right, I didn't get the whole story. All I know is, he wasn't doing it right and now they're saying there's no way of knowing for sure if it been Cappy or not."

There was silence on the cell block as the news was absorbed and processed.

"How can that happen?" Lester Ray heard himself ask as he, too, gravitated to the end of his cell.

"Beats me. That's just what I heard." Dan stood in the center of the hallway as if at center stage. "And I must have heard right, since Cappy's lawyer filed some kind of appeal with the court and it was heard this morning. Cappy's going home."

"Just like that?" Lester Ray's brows knit together as he tried to comprehend it. "Just like that, they're letting him go?"

"Judge said they couldn't hold him any longer. Gotta let him go since there was no way a' knowing if the test had been right. So, he'll be out of here as soon as he finishes signing them papers upstairs." Dan shuffled on down the hall, eager, no doubt, to spread the word beyond death row. "Don't that just beat all?"

"How'd he get them to do another DNA test?" Lester Ray called after him. "How'd they know to ask?"

"Somebody that worked at the lab ratted him out. And then somebody told a lawyer, Cappy's lawyer, and he went to the judge. Everyone downstairs is talking about it." Dan laughed dryly. "Me, I think Cappy's lawyer just played the odds. I'm thinking he figured, hey, some of the DNA got fucked up, maybe Cappy's was, too."

The guard paused, then half turned in the direction of Lester Ray's cell.

"Hey, you're the gambler, right? The hustler? You feeling lucky, Lester Ray?" Dan laughed again and continued on down the hall, talking all the way to the door. "Maybe talk 'em into giving you another test, maybe beat that date you got with the needle, Lester Ray. Warden's got your name on the calendar with a big red circle around it. Middle of June sometime, right? Be here before you know it."

Ignoring the taunt, Lester Ray called louder. "What lab was this, where this happened? You hear which one?"

"Fremont, I think it was," Dan said as he passed through the doorway. "Pretty sure it was the lab up in Fremont."

Lester Ray sat down on his worn, thin mattress, his forearms resting on his knees, and replayed the entire conversation with Armas and the guard over and over in his head.

Fremont.

Hadn't his own DNA been tested in the Fremont lab?

"Lester Ray?" Armas whispered. "How you figure this? You think this could be true?"

"Dan said it was."

"But Cappy say he done that woman. He *tole* us he done her, remember? Said he messed her up real bad."

"I remember."

"How could a test say he didn't, if he say he did?"

"I don't know." Lester Ray lay back on his mattress, his brows knitting together as he pondered that very thing.

First thing tomorrow, he was going to check into this. Call that lawyer the court appointed to represent him for his appeals. Find out what this lab thing was all about. If it was the same lab . . . if there was a chance, any chance at all . . .

Shit, he thought as he closed his eyes, maybe there was a way to beat his sentence, after all. He contemplated the odds.

The way things stood right now, his odds were a billion to one, definitely not in his favor. But if he could get them to retest him, too, the odds rose to fifty-fifty. Dead even. Didn't take a genius to decide whether or not to toss those dice.

Lester Ray mentally ticked off the number of times he'd bet the house—and won—on worse odds than these. Well, it was time to roll 'em one more time. God knew the stakes had never been higher.

Once a gambler, always a gambler. Lester Ray smiled to himself in the dim cell.

He lay awake long into the night thinking about how he'd spend his time, once he was out.

•   •   •

On Thursday afternoon, three days after hearing about the DNA debacle at the Fremont lab, Lester Ray sat across from Roland Booth, the attorney who'd been appointed by the Florida court system to walk him through his death row appeals.

"So what do you know about this DNA stuff?" Lester Ray folded his arms on the narrow table that stood between him and Booth, and turned his intense stare on the lawyer. "What are you hearing?"

Booth looked at him blankly, his expression a definite *huh?*

"Guy in here got out this week because of something being wrong with his tests." Lester Ray's calm whisper belied the urge to wrap the lawyer's tie around his neck and pull it as tight as he could. What the hell kind of a lawyer hadn't heard about the major fuck-up in the Fremont lab? Every inmate on every block in here knew about it. What kind of clown was Booth that he didn't know?

"The lab in Fremont." Lester Ray was practically growling, wondering, not for the first time, what the state of Florida had been thinking when they gave Booth a license to practice law. "They're saying the guy in the lab got the results all screwed up, then lied on the stand to cover it up, and some guys are getting out because of it. Don't you know what's going on around here?"

"Of course, I'm on top of it."

Lester Ray didn't bother to try to hide the smirk.

"So that means you have a plan?"

Booth nodded, his lips pursed, giving the appearance as always of listening carefully, though Lester Ray often wondered if he was maybe doing something else in his head, like making up a shopping list or thinking about what movie he was going to see that weekend.

The attorney's large, pale hands lay perfectly still atop the file that sat unopened on the table between them. His face was equally pale, with little sign of having been touched by the sun, odd for one who lived in the Sunshine State. He wore thick glasses with round tan frames that looked almost feminine. He always wore the same seersucker suit and dark blue tie.

"You do know that Fremont was the lab that did my DNA testing, right?"

"Of course. I know that."

Right.

"I want my DNA tested again. I want it done now."

"I'll certainly look into this for you, Lester Ray," Roland Booth told him solemnly. "But you understand, of course, that even if it is the same lab that tested your DNA, and even if the lab tech under investigation was the same one who testified at your trial, and even if we can prove there were some irregularities, there have probably been dozens of appeals filed already. This could be backed up for a long time."

"I don't give a shit about them." Lester Ray leaned forward, his dull eyes flat and cold. "And I don't have a long time. I'm on death row here. I have barely two months left and I don't give a crap about anyone but me, you understand? You're my lawyer. You're supposed to be working on my appeals. That means you work for me, right? I'm the client."

He was almost in Booth's face, as close to the lawyer as he'd ever been.

"I want that DNA test done over. ASAP. You find a way to make it happen, and make it happen fast. They're not going to put me down like some sick dog without a fight, you hear?"

"I hear you, Lester Ray." Roland Booth had tried to maintain his cool, but it was clear to Lester Ray that he'd rattled the attorney when he'd gotten too close.

Lester Ray made a mental note of that fact.

"I'll see what the criteria are for retesting, see if there are grounds to have your results reviewed." Booth looked as if he was about to break into a sweat.

"Reviewed, retested, reevaluated—whatever it is they're doing, I want mine done, too."

"I'll see what I can do, but I can't promise anything. Like I said, others have most likely filed already."

"I don't think we're communicating very well here, Booth. As my lawyer, you have a moral obligation to do whatever it takes to protect my best interests. The way I see it, my best interests are in staying alive and getting out of here. Now, you tell me what we have to do to get my name moved to the top of that list."

"I can request that, since the date has been set for your execution, your petition for review be given priority consideration, but there's no guarantee . . ."

"What else?" Lester Ray asked impatiently.

"That's about it. I don't know if the courts . . ."

"Then find out, for Christ's sake. If you don't know, find out. And fast." Lester Ray shook his head in disgust. "Maybe we need to go to the governor. What's the best way to get his attention?"

"I don't know, Lester Ray." Booth looked at him with growing irritation. "Maybe you should look for some celebrity to take up your cause."

"You mean, someone famous?" Lester Ray's eyes narrowed. "You mean, find some famous person and get them to talk me up?"

"Pretty much, but hey, I was only . . ."

"How do I do that?" Lester Ray ignored Booth's attempts to explain. He'd already figured out that Booth's suggestion had been made sarcastically. Lester Ray, however, saw the potential. "How do I get someone to go to bat for me?"

"I don't know. I guess you need publicity about your case. Then you need to convince him or her of your innocence. Then, I suppose, you . . ."

"That's it?" Lester Ray stared at the scratched tabletop as if the answer would be found somewhere in the midst of the random marks.

"Look, Lester Ray, it isn't going to be easy to get—"

"I don't give a shit about *easy*. You think it's *easy*, sitting here, every day and every night, thinking about what's gonna happen to me come the middle of June?" Lester Ray was about to explode. "Way I see it, it's your job to make sure it doesn't happen. So you go on TV, and you talk about how I'm innocent and I only have a couple more months and how the state of Florida has to let me have this chance to prove I'm innocent."

Lester Ray stared directly into Booth's eyes.

"You should be able to do that, piece of cake."

"Well, first I have to petition for the retesting. Then, I guess it would help to get someone to give me some print."

"Print?"

"Get a reporter to write the story, hope it gets picked up by the AP, get public opinion on our side."

Booth's long thin fingers stroked his chin.

"It's not going to be easy. The DA is going to fight this every step of the way. You know he believes you killed not only that Preston woman, but I heard he was looking at you for a couple of others, too. He's not going to stand by and let you walk without raising holy hell."

"Let him." Lester Ray snorted. "Look, all they had was this DNA test, right? The lab guy testified at my trial that the DNA in that girl matched mine. They had no eyewitnesses, no one to put me anywhere near that girl that night. They had no other evidence, Booth."

Roland Booth sat quietly, his face a mask of concentration.

"They had the neighbor who was out walking her dog," Booth reminded him. "She testified that she saw you outside Carolyn Preston's apartment."

"She said she saw a man who looked like me—medium height and build, had brown hair, and was wearing a khaki jacket." Lester Ray's smile was slow and sly. "How many men in central Florida do you suppose match that description?"

Booth nodded almost imperceptibly.

"Maybe. Maybe," he said. "I can try Harvey Crane from the *Journal*. Maybe he'll run with this. Maybe . . . if I can convince him . . ."

"That's your job, Booth." Lester Ray sat back against the chair and studied the younger man's face.

"I'll see what I can do."

"You'll give it your best shot?"

"Of course."

"Cross your heart and hope to die?" Lester Ray unexpectedly leaned across the table again, causing Booth to startle.

"Right." Booth broke eye contact, pushed his chair back from the table, and began to stuff the folder into his black leather briefcase. He stood abruptly and signaled to the guard at the door that he was finished and ready to leave.

"So I'll hear from you when?" Lester Ray stood as well.

"As soon as I know something."

"Next week. I want out of here, Booth."

"Everyone wants out of here, Lester Ray." Booth left the room without a backward glance.

"Yeah, well, for some of us, it's a matter of life and death."

Lester Ray paused, giving thought to what he'd just said.

"Life and death," he repeated softly. "Mine . . ."

One

Regan Landry sat cross-legged on the floor of her father's study and thumbed through the contents of a file, one of several she'd brought up from the basement in an unmarked cardboard box earlier that morning. Her father, Josh Landry, internationally renowned bestselling author of true crime books, had been the world's worst record keeper. Almost two years after his death, Regan was still sorting through the boxes of material he'd left scattered throughout his home outside Princeton, New Jersey. So far this past week, she'd uncovered newspaper articles in a box in the attic that related to cases chronicled in the file cabinets in the basement. Not for the first time, Regan rolled her eyes. The man had been the most unorganized person on the face of the earth.

When her cell phone rang, she had to move several piles of newspapers to find it. A glance at the caller ID screen brought a smile to her face.

"So what are you doing on this fine morning in May?" Mitch Peyton asked.

"What am I always doing when I'm at my dad's?" She laughed good-naturedly. "Sorting through files and trying to organize the mess."

"I'd think you'd be used to it by now."

"You'd think."

"I don't know why you don't just hire someone to do that for you."

"How would someone else know what to do with all this?" She glanced around the room and frowned.

"You'd tell them. You'd show them what you've done, point them in the direction of the materials that still need to be sorted through, and tell them to follow your lead. If a file exists, file the newly found material in it. No existing file, you make a new one."

"I wasn't aware that the FBI taught a class in Filing 101."

"You'd be surprised what they teach us down here."

"I've seen you at work, Mitch, up close and personal. There's little that you do that surprises me."

"I can see I'm going to have to work on my technique. Can't have the woman thinking she knows all my secrets."

Regan could have replied that Mitch had been an open book right from the start, but she let it pass.

As a special agent with the FBI, Mitch was a member of a distinguished team within the Bureau that sought out the best of the best. But when it came to Regan, there'd been no sign of the wily investigator with crack computer skills that had brought him to the attention of the team leader. Mitch was a man who wore his heart on his sleeve, and had since the first time they'd worked a case together.

"Maybe you're right." She sighed. "Maybe I should just have someone come in and make a list of the files we already have, then go through the other boxes, check the list for duplicates . . ."

"There you go." He didn't wait for her to run through the entire process as he knew her mind was already starting to do. "You've spent enough time on cleanup. You have a book due."

"Already turned it in to Nina last week, which is one of the reasons I'm here at Dad's now. I'm trying to decide what I want to do next."

"No ideas?"

"I have plenty of ideas, but none of them have struck my immediate fancy." She stood and went to the desk and flipped through one of the files she'd left out last night, thinking it might be a contender for the topic of her next book. "There are lots of possibilities, but nothing seems to be jumping out at me and demanding my attention."

"I always wondered about the process you writers go through," he said. "How you decide on one idea over another."

"The story that needs to be told decides for me. It's simply a matter of finding it. I'm just lucky that Dad did so much of the groundwork on several potential projects. There's no end to the number of books he'd wanted to write. Which, of course, explains why there's no end to the number of boxes and folders he left everywhere from the attic to the basement to one of the outbuildings."

"But until some idea grabs you by the throat . . ."

". . . I'll be sorting through files, hoping something does, sooner rather than later." She sighed. "I get antsy when I'm not working."

"I've noticed. While you're waiting for lightning to strike, move the search for an assistant to the top of your list of things to do. You know how things go with you: something lands on your radar, and you forget about everything else."

"You know me too well, Agent Peyton. Once I get started, finding an assistant will be the last thing on my mind. I shall put an ad in this week's *Princeton Packet* and one of the Trenton papers—maybe I should try New Brunswick, too—and see what kind of response I get. It would make more sense to have someone else doing this"—she stared around the room at the piles of files and boxes—"so that I can focus on my next project."

"Speaking of projects, anything new on your search for the elusive Eddie Kroll?"

"Not really." Regan sat in her father's oversized leather chair and swiveled around to stare out the window.

"Dolly Brown still not returning your calls?"

"No. She called me back, left me a message saying, effectively, she's told me everything she knows and to stop calling her. I can't for the life of me figure out what she's hiding, but she's lying about something." Regan paused. "I think if I work on her sister-in-law, Stella, I might be able to finally get some answers. But since her husband, Carl, died back in March, I've given Stella a pretty wide berth."

"Carl was Dolly and Eddie Kroll's brother?"

"Right. Stella always seemed to have something she wanted to say, but she was a bit wary of speaking up in front of Dolly, and Dolly was always around." Regan watched several ducks land feet-first in the pond behind the old farmhouse. "Maybe I should make a quick trip to Illinois, stop in and see if Dolly feels like chatting. While I'm there, I can stop at Stella's as well."

"Good idea. But put that ad for an assistant in the paper before you leave. Think you can be back in time for the weekend? I'm planning on a few days off, and I was hoping we could meet up at your place in Maryland. I miss you."

"I miss you, too. I was thinking about going to look at boats on Saturday. You can come with me and put in your two cents."

"I'll brush up on my boat-speak. Fore and aft. Avast and ahoy. Bow and stern."

"You're going to have to do better than that, if you're going to crew for me." She laughed. "I guess I'll see you . . . when?"

"Let's shoot for Friday night. I'm leaving this afternoon for Michigan, but I don't expect this case will go more than a day or so. I'll let you know if there's a change."

"Okay. I love you, Mitch."

"Love you, too, babe."

Regan closed her phone and slipped it into her pocket, hoping that Friday night would find Mitch on his way to her home in Maryland rather than the scene of some other heinous crime. She admired his work, was proud of his reputation as one of the FBI's top agents, understood the urgency of his job. But there were times when she needed him, too. Like now. She wished she could have his company for even an hour, right now.

Unfortunately, wishing alone couldn't make it happen, she reminded herself.

She forced her thoughts back to Sayreville, Illinois, and the mystery she'd found there a year ago, a mystery that remained unsolved.

She turned the chair around to gaze on the boxes she'd brought up from the basement. It had been in a box very much like any one of those that she'd first found report cards, dated from the 1940s, from Saint John the Baptist Elementary School in Sayreville, Illinois, for a child named Edward Kroll. From the comments written in the small, precise hand of Sister Mary Matthew, Regan had learned that Eddie Kroll had been an asset to the class, had shown an aptitude for mathematics, was inquisitive and an excellent reader. But there'd been no explanation of how or why her father had come into possession of these pieces from another boy's childhood, or why he had kept them hidden away. She'd searched through hundreds of files since her father's death, but the name hadn't turned up anywhere else. She'd even asked Mitch to run a check through the FBI computers to see if Edward Kroll had a criminal record, but he hadn't gotten any hits. The puzzle had led Regan to place ads in all of the newspapers local to Sayreville, Illinois. It had been one of those ads that had come to the attention of Dolly Brown.

Dolly Brown told Regan she'd been a neighbor of the Krolls, and how, at age thirteen, Eddie Kroll and two of his friends had lured another classmate to a vacant lot, where they'd beaten the boy to death. Eddie, as the youngest of the three, and the least culpable, had been sentenced to juvenile detention until he turned twenty-one, at which time he was released. No one knew what happened to him after that, Dolly Brown had said. Eddie Kroll had simply disappeared, and they'd heard a few years later that he'd died.

Dolly Brown had lied.

Dolly neglected to tell Regan that her maiden name was Kroll, and that she was the sister of the sought-after Eddie. It had taken Regan a while to figure that out.

She still wasn't sure why Dolly had lied about all that.

And there'd been that business about the other Kroll sister, Catherine. Dolly had shown Regan photos of Eddie as a child, but had insisted there were no pictures of their younger sister, Catherine, beyond early childhood.

Another lie of Dolly's.

Regan still had no explanation of why Dolly's sister-in-law, Stella, had quietly slipped a packet of old family photographs into Regan's purse during her last visit to Sayreville. There, amid photos of Eddie that had been taken prior his incarceration, were pictures of a pretty young woman identified on the flip sides as Catherine Kroll. The pictures were dated 1963. Regan had already determined that Catherine had been born in 1938, so she'd have been twenty-five years old.

Why had Dolly lied?

Regan had returned to Sayreville to discuss this very thing with Dolly, only to find she'd gone to Florida for the winter and had instructed everyone she knew not to divulge her whereabouts to anyone—especially to Regan Landry. When Regan had stopped at Stella's home, she found Stella's husband seriously ill, and she'd declined to press the matter. After a phone call to Stella in April, she learned that Carl had passed away several weeks earlier, and once again Regan chose not to question the woman.

"I guess the real question is why can't I let it go," Regan muttered under her breath as she reached for the file. It sat off by itself next to the phone on the corner of the desk, as if waiting for Dolly to call back with answers to all the questions the file seemed to ask.

Why *can't* I let it go?

Regan rested her chin in her hand. What difference would it make if she ever found out what happened to Eddie Kroll—where he'd gone, how he'd died, where he'd been laid to rest—or why Dolly had been so protective of him, even now, all these years later?

Questions without answers. Regan didn't know why it mattered. She only knew that it did, and that she was driven by something she didn't understand to take it as far as she could.

To that end, she went online and booked herself on a morning flight to Chicago. She could drop in on Stella, pay a sympathy call on Carl's widow. Of course, while she was in Sayreville, she'd drop in at

Dolly's as well, see what that crafty old bird was up to, see if she could figure out whatever it was Dolly didn't want her to know.

Her travel arrangements made, Regan turned her attention to her search for an assistant. She hunted up the phone number for the local newspapers' classified departments, and dialed the first number on the list.

Mitch was right. It was time. Time to get her father's files organized. Time to get on with her next book.

And once she'd hired that assistant, maybe she'd have time to figure out just what Dolly Brown was up to.

Two

Regan leaned back against her seat in first class and closed her eyes, wondering if she was wasting her time with an unannounced visit to Dolly Brown. Well, if Mohammed wouldn't come to the mountain, as the saying went, the mountain would have to go to Mohammed.

She just wished she had some reason to believe the trip would pay off. At this point, she'd be happy to come home with a little information, a little being preferable to none at all. Which was what her last two trips had netted, she reminded herself.

She'd called Dolly the night before, but this time she didn't leave a message. If Dolly was there—and screening her calls via caller ID—why give her a heads-up that she'd be having company soon? If Dolly was still avoiding her, why let her know in advance that Regan would be knocking at her door at around one the following afternoon?

Regan had it all planned. She'd park down the street and walk up to Dolly's house. She recalled a large picture window immediately to the right of the Browns' front door, so she'd stand on the left side of the door when she rang the bell. And she'd wear her hair up and tucked under a hat. A Chicago Cubs cap. Yeah, she could pick one up in the airport; they had been all over the place the last time she'd come through. She'd wear her dark glasses and a lightweight jacket. Dolly'd never recognize her, even if she happened to see Regan approaching on the walk.

I've really lost my mind, Regan told herself when she realized she was grinning just thinking about Dolly's expression when she opened the door and realized it was Regan behind the disguise. *I cannot believe I'm putting all this energy into fooling this poor woman into talking to me. God.*

Still, it would give her a certain amount of satisfaction.

Regan followed her script to the letter. She parked five houses away on the opposite side of the street, and approached from the blind side of the front door, all the while trying not to chortle gleefully at the thought of surprising an unsuspecting Dolly.

But Dolly's car was nowhere to be seen—not in front of the house nor in the drive—and after several buzzes on the doorbell, Regan had to accept that there was no one home.

Damn.

More than a little disappointed, Regan walked back to her car, determined to try at least one more time before she left for home tomorrow.

In the meantime, there was Stella.

Somehow Regan was certain that Stella would play a key role in unlocking the mystery of Eddie Kroll. Maybe she could even use whatever information she got from Stella to shake a little something loose from Dolly. There sure seemed to be a powerful undercurrent there. Regan was dying to find out what it was.

There was no reason to hide from Stella, Regan reminded herself when she hesitated next to the parking spot that stood empty in front of the Kroll house. She maneuvered her rental car into the space and grabbed her handbag from the front seat. This time around, she'd skip the Cubs cap, she told herself as she tossed the bag from the airport shop into the backseat. In the past, Stella had proven to be more straightforward than her sister-in-law. Regan hoped that would still hold true.

She followed the concrete path to the front door of the small twin house where Regan had first met Stella and her husband, Carl Kroll. A store circular in a transparent plastic sleeve lay on the top porch step, and Regan picked it up and tucked it under her arm while she rang the doorbell. On the second ring, she heard footsteps approaching. The inner door opened, and Stella Kroll looked out through the still-locked screen.

"Hello, Mrs. Kroll." Regan stood with her hands tucked into her pockets. "Do you remember me?"

"Why, yes. Yes, of course. You're Regan," Stella replied.

"I wanted to tell you how sorry I was to hear about your husband," Regan said.

"Thank you, dear, but you didn't travel all the way to Illinois to express your sympathy." Stella smiled gently. "And you had sent that lovely card . . ."

"Yes. You're right. I was hoping you could spare me a few minutes of your time."

"Time is something I have too much of, these days." Stella unlocked the door. "Please, come in . . ."

"Thank you, Mrs. Kroll."

Regan handed Stella the paper she'd picked up on the front step.

"Thank you." Stella closed the door behind them. "Let's sit out on the sun porch."

Regan followed her hostess to the back of the house, where a small glass-enclosed room overlooked a tidy backyard.

"Please, sit"—Stella pointed to the wicker sofa—"and I'll get you something cold to drink. Is iced tea all right?"

"Iced tea would be wonderful." Regan smiled gratefully and sunk into the sofa cushion.

"I just made a pitcher. I'm thinking it's going to be warm this afternoon. A good day to work in the garden." She gestured out the large picture window, which comprised most of the back wall. "It's still too early to plant, but it's a good day to start getting the ground ready. I thought I'd put in a few annual beds this year."

She smiled wistfully.

"I used to have such gardens, everyone admired them. I'd have flower beds . . ."—she waved her hand in the direction of the backyard—"all around the property line, both sides and across the back. I'd fill the house with bouquets and still have bouquets for my neighbors. The last few years, with Carl so sick, there just hasn't been time. It was all I could do to deadhead the roses . . ."

Stella's smile was almost apologetic.

"I'm sure it was a very difficult time for you, Mrs. Kroll."

"Carl didn't like to go outside, those last few years. Sometimes on nice days, I could get him out on the front porch, but for some reason, he just wouldn't come out back here. I just couldn't keep up with the gardens."

"Alzheimer's is a terrible disease," Regan said sympathetically.

"It takes so much and it leaves so little. Sooner or later, there's just nothing left."

"I'm very sorry, Mrs. Kroll," Regan offered softly, saddened at this glimpse of how much Stella's world had narrowed as her husband's illness had progressed.

"Anyway, Carl always did like having flowers in the house." Stella forced a bright note into her voice and a bit of a smile to her lips.

"I'm sure he'd be happy to see you working in your garden again."

"I like to think so." Stella nodded, then turned toward the kitchen. "Let me get the iced tea."

From the sun porch, Regan could hear ice clinking into glasses and the rustle of something papery. Within minutes, Stella had returned with a round tray with two glasses of iced tea and a plate of brownies.

"I made these last night, because I needed a little chocolate something." Stella smiled as she set the tray on the glass-topped table. "I don't usually bake for myself—I could do without the calories—so I'm really happy that you're here to share these with me. My daughter Elena usually stops by on Tuesday nights for dinner, but she's allergic to chocolate, so I made some of the blond ones as well, if you'd rather have them."

"I love brownies," Regan admitted, "but I can't remember the last time I had homemade. Chocolate is my favorite. Save the butterscotch for your daughter."

She chose one from the tray and took a bite.

"Delicious," she told Stella honestly. "This is such a treat."

"Thank you. My sister Mary's recipe. She's the baker in the family." Stella sat in a chair near the window and sipped her iced tea.

"Maybe while you're here, could I ask you . . ." Stella paused.

"Yes?"

"Would you sign my copy of *Fallen Angels*?" Stella asked with just a touch of shyness.

"You bought my book?" Regan's eyes widened.

"The day it went on sale." Stella nodded. "Read right through the night."

"That's some intense late-night reading. I hope it didn't give you nightmares."

"The crimes you wrote about were terrible, but I thought you handled them all very well."

"Thank you. That means a lot to me. And I'd love to sign your book for you."

"It's right here." Stella turned in her chair and took the book from a stack on the bookcase behind her. She handed it to Regan, saying, "I like to read out here sometimes at night, especially now that the weather's getting warmer. It helps fill my nights."

Regan searched her handbag for a pen, found the title page, and wrote a personal message to Stella before handing it back.

"That's nice." Stella smiled as she read the lines Regan had written. "Thank you."

"My pleasure." Regan slipped the pen back into her purse. "If you like to read true crime, maybe I could send you some of my dad's books. He was the master, you know."

"Oh, I have all of his books." Stella turned her back to Regan and returned the book to its place on the shelf. "I've been a fan of his for years."

"Really?"

"Oh, yes. Carl read them, too." Stella took another sip of her tea. "Terrible what happened to him. Just terrible. That awful little man who killed him . . . I saw the whole thing on television. It was just horrible."

Stella's sincerity touched Regan deeply. "Thank you, Mrs. Kroll. It was a great shock, losing him like that. So suddenly."

"It's never easy, losing a loved one, even when you've had time to prepare yourself. Even when you're expecting it." Before Regan could comment, Stella changed the subject. "I read in the back of your book that you grew up in England."

"Yes. My mother was English, and after she and my dad married, she wanted to live close to her family. I didn't come to the States until I was almost a teenager."

"Your father's books don't say much about your mother," Stella noted. "As a longtime fan of your father's, I've wondered what she was like."

"Very British, is the best way to describe her. Very proper and set in her ways." Regan smiled. "She was very beautiful, pale blue eyes and white skin and light blond hair. I think my father might have returned to the States sooner if she hadn't been so set against it. As it was, she was never very happy here, and she went back to England to be with her mother and her sisters every chance she had."

"I'm sure she missed her family very much."

"She did. As she got older, she spent more and more of her time there, less and less here. First her mother was ill, then her sister. So it was just me and my dad, most of the time." Regan paused thoughtfully, then added, "I'd have to say that I never knew my mother as well as I knew my father. He and I were really close, all of my life."

"You must have made a few of those trips with her."

"When I was younger, yes. We'd go as soon as school ended in June, and we'd stay until a week or so before school was about to start in the fall. She and I would go. My dad, almost never," Regan recalled.

"You have no British accent at all," Stella observed.

"Must have been my dad's influence." Regan smiled. "That, and the fact that, as a young child, I went to school with as many American kids as English. Frankly, it was fun to have an American accent, it was fun to stand out amongst all my Brit cousins. Then again, by the time I was in high school, I wanted to spend more time here, with my friends."

"Had you been to the States before your family moved?"

"Yes. I don't know how much you know about my father, but his earliest books were mysteries. They were published only in England, by a small British press. The publisher was a man named Everett Griffin, and his son, Bentley, inherited the company when his father died. A few years later, he moved it to the U.S. and renamed it Griffin Publishing." Regan paused to help herself to another brownie, having realized her usual lunchtime had come and gone. "My dad was one of their first authors. Griffin has the rights to Dad's entire backlist—his old books—and now they publish me as well."

She took a small bite, savoring the rich chocolate before continuing. "Originally, Griffin was based in Boston, and when my dad would go to see Bentley, I would go with him. Dad loved New York, and took every opportunity to visit, so we'd fly from London to New York, stay for a few days, then rent a car and drive to Boston. To this day, I love that city and all those little towns off Route Six we'd drive through along the coast on the way back."

"And you went to school here?"

"High school and college. I always thought I'd do something related to art—work in a museum, maybe, since my degrees are in art history—but then my dad asked me to work with him one summer, and I found I liked the research and found the subject matter fascinating. I was lucky to be able to learn from him."

"Well, he certainly taught you well. *In His Shoes,* the book you finished after he died, is one of my favorites."

"It makes me so happy that you've read his books." Regan grinned. "I know he'd have liked that. And he would have liked you, too. I wish you could have met him."

Stella smiled.

"Would you like some more iced tea?" she offered.

"I think I've probably taken enough of your time for one afternoon, Mrs. Kroll."

"Not at all. I'm enjoying the company. And please, call me Stella." She rose and took both glasses into the kitchen for refills. "Elena had to cancel this evening's dinner, some work meeting. I guess I didn't realize how much I'd come to look forward to Tuesday, and to having a guest."

"You mentioned you were planning on working in your garden this afternoon," Regan said when Stella returned to the sun porch. "Maybe I could give you a hand. I do have some experience, though not very recent. Gardening was my mother's favorite pastime. She had beautiful gardens at our home in England. I used to help her when I was little."

"The English are famous for their gardens. I always thought someday I'd go there, just to see."

Regan nodded. "There are the wonderful public gardens, the more famous ones, but some of the best are the ones you find in small villages, or the country estates. Mom's gardens in London were more restrained than the ones she had at our home in New Jersey. They were very much the classic English country garden you see in all the magazines these days."

"Oh, yes. That style is very much in vogue." Stella nodded enthusiastically. "I'm sure they're just beautiful."

"Not anymore. I'm afraid those beds have long since overgrown. My father never had much of an interest, and I'm afraid I've just never had the time," Regan explained. "I spend most of my time at my home in Maryland, and besides, I'm planning on selling Dad's property. So there's really no point in my spending any time out there."

"They say you can learn so much about a person from their garden. I'd have liked to have seen your mother's." Stella glanced out the window. "I'm afraid that, right now, the only thing anyone would learn about me from mine is that I've been neglectful."

"The offer's still open. I'd be happy to help."

"Oh, that's not necessary, dear, but I appreciate the offer. I'm sure you have better things to do."

"Not really. I'd wanted to spend some time with Dolly, but she hasn't returned my calls. I stopped at her house before I came here, but she wasn't at home."

Stella sat back in her chair without comment.

"Why do you suppose she's avoiding me?" Regan asked. "It just doesn't make any sense. I mean, *Dolly* contacted *me*. She answered my newspaper ad when I was first looking for information about Eddie Kroll, she sought me out. The first few times we talked, she had plenty to say. Talked about Eddie, told me what he'd been like as a kid, growing up. Of course, later I found out she'd been lying through her teeth, all that stuff about them being next-door neighbors." Regan shook her head. "Why do you suppose she did that?"

"I think you would need to ask Dolly that."

"I would, if I could actually talk to her in person. I just don't get it." Regan tapped her fingers lightly on the arm of the wicker sofa. "I don't understand why she responded to my ad if she wasn't going to tell me the truth. I had to figure out for myself that she was Eddie's sister, and I had to trick her into admitting that. Does that make sense to you?"

Regan watched Stella's face, but could read nothing there.

Stella averted her face from Regan's gaze, and grew quiet for a long minute. Finally, she said, "That's best kept between you and Dolly. I'm sure she had her reasons, but I don't feel it's my place to get into all that."

"Why not, if I might ask?" Regan leaned forward.

Stella patted Regan's knee and smiled. "I'm just an in-law."

Before Regan could ask what that had to do with anything, Stella stood.

"Now, I really do need to get on with my yard work, and if you still think you'd like to pitch in . . ."

"I'd love to give you a hand."

"Well, then, I suppose we could spend an hour or so working over those weeds."

"Or more, if need be." Regan touched her napkin to the corners of her mouth. "I have all afternoon."

"Perhaps I can talk you into staying for dinner, as well. I'd planned to cook for two."

"I'd like that. Thank you."

"Good. It's settled. Let me just get an extra pair of gloves for you, and we can get to work."

And maybe, Regan thought as Stella disappeared into the kitchen, *before I leave tonight, I'll have found a way to pry a little something out of your politely closed mouth. Like why "just an in-law" isn't entitled to an opinion . . .*

Three

Roland Booth stared at himself in the mirror, adjusted his tie, and unbuttoned the middle jacket button of his new gray suit. He tilted his head one way, then the other, before buttoning it again.

Buttoned? Unbuttoned?

He wished he had a better sense of these things.

He stepped into the green room to wait for his appearance on the hit legal show *And Justice for All,* the latest must-see TV, and pulled an anxious hand through his thinning hair. Four months ago, when he'd turned thirty-five, he'd felt used up, washed out by the legal system. Years earlier, having left the raw life of a Midwestern farmer, Roland had headed south with two things on his mind: warm weather and a lucrative career.

One out of two wasn't bad, he'd reminded himself wryly just a few months ago, when, on New Year's Day, he'd made his annual State of My Life entry in his journal.

Who could have guessed that so much could have changed in so little time? Two weeks, he reminded himself. It had been a mere two weeks since Lester Ray Barnes had demanded a meeting to discuss how he could avoid the death sentence that had been imposed following his conviction for first-degree murder. And here he was, about to make his national television debut on the hottest new show on cable.

Roland shook his head, marveling at how quickly one's fortunes could change.

A few weeks back, he'd pretty much shrugged off Lester Ray—Roland was certain the little shit wasn't worth the effort it would take to fight the DA and the courts, especially since he'd been thinking about applying for an opening in Lederer's office—but three days after their little sit-down at the prison, Roland had walked into Mattie's Diner and found himself standing in line waiting for a seat at the counter alongside Mack Ewing, the reporter who covered the county courts for one of the network affiliates. Seeing them engaged in conversation, the waitress asked if they'd like to share the table that had just been vacated.

"Fine with me." Roland had shrugged.

"Lead on," Mack instructed the waitress.

When in an attempt at casual conversation Roland had asked, "So, what's the hot news around town, Mack?" the last thing he'd expected was a lengthy diatribe against the DA.

"Shut me out, the bastard, all 'cause he didn't like a piece I did about that dumb shit ADA who blew the Kelly case a few months back." Mack's face darkened. "Malcolm Reed, you know him? Took offense to the spot and went whining right to his boss with it."

"I know Reed." Roland nodded affably. "What an asshole."

Mack opened a pack of crackers with his teeth and dumped them into his soup.

"Yeah, well, he who laughs last, and all that." Mack sneered. "I got a lead on a story that's so hot, it's going to smoke the hide right off the DA and everyone in his office. Friend of a friend's given me something big, and it's just about to blow."

Ewing leaned forward and lowered his voice.

"You know how Lederer is always talking about how tough he is on crime, and how high his conviction rate is?"

"Wasn't that his campaign slogan? 'Tough on crime, tough on criminals'?"

"Yeah, well, it's looking like there's a good chance some of those convictions are about to be upended. There's been a bit of *miscon-duct* discovered—good word, misconduct, don't you think?" Mack was all but chortling. "That guy that got out of the state prison last week—Capshaw? He's the tip of the iceberg."

Roland's fork stalled somewhere between his plate and his mouth.

"You're not talking about that lab over in Fremont?"

"You know about that?"

"I'm a court-appointed lawyer. Criminal defense, remember?" Roland sat up a little straighter and smiled benignly. "The story's been making its rounds."

"Oh, right, right. You're criminal defense," Mack said as if it had just occurred to him, and Roland realized right then and there that Mack had known all along what kind of law he practiced, and who his clients were, and that it was no accident that he found himself in line for a table with the reporter.

For Roland, it was as if those sky-high gates to the Emerald City had opened, and he could see clear down the yellow brick road to Oz.

He took a deep breath and said, "As a matter of fact, Mack, I'd been planning on calling you this week. You might remember my client, Lester Ray Barnes . . ."

"Sure, sure . . . say, wasn't he convicted strictly on DNA . . . ?"

"Yeah. DNA tested by the lab in Fremont. You might want to take a look at his case. It could add some meat to your story . . ."

And that was all it had taken for Mack to start the ball rolling, the ball that had led Roland Booth from his crummy, cramped little office to the green room waiting to take his place before the cameras with Owen Berger, host of *And Justice for All.* Roland was still pinching himself to think that he was really here. And from *here,* well, who knew how far this could carry him?

He fussed with his tie again, visualizing becoming a regular on the show, like that hotshot lawyer from Chicago, Amy Jensen. Or maybe he'd end up with his own show. Hell, maybe he'd even write a book about Lester Ray's case and how he, Roland Booth, had taken on the state, and fought to win justice for his innocent client who'd been railroaded by a DA hungry to keep his conviction rate up. Bet that would lasso a fat contract with a big-time publisher.

Hey, it could happen. Last he'd heard, this was still the land of opportunity.

Of course, once he'd won Lester Ray's freedom, he'd be suing the ass off the state of Florida, the DA's office, the lab. The thought of all those zeros made his head spin. He could hardly wait to begin writing up the complaint.

He glanced at the monitor as the show prepared for its next commercial break, the camera settling on the guest whose segment was just winding to a close, some lawyer from Boston who wore a handsomely tailored dark blue suit. Roland peered closely as the man stood to shake hands with Owen Berger, his attention not on the men's faces, but on their jackets.

Unbuttoned.

When in Rome, Roland reminded himself as he was ushered onto the set, his nervous fingers finding the middle button and releasing it from the buttonhole.

Regan stacked the pillows up behind her back and leaned against the headboard of the bed in her hotel room. Still not right. She threw the covers aside and went to the closet for the extra pillow she'd seen on the shelf. She placed it in front of the other two already on the bed and got back into bed.

Much better.

She opened the book she'd started reading a few days earlier, and tried to get into the story, but just wasn't in the mood. She closed it and got a notebook out of her handbag, which she'd dropped on the floor next to the bed. She opened it and made a few notes relating to her meeting with Stella, but realized she had little to add. Despite having worked in the garden together for the entire afternoon, and having spent another two hours preparing dinner and eating it, Regan had come away with precious little new information about the Krolls. Apparently, when Stella decided not to talk, she didn't talk.

Well, I admire her willpower. God knows I did everything I could think of to get her to talk about Dolly, but that woman's lips really were sealed.

Still, it was irritating to think that Dolly had proved to be elusive once again, that Regan would be returning to her Maryland home with no greater understanding than she'd had when she'd left. More than irritating. It wasn't as if Regan had nothing else to do with her time, between trying to focus on a new book and resolve the situation at her father's house. She just didn't have enough spare time to make fruitless trips back and forth across the country. Of course she'd swing past Dolly's on her way to the airport in the morning, but something told her Dolly wasn't there. She wished she'd probed Stella a little more about her sister-in-law's whereabouts. Would Stella have told Regan if she'd asked outright?

She'd give Dolly another month or so, then make another unannounced visit when she could fit it in. She didn't see where she had much choice in the matter.

Regan searched the nightstand and found the remote control for the television. Mindlessly, she channel surfed for several minutes before stopping at the movie channel on which a classic western was being shown.

She and Mitch had watched this one last week, she recalled, and she changed the channel.

Three more clicks on the remote landed her at one of her favorite shows. *And Justice for All* was half over. She'd always found Owen Berger to be slightly pompous, but she liked him anyway. As a fan of true crime, Berger had hosted her father many times over the years, and had invited Regan to appear on his show following the publication of *Fallen Angels*. She'd been unable to schedule an appearance as part of the promotion for the book, but Owen had graciously extended an open invitation for Regan to come on the show at her convenience. She'd forgotten about it until now.

"Nice shirt, Owen," Regan said to the television as the camera settled briefly on the host before shifting to the guest who was just being introduced.

". . . Roland Booth is the court-appointed attorney for convicted murderer Lester Ray Barnes, who is on death row in Florida. Welcome, Roland." Owen gestured to the man in the gray suit who sat on the opposite side of the desk. He looked uncomfortable and out of place. "Well, they sure do have a mess down there in Florida, don't they, what with all the allegations of deliberate misconduct by the owner and chief technician at the Fremont lab that tested DNA . . ."

"We sure do, Owen." Roland smiled as he nodded. "This laboratory has tested hundreds, if not thousands, of pieces of evidence over the years."

"And now it's come out that some of the test results are questionable . . ."

"More than questionable, Owen. The owner of the lab—who was also the head tech—Eugene Potts, has admitted that there were times when his methods were scientifically unsound. Further, he now admits to having been less than truthful when he was called as a witness to testify to his findings."

"He admitted he lied?"

"He admitted he lied." Roland nodded again. "Unfortunately for many people, he didn't keep records of which cases he lied about and in which cases he told the truth."

"What explanation . . . what excuse is this man offering for his behavior? What is he saying?"

"He's not saying much of anything right now, on the advice of his attorney, as I'm sure you can imagine. But I have heard there are cases where Potts didn't have a DNA match but said he did because the DA's office leaned on him so hard that he just found it easier to say yeah, he had a match, than it was to keep being browbeaten by the DA."

"Now, we want to make it clear that this is just speculation. Potts didn't actually say this himself . . . ?"

"Actually, he did say this. He told one of his techs that over a period of about six weeks, he was so backed up with the testing, he was in over his head." Booth shifted slightly in his chair. "During this period, he had several technicians quit on him, and he was getting a lot of pressure from the DA's office for convictions. He just couldn't keep up with the work, so he fudged some results, said what he thought the DA wanted him to say."

"How did this story get out?"

"The lab tech repeated the story to a friend, who told a friend—a lawyer, actually—who then gave the tip to a reporter, who started his own investigation."

"Now, let's look at the facts here. Doesn't it take more than DNA evidence alone to convict someone of murder?"

"In a case where you have no eyewitnesses, no other trace evidence, no proven nexus between the suspect and the victim, DNA evidence can speak volumes." Roland leaned on the edge of the desk. "It can be pretty convincing to a jury."

"Which brings us to your client, Lester Ray Barnes."

"Right. In Lester Ray's case, there was not one shred of evidence linking him to the murder of this unfortunate victim—Carolyn Preston, a beautiful, vibrant twenty-two-year-old woman, let's not forget her name, and let's not forget that her killer is still out."

"Okay. Stop right here, Roland. If there was no evidence, as you say, why was your client arrested? Why'd the police pick him up in the first place?"

Owen glanced at the monitor, then held up a hand. "Sorry, we'll have to wait until after the break to find out how Lester Ray Barnes ended up being arrested for murder. We'll be right back . . ."

Regan found herself leaning in the direction of the TV, caught up in the show. As one who made her living off true crime stories, she'd been intrigued by Roland Booth's allegations.

Wow, she thought as she eased back against the pillows. If what Booth was saying was true, this was a bombshell for the Florida justice system. She flipped her notebook to a clean page, and started to take notes. As she'd so often told Mitch, you never knew where your next book might come from.

When she finished, she reviewed the two pages of hasty notes she'd made from memory. This story appeared to have a bit of everything, she realized. An allegedly politically ambitious district attorney, the grisly murder of a beautiful young woman. An innocent man, unjustly accused, convicted and sentenced to death on the basis of false testimony given by a lab that may have mishandled the only evidence the police had . . .

If, of course, it was all true.

Wow indeed.

She lowered the TV volume, then reached into her bag and pulled out her cell phone.

"Turn on your television," she said when Mitch answered. "*And Justice for All.* Call me when it's over."

"What's the show about?" he asked sleepily.

"Oh, damn, you were sleeping. I'm sorry, sweetie."

"Hey. Had to get up to answer the phone anyway." He was awake now. "So what am I missing?"

"A really interesting story. A Florida prison inmate on death row who may have been convicted on bad testimony." In the background, she could hear Mitch's TV coming on.

"Oh. The Fremont lab."

"You know about it?"

"Sure." He yawned again.

"So?"

"So, what?"

"So, what do you think? Do you think this Lester Ray Barnes is going to get off?"

"I'd think he'd have to, if what his lawyer is saying is all true. But of course, we don't know that it is. This guy's job is to stir the pot, sway public opinion."

"Can you find out? Can you check into this and see if this man really was railroaded?"

"I could place a call or two."

"Oh, hey, the break is over, I'll call you after the show." Regan disconnected the call and turned the volume up.

"We're back with Roland Booth, a lawyer from the state of Florida who's here to talk about his client, Lester Ray Barnes, on death row and scheduled for execution, when, Roland?"

"In about six weeks. Lester Ray is running out of time, and that's one of the reasons I'm here tonight."

"You're trying to get his story out there."

"Yes."

"You've filed the appropriate papers with the courts."

"Absolutely. My brief contesting the conviction was filed at the end of last week."

"You're waiting for a decision."

"Holding my breath. Praying that the judge does the right thing."

Owen glanced down at the pad that sat in front of him on the desk. "You were about to explain how Lester Ray Barnes became a suspect, how your client was unjustly convicted due to the head of a laboratory deliberately giving false testimony regarding DNA evidence."

"Lester Ray was in the wrong place at the wrong time."

"Oh, come on, Roland. Isn't that what everyone says?"

"Yes, but in Lester Ray's case, it's the simple truth. He just happened to be walking out of a convenience store at the same time the investigating officers were pulling into the parking lot. They'd just come from the crime scene, where they'd been for hours. There'd been one neighbor of the victim's who'd been out walking her dog who'd said she'd seen a young white male, medium height and weight, light brown hair, wearing a tan jacket, leaving Carolyn Preston's apartment. And there was Lester Ray . . ."

"Let me guess. Young white male, medium height and weight, light brown hair, wearing a tan jacket."

"Exactly."

"Admittedly, that description fits a lot of young men. Where was this convenience store?"

"Two blocks from the crime scene."

"And he was seen here when?" Owen asked.

"Around seven the morning after the murder."

"What was Lester Ray doing in the neighborhood?"

"He lived there. He'd gone for an early morning walk, and he stopped in for a cup of coffee," Booth explained. "The police were pulling up in front of the store just as he was coming out. He fit the description, they brought him in for questioning, put him in a lineup."

"The neighbor identified him?"

"She said she believed he looked like the man she'd seen that night, yes."

"Then they tested his DNA against DNA allegedly found at the crime scene, it was declared a match . . ."

"End of story, as far as the DA was concerned." Roland shook his head.

"How'd they get his DNA? They asked for it, he gave it to them?"

"They got it from a paper coffee cup he'd tossed out."

"Well, that was convenient, don't you think?"

Roland shrugged. "I'm not making any accusations there. They said the coffee cup was found on the ground, he doesn't remember dropping it, but it was fair game."

"And you questioned the admissibility of this evidence at trial?"

"I wasn't his trial attorney. The lawyer who handled that part of the case moved to California about a month after the trial concluded, and I was assigned to handle the appeals. But the judge allowed the DNA, yes."

"Now, is this story too far-fetched to be believed?"

"I don't think so, not at all. Keep in mind that most of Potts's business comes from law enforcement—he had a lot on the line. And though I have heard of other labs messing up, I know of nothing on this scale, where you have potentially dozens of convictions that could be—should be—overturned because of one man's testimony."

"Couldn't that potentially release killers into the population?" Owen frowned.

"There is that potential, I suppose, but you have to weigh that re- mote possibility against the very real potential of sending an innocent man to his death."

"Is your client, Barnes, the only man on death row who is af- fected by this?"

"There is one other man on death row whose conviction was based on evidence from the lab in Fremont. And there was one man serving life for several rape convictions. He was the first to be released."

"The other inmate on death row: what are his circumstances?"

"Owen, I don't know all the particulars of his case, but I do know that his DNA still hasn't been found by the lab."

"So no one can really tell what was tested, where it came from, if proper procedures were followed, and therefore whether or not it was in fact his DNA that was found on the victim or at the crime scene?"

"Right."

"Aren't there controls on these labs?" Owen frowned.

"There are controls, and I'm sure that ninety-nine point nine percent of the time, the lab techs do their jobs, and testify honestly as to the results."

"Then what happened here, Roland?"

"I think what we had here was a man who'd been doing a great job for a long time, a man who'd established a very successful business for himself. All of a sudden, he can't keep up. In a very short period of time, he loses several key members of his staff, he finds himself with work backed up to the ceiling. He just can't get the work done on time."

"So he takes shortcuts . . . ?"

"He takes shortcuts, and in the confusion, he gets samples mixed up. Things get misplaced, mislabeled, even lost or tossed out. Then he gets called on to testify. What's he going to do, admit he's screwed up? That would cost him his business. He'd lose everything he's worked for all his life."

"So he decides to lie . . ."

"Right . . . tell the DA what he wants to hear on the stand. I've been told that there are cases where he lost the sample found on the victim, so he simply tested the DNA taken from the accused twice."

"Used two samples of the same DNA?"

"Yes."

"No question of match there." Owen threw up his hands.

"Right." Booth nodded. "Not when they were both the same sample."

"And all this took place over how long a period of time?"

"About six weeks. Apparently, Potts did manage to get caught up and he was able to hire some new technicians and get his work back on track."

"But in the meantime . . ."

"In the meantime, my client—among others—was tried and convicted on the basis of Eugene Potts's testimony."

"Barnes's DNA was tested during this six-week window when Potts's lab was in chaos?"

"Yes."

"How did all this come out? How did this story break?"

"A former lab technician saw Potts do several things she thought were questionable, and started watching him. She confronted him, he made some admissions, but told her he was back on track. But it bothered her—as well it should—and she contacted a lawyer with the story. He started looking into it, the rest is history."

"Why didn't she go to the police?" Owen asked. "Or the FBI?"

"She was afraid they'd go right back to Potts, she'd lose her job. She knew where most of the work came from."

"Now, you're not asking the state to have Lester Ray's DNA retested. You're asking that he be released."

"Absolutely. They can't retest at this point. Potts has admitted that the sample from the victim's clothing was lost. There's nothing to test against."

"Why not ask for a new trial?"

"A total waste of precious taxpayers' money, Owen. The DA had no other evidence, he can't produce valid DNA testing at this point, so the state has no choice but to let him go. We already know that the first testing was scientifically unsound."

"District Attorney Lederer, on the other hand . . ."

"Still believes that Lester Ray is guilty."

"What's he basing this on?"

"He says his *gut* tells him that Lester Ray killed Carolyn Preston." Roland shook his head slowly, as if to emphasize the preposterous nature of the DA's relentless pursuit of Lester Ray. "Can you imagine, sending a man to his death because your *gut* tells you he's guilty?"

"Well, how about this eyewitness, the one who said she saw Lester Ray coming out of Ms. Preston's apartment that night? Won't she be called back to testify again?"

"No one's been able to locate her, though I understand the DA's office has pulled out all the stops to find her." Roland looked directly into the camera. "So, Tamara Evans, if you're out there, please contact the district attorney's office immediately. A man's life could be in your hands at this very minute."

"I might add here, if anyone knows Tamara Evans, the witness who claimed to have seen Lester Ray Barnes leaving Carolyn Preston's apartment . . . how many years ago was this?"

"Almost four," Booth told him.

"Call the district attorney's office, call the station here, I'll give you my number here . . ." Owen motioned to someone off stage, and the phone numbers began to run across the bottom of the screen. "We'll be right back, and we'll be taking your calls to Roland Booth right after these messages . . ."

Regan wrote swiftly, trying to recall Booth's comments, detail by detail. When she finished, she read back over her notes. If what Booth had said was true, a man was less than four weeks away from being put to death for a crime he didn't commit.

Her heart began to beat a little faster as she contemplated the possibilities.

The scenario laid out by Booth was fascinating, explosive, and certain to be controversial if proven true. Being imprisoned and sentenced to die for something you didn't do had to be right up there near the top of the list of man's deepest fears. Helpless, abandoned, all avenues of hope cut off . . . your pleas of innocence disregarded, left to count down your remaining days . . .

Regan shivered.

Owen returned to the screen and she increased the volume to hear the first caller, not wanting to miss a word.

It went without saying that if Mitch could tap into information that could corroborate Booth's story—if Roland Booth was telling the truth—Lester Ray Barnes's experience with the Florida criminal justice system and his close brush with death would make one hell of a book.

And if the case lived up to its hype, Regan wanted to be first in line to write it.

She stared at the screen, her mind racing. When the show concluded, she redialed Mitch's number.

"Hey," she said after he'd picked up. "What are the chances your impeccable skills could locate Tamara Evans . . . ?"

Four

Regan stood in front of the small house that sat on a short lot on a narrow street in a one-horse Texas town.

"You think she's home?" she asked Mitch as he walked around the car.

"Car's in the driveway." He shrugged. "I think the real question is, will she talk to us?"

"Let's go find out." She tugged at his sleeve. "She could close the door in my face, but God knows it won't be the first time that's happened."

The sidewalk cracks had been badly patched, and loose bits of aggregate skittered into the spotty grass. The steps were in little better condition than the walk, and the screen door hung at an odd angle to the front door. Regan rang the bell, then stepped back.

"You going to flash your badge?" she asked Mitch.

"If I have to. But you never know. She might . . ."

The door opened abruptly.

"Yes?" The woman inside the screen looked from Regan to Mitch and back again.

"Tamara Evans?" Regan asked.

"You are . . . ?"

"My name is Regan Landry, and this is Special Agent Peyton, from the FBI."

Regan elbowed Mitch, who held up his badge.

The woman in the doorway sighed deeply.

"I figured someone would show up sooner or later. Might as well be today, I suppose." She opened the door wide and stepped aside. "Come on in . . ."

Regan and Mitch exchanged a look of quiet surprise as they followed her into the tiny front room. The house was sparsely furnished but immaculately clean. A handful of wildflowers in a jar stood on a table next to a tired wing chair, and a pile of worn paperback books was stacked on a table in front of a sofa, the cushions of which were slip-covered in a pale green and white fabric. A large basket overflowed with stuffed animals, and a white cat with gray markings sunned itself along the back of the sofa.

"This is about that guy over in Florida, right? The guy who's in prison?" Tamara Evans shooed the cat away and gestured for Regan and Mitch to be seated on the sofa. She was a thin woman of medium height, with frizzy brown hair and an air of resignation.

"Yes." Regan nodded. "I guess you've seen the news."

"Some." Tamara perched on the arm of the chair. "I work two jobs and have a four-year-old, though, so I don't have a lot of time to watch TV."

"You said you figured someone would come looking for you. Why is that?" Regan asked.

"I was the only person who said they saw that Barnes guy near that girl's apartment," Tamara said. "I figured someone would be digging up the statement I originally gave the police and would be wanting to know."

"Know what?" Mitch leaned back against the sofa cushions.

"About why there were two statements." Tamara shook her head. "I told that woman from the district attorney's office about that cop and she said she'd look into it, but I know she didn't. I mean, when I showed up to testify at the trial, the cop was sitting right there, in the front row, staring at me. Making sure I didn't forget what he told me."

"Which was . . . ?" Mitch asked.

"He told me that I couldn't use words like *maybe* and couldn't say things like 'it could have been,' or 'it looked like him.' He said I had to say, 'it was him.' 'I saw him,' not 'someone who *looked* like him.' I told the cop, and I told the DA, I didn't really see the guy's face. I mean, I *saw* him, but I didn't see his face. I really didn't want to say it was positively him."

"Then why did you?" Regan asked.

Tamara bit the inside of her cheek, obviously debating what to say.

"I'll probably have to go to jail if I tell you," she said finally. "You're the FBI. You could arrest me."

"Are you saying you were coerced?" Mitch was pretty sure he knew what she was going to say next.

"I had a couple of outstanding tickets—one for speeding and about five parking tickets. I hadn't paid them because I didn't have the money. This cop told me if I changed my statement to say it was this guy, Barnes, instead of it could have been Barnes, he'd make the tickets go away."

Her eyes filled with tears and her voice quivered.

"He said that they all knew Barnes killed this girl, but if I didn't say it was him, they were going to have to let him go. And then when he killed someone else, it was going to be my fault."

"So you changed your story and he made your tickets go away," Regan said.

"Look, I had a baby. I didn't want any trouble with anyone. They told me he was the killer. They said they were positive he'd killed that girl and maybe a couple others."

Tamara looked at Mitch.

"Am I going to go to jail?"

"Not if you make good on this now," he told her. "I'll make sure you don't go to jail, if you tell the truth now."

She nodded.

"Okay, yes. Sure." She nodded. "I'm glad you came. It's bothered me, these past few years. I mean, if he killed that girl, he should be in jail. But if the only thing that put him there was lies, that's just not right. Maybe he didn't kill her. And now they're saying he didn't. I've been feeling like shit over it."

"You can change all that right now," Mitch said.

"Just tell me what I have to do."

"You're going to have to give me a statement, and you're going to have to come back to Florida at some point."

"I don't know . . ." She shook her head. "I can't just pick up and leave. I work at the supermarket down the street during the day, I pick up my daughter from day care in the afternoon, and my mom watches her for me while I work at the diner at night. I can't just leave town."

"You're going to have to work that out with the district attorney, Tamara. Your testimony is going to be very important."

"You're sure they won't lock me up? Positively sure?"

"I'm sure."

"Let me get a piece of paper, then." She rose and went into the next room. "Just tell me what you want me to say."

"I want you to write the truth, just as it all happened."

Tamara came back into the room with a notepad and a pen.

"Can I just start writing?" she asked.

"Go for it," Mitch told her.

And write she did. By the time Tamara Evans had finished her seven-page statement, there would be no doubt in anyone's mind that the man she'd seen outside Carolyn Preston's apartment could have been any one of a number of men, and could have been, but wasn't necessarily, Lester Ray Barnes. Mitch looked it over for omissions, asked a few questions that led Tamara to add a few lines at the end, but otherwise the statement was just an in-your-face accounting of what had transpired between the witness, the cop who interrogated her, and the ADA. The press was going to eat it up with a spoon.

"Don't take this the wrong way, but I'm thinking I should take this statement directly to the DA myself," Mitch said as they settled into their seats on the plane that would fly them to Jacksonville. "All things considered, I think this is going to be a very bitter pill. I'd like to handle it as professionally as possible."

"And you think I would not be professional because . . . ?" Regan bristled.

"This has nothing to do with you," he told her. "It has everything to do with this being a highly sensitive situation, one that will prove to be very embarrassing to the DA as well as the police department once it's out. I think having the statement brought in to him by a writer"—he held up a hand to ward off her protests—"regardless of how professional and well regarded and respected that writer might be, would be salt in the wound. A cop coercing a witness to elicit false testimony is a very serious allegation. Add to that the complicity of a member of his staff, and he's going to be one pissed-off DA. I can tell you, from my own experience, it won't be pretty."

"He should know I'm working on this, and that I'm planning to give a copy of Tamara's statement to the attorney for Lester Ray Barnes. Booth will need this statement to present to the court as part of his brief."

"Lederer will know that you're in on this, and he'll be made aware that you have a copy and he'll know exactly what you're doing with it. But he isn't going to be happy about any of this. And sooner or later, you will need to speak with him, Regan. If you go past him and go directly to Barnes's lawyer with this statement, I can pretty much guarantee that no one in law enforcement in the state of Florida will give you the time of day. Ever."

She rested her head against the back of the seat and gripped the armrests as the plane began to move forward ever so slightly.

"You're right. Of course, you're right." Regan sighed. "You give him a heads-up, it will give him an opportunity to deal with the police officer who bullied Tamara before this gets public. Then he can say to the press, yeah, we know all about it, and we've suspended the cop, or whatever he decides to do. He saves face. The police department saves face."

"And it keeps the doors open for you," he reminded her. "Assuming, of course, that he even releases it."

"You can get through to him fast? Today?" she asked. "I want to get this information to Booth as soon as possible."

"I'll need a few hours, once we land."

"I'll use the time to figure out how I want to approach Booth."

She closed her eyes as the plane began its ascent. "Think we'll make it to that marina this weekend?"

He covered her hand with his and leaned close to her ear.

"Aye, Captain," he said in a gravelly voice. "This time tomorrow, we'll be hoisting the Jolly Roger and setting sail for the open sea."

She laughed softly, her eyes still closed. "Or at the very least, checking out the new boats at Henderson's Marina."

"Same thing." He settled back into his seat, his hand still on hers, and he too closed his eyes. But there'd be no sleep for him. Somehow, between now and the time they landed in Florida, he was going to have to figure out a way to tell District Attorney Patrick Lederer that a cop had coerced a witness to lie under oath, and worse, that one of his assistants had been told about it and failed to follow up.

Like he said, it wasn't going to be pretty.

"So what exactly is the DA saying?" Regan asked Mitch when he finally returned to their hotel room after a private late night meeting with Patrick Lederer.

"In a nutshell? After he read Tamara's statement and finished cursing me out and throwing things at the wall? He's saying Lester Ray Barnes is a cold-blooded killer whether or not Eugene Potts lied on the stand, and regardless of which of Tamara Evans's statements was the correct one."

"What does he have to support his opinion?"

"You mean, hard evidence? Not much. There was no trace evidence, no fingerprints, no confession . . ."

"So there's nothing to tie this guy to the murder scene."

"Nothing that I can see."

"And yet Lederer is going to continue fighting the petition Booth filed with the court? Is he crazy?"

"He's committed. And he's not one to back off a fight. Look, he's been convinced from day one that Barnes is the man. He believes that Barnes is guilty and has held on to that belief for years."

"So he's going to ignore Tamara Evans's statement?" She frowned. "Even when he knows I'm giving a copy to the defense attorney?"

"He's not going to ignore her, no way could he do that. After he finished blowing off steam, he calmed down a little. He'll be making a personal visit to Tamara, probably want a lie detector test for her if the ADA doesn't back her story."

"And if the ADA does?"

"Then I think Pat Lederer is going to be in a very uncomfortable position come Thursday's hearing."

"Think he'll withhold the statement from the press for that long?"

"I think he'll try."

"How can he do that if I give a copy to . . ." She stared at Mitch. "Are you asking me not to give a copy of the statement to Barnes's lawyer?"

"I'm not asking you to do anything."

She stared at him for a long minute, then said, "Okay, what do you think I should do?"

"I'd like to see you give Lederer a few days to deal with this. To talk to Tamara himself, to talk to the ADA and the cop. Before I handed that statement over to anyone, I'd want to make sure it was the truth."

"I don't think she was lying, Mitch."

"Neither did the members of the jury when she took the stand during Barnes's trial," he reminded her.

"Shit." She got up and paced slowly. "Think the judge will let Barnes out once he sees Tamara's statement?"

"I don't think he'll have a choice. The guy was wrongly convicted . . . even if he is guilty."

"You think he's guilty?" she asked. "You think Lederer's right?"

"Truthfully, I don't know what to think. Lederer's no fool; he's been around a long time. I'd expect him to be able to read this guy, you know? But then you look at what he's got that he can take into court, and you know that without the testimony from the lab and Tamara's statement, this guy would never have been convicted."

"What do you mean, what he had that he could take into court? What else was there?"

"Barnes had some priors, not admissible. Two arrests for sexual assault, both times the charges were dropped when the victim refused to testify against him."

"You think Barnes got to them?"

"Maybe. I haven't seen the files myself, so I can't say."

"But you think he'll beat this?"

"Don't see it happening any other way, at this point."

"Will Lederer talk to me?" she asked.

"He will if you sit on that statement for a few days." Mitch ran a hand through his hair. "I know he won't be talking to the press right now."

"I'm not press," she pointed out. "How about this? I don't go to Booth until Lederer has talked to the cop, the ADA, and Tamara. But he gives me a heads-up before he goes public. I need Booth to know that this came from me."

"Seems fair. I'll talk to Lederer first thing in the morning."

"You think the hearing will still go on as scheduled for Thursday?"

"Probably. The judge has just about run out of patience with this situation, from what Lederer tells me."

"I have to be in New Jersey on Tuesday to interview a possible assistant. But if I hop a plane later in the day, I'll have time to talk to Lederer, Booth, maybe Barnes, before the hearing."

"Have you thought this whole thing through?"

"Thought what through?"

"This isn't the type of thing you've done before. You don't really have experience dealing with people like Barnes," he said. "Just because he got the shaft doesn't necessarily make him a nice guy."

"I've been in the company of killers before. I've interviewed serial killers, I've . . ." Her voice was beginning to take on an edge.

"They were all behind bars," Mitch interrupted, "with no chance of getting out."

"I'm really intrigued by this, Mitch. I think it has the makings of a great book. I think I could do it justice."

"Hey, I'm not doubting for a minute that you'd write a great book. I'm just saying, this might not be someone you'd want to get up close and personal with."

"You think he's guilty."

"I think he's guilty of something, I'm not sure what."

"And that's your gut speaking? After talking to Lederer?"

"Yeah. My personal opinion? He's bad news, babe."

"Mitch, someone's going to write Barnes's story—and Carol Preston's. Why not me?"

"I think you should speak with Lederer before you make up your mind. Get a feel for the case from him."

"Trust me, I have no intention of going into this with my mind made up either way." She waited, but when he did not respond, she said, "Have you ever known me to do something stupid, or put myself in harm's way for a story or anything else? I just want to find the truth, Mitch. I just want to write the story."

"Just be careful," he told her.

"I'm always careful. You know that." She paused, then said, "Okay, what's really on your mind? What's bothering you about this case?"

"Nothing I can put my finger on. I just feel there's something else going on here. I don't know what it is, but something's off."

"I won't be going to see Barnes by myself, if that's bothering you. I won't be alone."

"I can have an agent watching your back if you want. And you know I'll only be a phone call away."

"I'll be fine, but it's good to know you're there. And of course if I feel something isn't right, I'll walk away from the story. You'll be the first to know."

"I'm going to hold you to that."

"And right now, I'm going to hold you to that fabulous dinner you promised me." She stood and tugged at his hand. "I'm about to starve. And after dinner, maybe we can take a romantic walk on the beach . . ."

Five

"What experience do you have?" Regan balanced the phone on her shoulder while she poured her third cup of coffee of the morning. "I'm looking for someone who is extremely organized . . ."

It was Monday morning, and Regan had to force herself to keep her mind on the task at hand. She paced back and forth while the caller—a retired woman who'd seen her ad in the Windsor Hights *Herald*—enumerated her years of office experience. When she'd finished, Regan admitted that she had outstanding credentials. Unfortunately, she wouldn't be able to start until August, which, as far as Regan was concerned, was two months too late. She needed an assistant now, so that she could turn her full attention to the case that had consumed her even more since she and Mitch had landed in Texas on Saturday.

She had been thinking a lot about Lester Ray Barnes and his impending death sentence, Tamara Evans and the cop who'd bullied her, and she was itching to dig even further into the story. In two days, she'd be in Florida, for her one-on-one with Patrick Lederer, and a few hours later she'd be meeting with Roland Booth, and she hoped to get in to see Barnes himself before Thursday's hearing. Once he was a free man, every journalist in the country would be after him. If she was going to do this, she had to nail it down now. And that meant wrapping up this bit of business here so that she could get on with her work.

"I'm sorry, I need someone who can start as soon as possible," Regan told the woman. She thanked her for her time, then hung up the phone and checked the time. She'd scheduled an interview for ten A.M., which gave her twenty minutes to return the other calls that were left on her answering machine over the weekend. The calls had consumed her time and attention since she'd returned from Florida on Sunday afternoon.

By the time the doorbell rang promptly at ten, she'd spoken with eight more candidates, only two of whom sounded even vaguely qualified. Discouraged, she returned the phone to the base and answered the door on the third ring.

The young woman who stood on the brick porch immediately brought the word *waif* to Regan's mind. She was no more than twenty-five if that, small and thin, with straight light brown hair and large brown eyes. Her blue shirt was tucked neatly into the waistband of her matching cotton skirt, which hit right around mid-calf, and her flat shoes had more than a few miles on them.

"Miss Landry?" She tilted her head slightly to one side. "I'm Bliss McKinley. We spoke last night on the phone?"

"You're right on time. Please come in." Regan stood back to permit the woman to enter.

"Your house is beautiful." She looked over her shoulder as she stepped inside. "The house, the grounds, the fields . . ."

"Thank you. Actually, the farm belonged to my father." Regan gestured for Bliss to follow her down the hall and into Josh's study. She held the door aside while Bliss entered. "Please sit anywhere."

Regan sat on the leather sofa and waited until Bliss appeared comfortable.

"You have your résumé with you?" Regan asked.

"Yes. Right here." The young woman removed several typed pages from a folder that stuck out the top of her cloth handbag.

Regan spent several minutes looking over the pages.

"I think you told me on the phone that your husband is a student at the seminary in Princeton. Is that right?" Regan asked.

"Yes. This is his first year." Bliss smiled.

"And you're pursuing a master's in . . ." Regan's eyes scanned the résumé.

"Anthropology. I'd planned to continue in the fall, but then I found out I was pregnant, so I thought I'd be better off working for a while, to put some money away for when the baby comes. When I saw your ad, I thought it might be a good fit, since you only want someone for three to five months."

"Well, that will depend on you," Regan told her. "On how fast you work, on how many hours you can work each week."

"I can work whatever hours you need, four days or five. I can start early, I can stay late." Bliss nodded eagerly. "You said you needed someone who is very organized, and that's me. I worked all through college as a research assistant for professors, some of whom were notoriously careless and messy. I'd be happy to give you references."

Bliss paused for a minute, then reddened. "Not to imply that your father was careless or messy . . ."

"Oh, but he was. I think I mentioned that on the phone." Regan laughed. "Let me explain to you what we have here."

She waved a hand in the direction of the boxes that lined the floor and stood in uneven stacks around the room.

"My father was a writer. I am too. I need to organize his files, once and for all." Regan stood, unable to hide her frustration. "He left piles of newspaper clippings, police reports, interviews, letters . . ."

"What kind of books do you write, Miss Landry?" Bliss asked.

"True crime. I research crimes and then write about them. About the victims and about the perpetrators. I should warn you, some of the material is very . . . graphic."

"Oh." Bliss appeared to consider this.

"Will that bother you?"

Bliss went to the box nearest her chair and opened it. She took out several files and flipped through them. Regan noticed she sped past the packet of photographs without looking.

"I guess I won't be expected to look at all the pictures?" she asked.

"No. Unless it's necessary to identify some that might be un-marked." Regan thought about that, then added, "Though in a case of loose or unmarked photos, you'd put those aside for me."

Bliss nodded, then knelt on one knee and thumbed through the contents of another box. "The files are not in any particular order?"

"No order whatsoever."

"And all the boxes are like these?"

"Exactly like that." Regan nodded. "The ones in here, in the basement, the attic, the small barn . . ."

"And some material from the barn boxes might go with some of the files in the attic . . . something from the filing cabinets in here might match up with something else in the barn?"

"You catch on very quickly."

"So it's like a big puzzle . . ."

"What a unique way of looking at it." Regan sat on the edge of the desk, and made a quick decision. How likely was it she'd find anyone better qualified for the job than this young woman? Besides, she liked Bliss. There was something about her that made Regan want to smile. "Think you'd like to take it on?"

"Sure." Bliss dropped her bag on the floor. "When would you like me to start?"

"Could you start tomorrow?" Regan was only half joking.

"I'm already here." The young woman shrugged. "Why not today?"

"Great." A smiling Regan stood. "That would give us a little time to get acquainted and for me to give you a tour of the house, and to show you what I've already done as far as the files are concerned. Let's start in the kitchen, grab a cup of coffee—decaf for you?—and I'll give you the rundown on where things are. I'm going out of town tomorrow afternoon and I'll be gone the rest of the week, so after this, I'm afraid, you'll be on your own for a while . . ."

Regan looked out the window and squinted as the bright sun re-flected off the wing of the plane that had just landed in Jacksonville.

She rummaged in her handbag for her sunglasses and slipped them on top of her head, pulled her carry-on bag from under her seat, and joined the queue that was making its way slowly to the door. Having no luggage to collect once off the plane, she headed straight for the exit and searched for a cab. She was just about to raise her arm to get the attention of an approaching driver when she heard someone calling her name.

"Regan Landry?" A tall woman with long red hair stepped out of the crowd and touched her arm.

"Yes?" Regan turned.

"Dorsey Collins. FBI." The redhead pointed to the quilted bag slung over Regan's shoulder. "That's it? That's all you have?"

"I'm not planning on staying long," Regan told her.

"I'm parked right down here." Dorsey pointed to a black Mustang that sat by itself in front of a NO PARKING sign. She gestured for Regan to follow.

When they approached the car, Dorsey waved to the uniformed police officer who stood nearby, as if on guard.

"Thank you, Officer," Dorsey called to him.

"Any time, Agent Collins." He smiled. "Any time . . ."

"So you know Mitch," Regan said as she tossed her bag into the backseat of the Mustang.

"Sure."

"Nice of you to pick me up."

"Nothing would do but an official welcome for Mitch's lady friend." Dorsey smiled and slid behind the wheel.

"Mitch asked you to pick me up?" Regan frowned. He'd not mentioned it.

"No, he did not. But District Attorney Patrick Lederer did." Dorsey eased the car into the line of traffic. "He thought better of having you come to his office. The media's been all over him since that clown Roland Booth went on TV last week and ran off at the mouth about Lester Ray Barnes. Since the DA has turned down every request for an interview from every reporter on the planet, he realized it wouldn't look good to have you seen coming and going from his office, especially since . . . well, apparently there's more in the wind. Anyway, he called Mitch back this morning, but your flight was already in the air. When Mitch couldn't get you on your cell, he called me, I called the DA and arranged to pick you up, take you to meet Lederer, and then I can take you wherever you want to go next."

"I'm surprised Lederer went to all that trouble."

"He owes Mitch a favor."

"How do you know that?" Regan turned to study Dorsey.

"Because I know what Mitch did for the DA." Dorsey grinned. "And if you want the skinny on that, you're going to have to ask Mitch yourself."

"I just might have to do that," Regan told her.

Dorsey laughed. "Mitch is a good guy, a great agent. He has a lot of friends who are cops. Not just here, but other places as well. We keep telling him there's something unnatural about an FBI agent being so well liked by the locals, but there it is."

"He is a pretty nice guy," Regan agreed.

"We're all wondering how you managed to snag him." Dorsey put on her turn signal.

"Excuse me?" Regan tilted her head.

"Just curious, that's all." Dorsey smiled. "He's always been such a loner. All business all the time, but cute in a slightly geeky way. We were just wondering how you got him to sit up and take notice."

"I have no idea. We just clicked right off the bat," Regan told her honestly, then laughed. "But you see the geek factor in him?"

"Oh, yeah. You should have seen him before he got his contacts. Definitely geek-hot. Tough to get his attention, though. And God knows we all tried."

"I hadn't realized he was such an elusive soul."

"Well, now, that's a nice way to describe him. An elusive soul. I'm going to have to remember that the next time I try to get someone's attention and can't."

Regan seriously doubted that Dorsey Collins would fail to get anyone's attention, but she let it go.

"So where will I be meeting Lederer?" Regan changed the subject.

"Diner a few towns over from Fremont, a place where he's not likely to be bothered by anyone."

"Speaking of elusive souls," Regan commented.

"He has a right to be. This whole thing with the lab is blowing up in everyone's face. Mine included."

"You worked with the cops on the Barnes case?"

"No, another case. Erwin Capshaw. Bastard. He's already out." Dorsey's face hardened. "No way should that slime be out of prison. He's going to hurt someone, and you can quote me on that."

"He was on death row?"

"No, he had a life sentence. As far as I'm concerned he should have gotten the death penalty." She shook her head.

Dorsey turned off the highway and headed out a long stretch of country road.

"Capshaw's lawyer was the first to find out what was going on at Potts's lab. He got the story from the girl who caught Potts doctoring up a file the night before he was supposed to testify at someone's trial. The lawyer was dating the lab tech's sister, that's how he got a jump on this thing before anyone else knew what was happening. Filed his brief contesting the conviction, went in and had a heart-to-heart talk with the judge, had Potts subpoenaed . . ."

"And the ball started rolling from there?"

"Hasn't stopped yet."

"How do you know Capshaw wasn't innocent?"

Dorsey flashed an indignant look.

"Look, I'm not questioning your expertise, or your judgment," Regan told her. "I'm simply asking how you know. I'm not familiar with the case, I don't know what he was arrested for or anything else about him. You brought him up, I'm just asking for the details. I've never heard of him."

"Ah, and that's something his lawyer, Bob Shotwell, will never forgive Roland Booth for. Booth got the media all hyped up over Barnes before Shotwell could make his big announcement. By the time Booth started holding press conferences, Capshaw—and therefore, Shotwell—was already old news. Shotwell's client was out of prison, safe and sound. But Barnes was still in, still vulnerable, his execution less than two months away. Lots of drama there, you know, but the guy who's already slipped out quietly, hey, who cares."

"Stole Shotwell's thunder?"

"Right out from under him." Dorsey grinned. "I heard there was a big to-do over it in the courthouse the other day. Booth on his way up the main stairwell, Shotwell on his way down. I heard it wasn't pretty."

"You could pretend to be horrified."

"Hey, why bother? I loved it. They're both weasels, as far as I'm concerned, and both their clients are scum. If they want to pound on each other, I'm going to watch and cheer them both on."

"So tell me about Capshaw."

"Erwin Anderson Capshaw. Age forty-three. Has a sheet from the Keys straight up through to Virginia. Started out his long and illustrious career as a peeper—at age nine. Juvie record is sealed, but I've been told on good authority that if we could get a peek, we'd see reports of sexual assault that go back as far as junior high. Accused of rape at age sixteen—he beat that, the victim changed her mind about testifying—and it all went downhill from there."

"What earned him the life sentence? What was he convicted of?"

"Kidnapping, rape, and torture of a woman in Tallahassee."

"Why no murder charge?"

"She didn't die. She's been institutionalized since the attack."

"So she couldn't testify against him?"

"Doesn't even know her own name."

"What did the DA have to get the conviction?"

"DNA. His semen, her leg."

"Don't tell me. The lab lost his sample."

"Better than that. Potts lost *both* samples. Hers and his. It was as if they never even had it."

"That's crazy."

"Tell me about it." Dorsey shook her head in disgust.

"So Potts spilled to his tech, she tells her sister, who tells her boyfriend . . ."

"Who just happens to be Capshaw's lawyer. Yup, yup, and yup." Dorsey made a right onto a side road. "Seems the tech came back to the lab one night to pick up something she'd left, and found Potts sitting in the lab, files all over the floor, crying. At first he didn't want to tell her what was wrong, but he finally broke down and told her he'd been fudging reports, fudging results, for the past five or six weeks."

"Holy shit."

"Exactly. Imagine his surprise when he's subpoenaed to testify. He breaks down on the stand, and it's all over. Shotwell files his motion contesting Capshaw's conviction, now there's not even evidence for a retrial. The DA has nothing. Capshaw walks." Dorsey's grin was evil. "And right on his heels comes Booth and his poor, pitiful condemned client to garner the most sensational attention from the press. But since Capshaw wasn't on death row, both he and his lawyer miss an opportunity to appear on TV and get their picture on the cover of *Time*. Too bad."

Dorsey pulled into the parking lot of a small white diner identified by a large purple sign bearing the single word PANSY'S. She turned to Regan.

"Hope you have your shit together, because he's only going to give you about twenty minutes. Make 'em count." Dorsey got out of the car and waited for Regan to come around to her side. "And be forewarned, he isn't in a happy frame of mind right now."

"Thanks for the heads-up."

Regan followed the agent into the diner, where a woman in her seventies nodded to them as they entered. Dorsey headed for the only booth that was occupied. As the women approached, two of the three men in the booth rose. They greeted Dorsey curtly, then looked Regan up and down before taking seats at the counter nearby.

"District Attorney Patrick Lederer, meet Regan Landry." Dorsey made the introductions, then joined the two men at the counter.

Lederer motioned for Regan to have a seat.

"I really appreciate your taking the time to speak with me," Regan said as she sat across from the DA. He was a large man with pale blond hair just this side of gray, and piercing blue eyes that held no welcome.

"I knew your father. I have fond memories of him," Lederer told her. "I understand you're continuing his work."

"Yes, sir, I am."

"You have big shoes to fill."

"There's no argument there."

"So you're going to write a book about Lester Ray Barnes." Lederer all but spit out the names.

"I'm considering it, yes. Right now, I'm just trying to gather enough information to determine if it's a story I want to write."

"Does it need to be told? Should it be told?" Lederer looked disgusted at the very thought. "Personally, I wouldn't give that little rat bastard two cents' worth of ink. Ever since the story broke about the Fremont lab, the press is making him out to be some poor oppressed little man who was screwed by the system. Let me tell you about that poor little man, and what he did to Carolyn Preston . . ."

"For the jury to have imposed the death penalty, it must have been atrocious . . ." She paused.

"But . . . ?" He motioned for her to finish her sentence.

"But if Eugene Potts lied on the witness stand when he testified that Barnes's DNA matched the DNA found on the victim . . ." She swallowed hard, knowing he knew this, that he'd heard it a hundred times in the past week and he wasn't going to want to hear it from her now. It was on the tip of her tongue to bring up Tamara Evans's name, but she decided against it. Her instincts told her now was not the time. "In the absence of any other conclusive evidence, how can the courts fail to release him?"

He waved a hand in her direction, as if to wave away the facts.

"I know this bastard. I know he's guilty. It's killing me to know that before this week is over, he'll be back on the streets. And I'm telling you this, Ms. Landry." He leaned across the table and lowered his voice to a growl. "He'll do it again. I give him a month. If he lasts that long. He might make nice for a time, while the spotlight's still on him, but you mark my words. The minute he's off on his own, he's going to kill again. Then I'm going to be asking you and everyone else who thought to make a buck from the story to sit down with the family of his victims and tell them why it was a good idea to let him out of prison."

"If Lester Ray Barnes is going to go free, it isn't going to be because I did—or didn't—write about him. It's going to be because Eugene Potts screwed up, and lied about it. I'd think you'd be having this conversation with him."

"I already have." Lederer ran a hand through his hair. "He'll be an old man before he gets out, probably die behind bars. Like Barnes should have."

Lederer blew out a long breath. "And then, of course, there's the elephant in the room."

She glanced over at him and he smiled wanly.

"I appreciate your restraint in not bringing up Tamara Evans. Or Ted Keaton. Or Felicity Runyon."

"I figured we'd get to Evans sooner or later. I thought I'd follow your lead on that."

"Appreciate that."

"But who are Keaton and Runyon?"

"Keaton is the cop who got Tamara Evans to twist her testimony," he told her. "Runyon is the former ADA who knew about it and chose to pretend she didn't."

"Any chance I can speak with Keaton?" she asked.

"Not a snowball's chance." Lederer shook his head firmly.

"But if I'm going to write the whole story . . ." Regan frowned.

"You're going to have to do it without speaking with Keaton. First off, his lawyer would never permit it." He lowered his voice again, fire in his eyes. "But don't feel bad. He won't speak with me, either."

"You haven't discussed this with him?"

"He isn't talking to anyone."

"ADA Runyon?" she asked hopefully.

"Former ADA Runyon," he corrected her coolly. "Not a chance."

"Let me just ask you this. Has she corroborated Tamara Evans's story? Has she admitted that she knew about Keaton's strong-arming the witness?"

"In another forty-eight hours, it isn't going to be a secret." He shrugged. "Yes. Runyon admitted that Evans contacted her but says she didn't follow up because Keaton never returned her phone calls."

Regan raised a skeptical eyebrow.

"Yeah." Lederer nodded. "That was pretty much my reaction, too."

"I'm assuming Keaton will be prosecuted," she said, "but what about Runyon?"

"Stupidity is not a criminal offense," he said dryly. "What she did was stupid and it was negligent, but criminal? I'll never be able to prove it was a deliberate attempt on her part to bury the information. She says now it was an oversight, that yes, she should have kept after Keaton or brought it to someone else's attention—such as mine—for follow-up, but the case was so complicated, there was so much going on, she just forgot to follow up."

"How do you forget an allegation like the one Tamara Evans made?" Regan persisted.

"Well, obviously." Lederer's temper was starting to get the best of him. "On the other hand, how do you prove she made a conscious decision to discount it? Look, had Evans's statement been the only piece of evidence that the jury had to convict Barnes, I might feel a little differently. But it was Potts's testimony that convinced the jury. We polled every one of them after the verdict was announced, and every single one of them said it was the DNA. I'm not going to waste my time prosecuting Runyon for her stupidity, but I can tell you this, she'll never practice law again."

"Okay, Runyon's off my list, Keaton likewise." Regan sighed. "What are the chances I can get a copy of the police file?"

"You're really pushing your luck today, aren't you?" he asked without humor. "I agreed to speak with you out of a courtesy to

Agent Peyton and out of affection for your father. But I have to tell you, I'm a little sick of journalists who glorify the likes of Lester Ray Barnes. Who revel in putting all the gory details out there, and . . ."

"Sir, with all due respect," she interrupted him. "I'm not here to argue with you or put you on the defensive. I don't even know if I'm going to write about Barnes. I wanted to hear about the case from you. There's no attempt to glorify what he did—if in fact he did it. I know you have strong feelings on that issue, and you may very well be right. My job isn't to make assumptions either way, guilt or innocence. My job is to tell the true story."

She watched his face. It told her nothing.

"Look, I know I can get my hands on the file, and if I decide to go ahead with this project, I will. I'm going to want to see what the cops saw, that's standard procedure for me. I thought I'd ask you for it, but we both know I can get it if I want it." It was time to turn the conversation to another direction, so she softened her tone. "But there are things you know that won't be reflected in the file, and I wanted to get a sense of Barnes from you. You prosecuted him. You got the conviction. What was there about him, right from the start, that told you he was guilty?"

Lederer sighed heavily.

"The man has no conscience. There is nothing in his eyes. I watched that man's face when he was looking at the photos of the crime scene, and I'm telling you, the man has no soul. He was totally impassive." He paused, then asked, "You know what he did to her, right?"

Regan shook her head.

"He raped her, left her stretched out flat on the floor just as if she was in a coffin. Arms crossed over her chest, a plastic flower in her hands. He'd slit her throat, then taken her blood and smeared it around her mouth, like lipstick, like a big happy grin." Lederer shook his head. "Grotesque. But Lester Ray, he flipped through the stack of photos from the crime scene like nobody's business. Never blinked."

"But there was no blood on him? No bloody clothes, no bloody footprints?"

"Not a damned thing. He knew what he was doing, knew how to clean himself up, how to dispose of the evidence. We never found anything." Lederer tapped on the tabletop. "Of course, he'd had practice."

"What do you mean?"

"Over the years, he'd been accused of rape twice, had several charges of assault—including beating a fifteen-year-old girl—but the charges always ended up getting dropped. Victims always disappeared or failed to appear or refused to testify against him."

"And there was no DNA to test from the previous cases?"

"None were in our jurisdiction; several took place before DNA typing was utilized as widely as it is now. But of course in the end, it wouldn't have mattered much, since the evidence was lost anyway."

"I can't even begin to imagine how frustrating this must be for you."

"No, you really can't." Lederer nodded to one of the men that he was ready, and started out of the booth. "So, are you going to try to get in to see Barnes?"

"I'm going to meet with Roland Booth first thing in the morning. I'd like to get in to speak with Barnes in the afternoon. His hearing is the day after tomorrow. If he's released, he could take off. There's nothing to hold him here."

"Nothing but the thought of how much money's going to fall into his lap once he's exonerated and sues the state, the lab. Oh, and of course me." The DA stood. "Not to mention the book you're thinking about writing."

"Money hasn't been discussed."

"Oh, it will be, Ms. Landry." Lederer shook her hand, then nodded his good-bye to Dorsey. "Trust me on this. It will be."

Six

"What time is your meeting with Booth?"

"Nine-thirty." Regan opened her eyes and looked up. Mitch was leaning on one elbow, looking down. "How did you know I was awake?"

"The sun's up." He nodded in the direction of the window where light slanted into the room just enough to let them know they hadn't completely closed the drapes the night before. "You're always up with the sun, if not before. And you never sleep past six in a hotel."

"Lucky for you this wasn't my annual sleep-until-seven morning."

"You only do that at home."

"True." She pulled the pillow to a better fit under her head. "Mitch, did you come down here to protect me from Lester Ray Barnes?"

"Nope." He leaned down and kissed the side of her mouth.

"Want to tell me how you just happened to arrive down here last night?" she persisted.

"Wasn't my idea." He shrugged. "I just go where I'm told."

Regan rolled her eyes and he laughed.

"Seriously. It was John's idea. The local office needed some helping hands in going through Potts's lab. I merely volunteered to be part of the team."

" 'Cause you're such a team player.' "

"You got it, Ace." He pushed back a blond curl that had fallen across her face and eased it back into place. "The fact that you were here had hardly anything to do with it."

"Are you going to be meeting with Lederer?" she asked.

"Later today. Maybe he'll have calmed down a bit by then, since he was obviously in high gear when you saw him yesterday."

"I can't blame him for being upset, especially since this scandal broke on his watch. He's really vehement about Barnes, though. He is convinced he's guilty."

"Maybe he is."

"There's a damned good chance he is. But you can't execute a man on the basis of bad evidence. Now, if new evidence could be found, that's something else, right? Could he be tried again? Would double jeopardy apply, if the first trial was ruled invalid?"

"I don't know. I'm not a lawyer, and I don't know Florida law on this point. I can ask, though." Mitch lay back against his pillow, his arms folded behind his head. "But I don't think it's going to matter. There just isn't any evidence left to test. So, short of an eyewitness coming out of the woodwork, or finding Carolyn Preston's blood on something of Lester Ray's, or the original DNA turning up, I don't see how Lederer can bring charges. It's costly, and without something concrete, he can't win. Plus, the man has been more than a little embarrassed by the entire situation."

"So you're here to do what?"

"Get as much information as we can about Potts and his activities. Meaning details on all the cases he was involved in during that period of time when he admitted to having screwed with the evidence."

"Checking his computer data?"

"That's why they sent the best." He wiggled his fingers across an imaginary keyboard.

"Your legendary computer skills aside, why isn't the local office handling the investigation?"

He hesitated before replying, "There is some question about whether or not someone in the local office might have known about what was going on and might have looked the other way."

"Why would someone do that?"

"Any number of reasons."

"Just tell me it isn't Dorsey Collins."

"It isn't Dorsey Collins."

"Seriously?"

"Seriously. We're looking at two people, but she isn't one of them."

"Good. I liked her." Regan sat up and pulled the sheet around her. "Did you ever go out with her?"

"Huh?"

"Dorsey. Did you ever go out with her?"

"Why would you ask me that?"

"Because I want to know."

"Uh, maybe once or twice, a few years back. Long before I met you." He frowned. "Why, what did she say?"

"Nothing." Regan laughed. "Don't look so freaked out. I was just curious. She's really attractive and she seems to be smart and fun and she's probably good at her job."

"She is. She's all those things, but she's not really my type."

Regan narrowed her eyes. "I think you might want to rephrase that."

"Uh . . ." He shifted uncomfortably, obviously trying to figure out what he'd said that had been objectionable.

His cell phone rang.

His mouth eased into a smile. "Saved by it . . ." Regan laughed.

Regan went into the bathroom and turned on the shower. When she finished, she wrapped a towel around her and went to the closet for the clothes she wanted to wear that day, noting that Mitch was still on the phone. She went back into the bathroom, taking along the conservative pantsuit and the shirt with the high neckline selected with a visit to the prison in mind. She'd also packed low-heeled

shoes, and would wear no jewelry except a plain ring on the third finger of her left hand. ("Don't even let them wonder if you're single,"
one of her FBI girlfriends had once told her. "Don't feed anyone's
fantasies.") She pulled her long curly hair back into a low ponytail.

By the time she'd dressed, Mitch was off the phone and getting
dressed as well.

"You look like a librarian from the fifties," he told her. "Or possibly a nun. A contemporary one."

"That's the idea."

"I'll be at the Fremont lab most of the day, but I'll have my cell
phone with me."

"I think I should be back by four or so," she said. "Maybe we
can find someplace fun for dinner."

"If you're in the mood for seafood, I know just the place."

"I'm always in the mood for seafood. That's why I live on the
Chesapeake." She checked the time as she strapped on her watch. "I
think I'll give Bliss a quick call before I leave, see if everything's
okay."

"So you think she'll work out?" Mitch rubbed his chin. "I think
I need to shave . . ."

"I think she's going to be perfect. I spoke with her last night before you got here, and she already had a database started and was
halfway through one of the file cabinets in the study."

"Aren't you sorry you didn't hire someone sooner?" he called
from the bathroom.

"Nope. I probably wouldn't have gotten Bliss, and I like her."
Regan checked the contents of the large shoulder bag she preferred to
a brief case. Satisfied that she had everything she'd need for the day,
she closed the flap and walked to the bathroom door. Mitch was just
about to turn on his electric razor.

"You leaving now?" He paused, razor in hand.

"I'm not sure how long it will take me to get to Booth's office,
and I don't want to be late."

She leaned through the doorway to kiss him good-bye. He met

her halfway. She rubbed the rough side of his face with hers. "You're sexy with a little stubble."

"Why didn't you tell me that before I started shaving?" He frowned at his reflection in the mirror.

"I'll see you later." She laughed. "Hope you find whatever it is you're looking for at Fremont."

"Part of me hopes I don't." He met her eyes in the mirror. "I hate to think that someone I know, probably someone I've worked with, would encourage anyone to screw around with evidence."

"Well, maybe it's just a rumor." She kissed him again. "Remember what you told me about keeping an open mind."

Regan grabbed her bag from the foot of the bed and left the room, checking her pockets for the keys to her rental car. She opened the door of the Maxima, slid behind the wheel, and backed out of the parking space.

Roland Booth's office was sixteen miles from the motel, and she made the trip in under twenty-five minutes. She parked right out front, then sat for several moments to study the locale. Booth's office was in a small strip mall, the blinds in the storefront windows closed, though the sign on the front door said the office was open. ROLAND ALFRED BOOTH, ATTORNEY AT LAW was painted in black across the window, followed only by the phone number. A pot of dried-up gardenias stood near the door. The overall impression was that of a lawyer who either wasn't practicing all that much law, or wasn't charging enough for the law he did practice.

Regan got out of the car and walked to the door. The strip mall, much like Booth's office, didn't appear to have much business. Only a handful of parking spots were occupied, and few of the stores showed any sign of activity. Several had FOR RENT signs in the windows.

She opened the door and stepped inside.

"Mr. Booth?" she called out.

The reception area—if one could call it that—was an eight-by-eight space furnished with two orange plastic chairs and another gardenia, this one only slightly healthier than the one that stood sentinel outside. Two doors—both closed—were set in the back wall. At her call, one door opened and a tall rangy man with large hands and surprisingly pale skin came out.

"Miss Landry?" he asked.

"Yes. Are you Roland Booth?"

"I am, yes. Come in, please." He gestured to the open door, apologizing for the boxes that stood on the floor between her and the office. "Sorry about the mess here. I'm moving to another office and just haven't had the time to finish up here."

He stepped aside for her to enter, then hastened behind her to remove a box from the one side chair that faced the worn wooden desk.

"Sorry," he said again. "I thought this would be the best place for us to talk, since I've been giving the new address and phone number out for the past week."

"I wondered why there were no reporters hanging around," she said. "I would have expected to see at least one or two, since your client's case has garnered so much attention recently."

"You have no idea." He shook his head of thinning pale brown hair. "It's been crazy. I never imagined it would be like this."

"The press can be relentless." Regan smiled as she took the seat. "I've seen my share over the years."

"Oh, of course. Josh Landry was your father." Booth pulled his chair out from the desk and sat. "That was terrible, what happened to him. I was a fan."

"Thank you. I appreciate you telling me."

"Think your father would have been interested in my client, Miss Landry?"

"It's Regan," she told him, "and yes, I think he'd be interested. It could be a very compelling story."

"It's a great story," Booth told her confidently. "And both Lester Ray and I are thrilled that you're going to be writing it with him. It's going to be a huge bestseller, don't you think?"

"Ahhh . . . Mr. Booth . . ."

"Roland."

"Roland. I haven't decided whether or not I want to write your client's story. And if I do, I will be writing it alone. I won't be writing it with Lester Ray, or you, or anyone else."

"How do we . . . how does he . . . get compensated for his story?" Booth frowned.

"If I decide to pursue this, we'll try to come to some sort of agreement based upon his personal involvement in the actual writing of the story. Generally, I work alone. However, there have been instances in the past where my father had wanted certain sections written in the subject's own words. We may want to do some of that here. But right now, compensation is a non-issue. I'm only starting to look into this. I don't know if it will ever become a book."

"I see." Booth rubbed his chin and looked thoughtful. "Maybe you should meet with Lester Ray right off the bat. You'll see what kind of a man he is, you'll be able to tell right away how badly he's been maligned by the press, how he's been misjudged by the DA."

"The DA didn't judge him, Roland," Regan pointed out. "A jury did that."

"True." The lawyer stood. "But the DA did everything he could to paint the most vile picture of Lester Ray. He's really a sweet guy. So what do you say, you game? You want to meet him this morning?"

"Oh, sure." She stood also. "I'm looking forward to it."

"Just let me make a quick phone call to the prison and let them know we'll be there a little earlier than we'd planned. Normally, you'd need thirty days notice to get in, but since you're with me, and the warden's such a good guy, we shouldn't have a problem."

Booth dialed the phone on his desk, and Regan went back into the lobby to wait. There were dark rectangles on the walls where something had hung for a long time. Bare walls, bare floor—the rug had recently been removed too, she thought, judging by the condition of the floor.

"We're all set," Booth told her as he joined her outside the office door.

"Fine."

They left the building, and he paused to lock up. He looked at her car, then back at the old station wagon parked next to it.

"This yours?" he asked, pointing to the car.

"A rental."

"Nice." He looked it over longingly, front to back, then glanced from the station wagon to her rental. "Maybe you'd like to drive. The A/C doesn't work very well in mine."

"Sure."

"I'm looking for something else, though, as soon as I have time," he said as he got into the passenger's seat. "Something like this might be nice."

New office, new car? Regan figured Roland Booth for a man who thought his ship was just about to dock, between all those lawsuits Lederer suspected the attorney would be filing.

"I heard there were two other prisoners on death row with your client whose DNA results were—or could have been—compromised. I know that the one—Capshaw?—has already been released," Regan said. "What about the third man? What do you know about him?"

"Oh, Armas Dunmore." Booth nodded. "He won't have grounds for appeal. Turns out he confessed midway through the trial. Old Armas isn't the brightest guy, from what I hear from Lester Ray."

"Did he confess before or after Potts testified?"

"I don't know. I didn't handle his case." He shrugged. "What difference would it make?"

"Well, if he's of diminished capacity, and he confessed after the so-called expert testified, couldn't a smart attorney make a case that Armas confessed because he was intimidated by Potts's testimony, figured the jury would convict him on the basis of what Potts said?"

From the corner of her eye, Regan could have sworn she saw the whole scenario playing out in Booth's mind. Finally, he said, "Maybe."

She figured he was still thinking about it, though, as they drove on for another ten minutes without his speaking, except to give her directions.

When they arrived at the prison gates, she and Roland both handed over their IDs, had their names crossed off the list, and were waved through. Regan parked in a visitor's spot, and they went inside. They signed in and followed a narrow corridor accompanied by a short stocky guard. When they reached the room where they'd meet with Lester Ray, the guard opened the door for them without speaking, then closed them in.

Lester Ray Barnes was already seated at the worn table with the chipped Formica top. He wore an orange T-shirt and blue pants.

"It's okay, Lester Ray." Booth waved him back into his seat when the inmate started to stand. "You don't need to get up."

Lester Ray looked directly at Regan. "I like to stand when a lady enters the room."

"It isn't necessary, but thank you." Regan took one of the two wobbly chairs. "I'm Regan Landry, Lester Ray."

"I know." He smiled broadly. "I was so excited when Mr. Booth told me you were coming to see me. You're, like, famous. A celebrity. Just thinking about you coming to see me . . ."

Regan smiled weakly at his attempt to flatter.

"And I read all your books, all your father's books. At least, I did when I was outside. Not so much since I've been in here." He continued the chatter.

She was about to ask him which had been his favorite but he never slowed down.

"But I'm going to be out of here soon, you know? I'll catch up on all the books I've missed. All the books, all the music . . ." His eyes filled with tears. "I've missed so much since I've been in here, but I'll make up for it. I'll have my whole life ahead of me, right, Mr. Booth?"

"That's right, Lester Ray. Pretty soon you'll be walking out that door for the last time."

"I can hardly believe it myself." Lester Ray looked as if he was about to pinch himself.

It was all Regan could do to keep from grinning at his performance, which wasn't all that good.

"And to think there's going to be a book about *me*. When Mr. Booth told me you were going to write a book about me, I just couldn't believe it. I mean, you are a famous writer, and . . ."

"Whoa, hold up there, Lester Ray." Regan shook her head. "As I told Mr. Booth this morning, I never said I was going to write this book. I only asked if I might speak with you, and him, as a means of exploring the subject, to see if this case was one I'd like to write about. You need to understand that if I decide to do this book, it isn't going to be about you."

"Why wouldn't you want to write about me?" Lester Ray frowned. "Mr. Booth said the story has everything."

"That being the case, I should tell the entire story, don't you agree? I should write about the victim, I should write about the system that permitted you to be convicted on bad evidence, and the system that set you free. After I've learned all I can, perhaps I'll decide to write the story, and perhaps I'll pass. Right now, we're just talking, Lester Ray." She tried to sum up the situation as simply as possible. "Is it all right if I call you Lester Ray?"

He hesitated for a moment, then asked, "Could you call me Darren instead?"

"Darren? Is that your real name?"

"No. I just like the name. That's the name I would have picked if I coulda named myself. It's a great name, don't you think? Kinda suave?"

"Very nice." She nodded.

"I'm thinking about changing my name, all legal like, once I'm out of prison." He leaned forward as if sharing something confidential. "Lester Ray just shouts *redneck,* don't you think? I don't think that Florida jury would have convicted Darren, but they sure didn't like Lester Ray."

"I don't really think your name played into your conviction, Lester Ray," she told him.

"Darren."

"Right. But I do think that you were convicted on the basis of Eugene Potts's testimony."

"Yeah, what do you think of that, coming into court and just flat-out lying about me." Lester Ray's eyes darkened. "Made up shit . . . I mean, stuff . . . about me. Said he found my DNA on that girl."

He leaned closer still, his voice soft, sincere.

"Miss Landry, I did not kill that girl. I swear on my mother's grave, I did not kill that girl. I never saw her before they showed me her picture, the one they took of her on that couch, with the blood all around her mouth?" He shivered. " 'Bout made me sick. What kind of a sick person would do something like that to such a pretty girl, then smear her up like that, lay her out like that?"

He shook his head, quietly horrified at the very thought.

"I've done some things in my life I'm not proud of, but I never done nothing like that to no one. I couldn't even think of something that evil, Miss Landry. Whoever did that to that girl is evil through and through, but it wasn't me."

His gaze was steady, his expression solemn.

"I swear, Miss Landry. It wasn't me."

He appeared to be waiting for her to react, and when she did not, his eyes filled with just the barest trace of tears.

"You cannot imagine what it is like to be in this prison, counting down the days you still have left, knowing that everyone else is counting them down, too. And no one cares. There's stuff that has to be done, official stuff, before you execute a man, and that's all that's been on anyone's mind around here. The paperwork. The stuff they have to do before they kill me." A tear dropped from each eye. "If I'd done what they said to that girl, it would be right. It would be justice. But there's no justice in killing me, since I didn't kill her, and I didn't kill anyone else."

Lester Ray began to sob.

"I do not want to die, Miss Landry. I want to live honorably for a long time. I want you to write my story, whether they execute me or not. Either way, I want you to be the one to tell it. Someone should." He looked up and wiped his eyes with the back of his fore-arm. "Someone has to . . ."

Seven

The courtroom was filled to capacity. Regan stood in the back to survey the crowd and sort it out. The reporters were, for the most part, obvious. She figured that the two young men and the even younger woman crowded around the prosecutor were members of the victim's family. Lester Ray sat calmly next to Roland Booth, his head down, as if an incidental witness to the proceedings.

Regan started up the aisle, looking for an unoccupied seat close enough to hear what was said. Five rows from the front there was one small space on the end, just about right for a body as petite as hers. She was just about to sit when Lester Ray turned around and saw her.

He smiled brightly and waved, then tapped his attorney on the arm excitedly. Roland Booth, too, turned and smiled broadly.

Every eye in the courtroom followed his gaze and stopped when they reached Regan.

She pretended not to notice the buzz that went through the reporters in the back of the room.

The judge entered and all stood until he seated himself. He gestured for both the defense and the prosecutor to approach the bench. Everybody in the room leaned forward, every ear straining to hear what was being said. At one point, the judge pointed to the district attorney and seemed to growl, but his voice was low and the words indistinct.

She had to give Patrick Lederer credit for showing up himself. He could have passed this off to his first assistant and avoided the scrutiny. He had to know that every reporter in the place was itching to stick a mike in his face.

Elvis Franklin, the attorney representing Eugene Potts, was called to the bench, and after some heated discussion, the judge banged an angry hand on his podium.

A man in the front row began to weep.

"Frankly," the judge said sharply, "it's a little late to worry about your client's Fifth Amendment rights. Your client has already incriminated himself, Mr. Franklin. Your client is facing perjury charges because of his admission. Mr. Barnes is facing execution." The judge stood abruptly. "I want you—all of you, including the defendant—in chambers."

"And you." He pointed to Franklin. "Bring your client."

The attorney gestured to his client—the sobbing man from the front row—and they disappeared into the judge's chambers.

There appeared to be a simultaneous sigh in the courtroom, as if everyone had exhaled at the same time. Everyone who'd been leaning forward now leaned back against the seats.

"Miss Landry. Joe Mustin, AP." An overweight dark-haired man with a notebook and an impatient smile appeared to Regan's right and knelt down in the aisle next to her. "I understand you're going to be writing a book about the Lester Ray Barnes case. Do you have a title yet? Can we assume your publisher has already purchased the rights to the story?"

"I wouldn't be too quick to assume anything, Mr. Mustin. I'm here strictly as an observer." She met his gaze but did not return his smile.

"Word is that you've agreed to work with Lester Ray and Roland Booth to . . ."

She shook her head. "I haven't agreed to anything with anyone. I really don't have anything to say."

He appeared to be about to protest, and she waved him off. "Please. I'm simply watching the proceedings."

"Strictly in the interest of justice."

"Always." This time she did smile.

"So you have no particular thoughts about Lester Ray's guilt or innocence? Word is that you met with him yesterday."

She had plenty of thoughts on that subject, none of which she was about to share with a reporter.

The reporter leaned on the back of the seat in front of Regan's and used it to push himself up.

Before he could say anything else, the door to the judge's chambers opened and those in the courtroom rose. The three attorneys, the defendant, and the witness all filed back to their seats.

"I've gone over all of the evidence, I've spoken with all the parties. I apologize to the family of the victim for all the delays we've experienced. I can only imagine what this must be like for you. You have my deepest sympathy." The judge turned to the defendant's table. "Lester Ray Barnes, I do not know if you are guilty of this crime or if, as you claim, you are innocent. I only know that you have been denied your right to a fair trial, and that the evidence upon which you were convicted and sentenced was fabricated. That goes against the very foundation upon which our system of justice rests. If you are in fact innocent, you have my most sincere apology. If you are guilty, may God have mercy on your soul."

He cleared his throat and stared at Lester Ray for a long minute.

"Inasmuch as the state of Florida has failed to produce enough credible evidence to sustain the conviction, this court has no choice but to reverse the conviction." He addressed Lester Ray one last time.

"You are free to go, Mr. Barnes. But God help you if you ever again appear before me in this court."

The judge struck once with his gavel, and left the courtroom without a backward glance.

Eight

The courtroom fell silent for several seconds—the calm before the storm, Regan would later reflect—then burst into a flood of voices. Reporters scrambled over each other, some aiming for Lester Ray, some for the prosecutor, others for the victim's family members, one of whom had shrieked as if in pain.

Regan turned for the aisle and tried to ignore the calls for her attention from Roland Booth as well as from several reporters. She worked her way to the door, and to the courthouse steps, where a reporter from one of the local network affiliates stuck a microphone in her face.

"I'm outside the courthouse with noted true crime author Regan Landry." The aggressive blonde held her ground despite Regan's attempts to walk around her. "Roland Booth announced right before they went into court this afternoon that he and his client are going to be working with you on a book about Lester Ray's experiences. This will be a departure for you; as we all know, your previous books—and those of your father—have all been centered around cold cases. Lester Ray's case couldn't be hotter. How different will this book be for you? And how much of the book will be written by you, how much if any by Lester Ray and Roland Booth?"

"I . . ." Regan started to respond, but before she could get a word out, something struck her in the middle of her back.

Regan fought to keep her balance even as a young woman spun

her around and screamed, "How could you? Why would you waste one second of your time even talking to him? You're going to tell his story?" Regan recognized the woman from the courtroom. Carolyn Preston's sister. "What about Carolyn's story? Who's going to tell her story?"

Regan opened her mouth to explain that she hadn't agreed to write anyone's story yet, but the woman screamed over her.

"Do you know what that bastard did to my sister?" She lunged forward but was restrained by two young men, one on either side.

The brothers, Regan thought. She'd seen them all in the courtroom.

"I know what someone did to your sister," Regan said softly. "I don't know that it was him. I'm terribly sorry for your loss. I know you want someone to blame."

"What could you possibly know?" The woman began to sob. "You don't know what it's like to have someone you love murdered. You don't know how it feels."

"I do know what it's like," Regan told her. "I know exactly how it feels."

The woman froze, her eyes challenging Regan.

"Two years ago, my father was murdered." Regan reached out a hand to the woman and touched her arm gently. "We know for certain who murdered my father, but if there'd been any question—any question whatsoever—I'd have wanted it answered, once and for all. I'd want to know, beyond a shadow of a doubt, who was responsible. I'd have wanted justice for my dad. I'd think you'd want to know the truth, too."

"We all know it was him." The woman was crying softly in the arms of one of her brothers. "If that lab tech hadn't lied, if he hadn't messed up the evidence, there'd be no question now. Barnes would still be in prison, where he belongs."

"But Potts *did* lie. He *did* mishandle the DNA. And that is on Eugene Potts, not Lester Ray Barnes."

"You're defending him because you're going to write a book about him and get rich off my sister's death." The woman's voice began to rise, and the young man holding her pulled her back again, his eyes dark with rage even as he tried to calm his sister.

"I'm not defending him, I'm stating the facts. I haven't made any decision about this book. I don't know enough yet to know if it's something I want to write about. But if I go ahead with this project, I promise Carolyn's story will be told." Regan took a deep breath. "The true story, whatever that may turn out to be."

Carolyn Preston's grieving sister stared at Regan through red-rimmed eyes, then turned her back and walked away, a brother on either side.

"I'm so very, very sorry for your loss," Regan said softly, knowing there was nothing she could say that would evoke a rational response. Best to walk away, she told herself. There was nothing she could say that they would want to hear.

She eased her way through the crowd, her cheeks burning, ignoring the reporters and Roland Booth's attempts to catch her attention. Her cell phone was ringing by the time she got to her car. She checked the incoming number before answering.

"You okay, babe?" Mitch sounded far away.

"I'm okay. I just want out of here." She locked the doors and turned the key in the ignition. "But how did you know . . ."

"Someone put the TV on in the lobby, and there was live coverage. It looked like you were being mobbed."

Regan frowned.

"What exactly did you see?"

"I saw a woman—apparently the victim's sister—screaming at you. But I have to say, you were cool, very understanding, very gentle with her. Anyone else might have—"

"Are you telling me that the confrontation by the Preston family was televised?"

Mitch sighed, painfully aware now that she hadn't known, and wished he hadn't been the one to tell her. "The camera was rolling from the minute the reporter stuck that mike in your face. The entire conversation—if you could call it that—was broadcast live. The cable news channels are just starting to run it now."

"Great." She pulled away from the curb, and immediately a dark car pulled behind her. She stopped at the stop sign and glanced at the rearview mirror. "That's just fucking great."

She watched the car turn when she did.

"I think someone's following me. I saw him in the courtroom. I think it's a reporter," she told Mitch.

"I'm on my way back to the hotel room. I'm going to pick up our things and I'll meet you. We'll stay someplace else tonight, just in case you were followed yesterday after you dropped off Booth. Can you drive around for a while?"

"Yes, but I don't know where to go."

"Where are you now?"

She named the cross street she'd just passed.

"Go three more lights, then take a right. Five blocks down from there, make another right into the parking lot on the corner."

"And from there I should go where?" She passed through the first light.

"From there you'll go inside the building on the corner. I'll call ahead and let them know you're coming."

"What building?" She frowned. Light number two was straight ahead.

"The local office of the FBI." She could almost hear the note of satisfaction in his voice. "That guy who's following you will never make it past the lobby."

"You think he's still sitting in the parking lot?" Regan asked Mitch as she hung her clothes in the closet of their new hotel.

"Probably." Mitch grinned. "He's probably made a bunch of calls back to his office."

Mitch held an imaginary phone to his ear.

" 'Yeah, she's still in there, she's been in there for hours. You hear anything about her being with the FBI? Or anything about the Bureau being in on this? No, I have no idea what's going on in there, but I'm not leaving till she comes out.' "

Regan laughed. "I had no idea there was parking under the build-ing."

"Unless you see the building from the back, you wouldn't know. And of course, that's a restricted area."

She smiled, pleased at having made a getaway in Mitch's car, happy to have some time alone with him, for some peace and quiet.

He stood behind her and rubbed her shoulders.

"Tough day?"

"Crazy." She nodded. "A little lower, on the right. Yeah, right there . . . perfect."

He reached around her for the remote and turned on the televi-sion.

"Am I going to have to watch myself being verbally accosted by the Prestons?"

"Might as well see what everyone else is watching."

"Thanks," she said dryly. "I can't wait."

He turned on the news.

"How about I call room service, and get us a nice bottle of wine and some dinner." He nuzzled the back of her neck. "What did you eat today, by the way?"

"I had a burger from a drive-through place on my way to court this morning, and Dorsey got me a package of peanut butter crackers and a soda from the vending machine while I was waiting for you to pick me up."

"No wonder you're tired. Your body hasn't had any decent fuel all day. How 'bout a big salad and a steak? Or some fish? They have a nice menu here." He went to the desk and brought her the menu to look at.

"Do they have any good desserts?"

"Well, they have crème brûlée, and . . ."

"Oh, shit, Mitch." She grabbed the remote and raised the vol-ume. "What are these idiots up to now?"

Roland Booth and Lester Ray Barnes were being interviewed on the steps of the courthouse. Guards held back the crowds, including,

Regan supposed, the Preston family. She could only begin to imagine what they'd had to say to the newly released Barnes and his lawyer.

". . . and thank my lawyer, Roland Booth, who believed in me from day one," Lester Ray was saying in that soft voice. "And the judge for making the right decision."

"Lester Ray, did you have any family in court today?" the reporter asked.

"No, sir, I did not. I have no family." There were tears in his eyes. "But my friend, Regan Landry, was there today, and I am grateful for her support."

"Oh, for Christ's sake." Regan grimaced.

"It's rumored she's basing her next book on this case," the reporter continued.

"Fuck!" Regan snapped.

Roland Booth leaned forward before Lester Ray could respond.

"Shut up, Roland," Regan said to the image on the TV screen. "Don't say it."

"We'll be meeting with Ms. Landry over the next few days to work out the details," Roland said. "We're very excited about the prospect of getting Lester Ray's story out there. It's a real triumph, an inspiration. She's the one to write it, she's our first choice. And as Lester Ray said, we're grateful to her for being in the courtroom with him. Her presence was even noticed by the judge."

"Did he mention . . . ?" the reporter asked.

"Oh, yeah." Booth nodded enthusiastically. "When we went into chambers, he even asked Lester Ray if she was there to take notes for a book, and we told him she was. I can't help but think that could have impressed him, you know? That someone with her credentials was behind Lester Ray . . ."

"Oh, that is such bullshit, Roland," Regan yelled at the screen. "Just shut the fuck up!"

"Calm down," Mitch told her.

"No way would a judge be influenced by who was or was not in the courtroom." She turned to Mitch. "Least of all a writer, for Christ's sake. That's just crap."

"But it's apparently crap that Booth believes. Or at the very least, he wants other people to believe it. Wants everyone to know that he's rubbing elbows with the big-time author."

"That's bullshit," she repeated. "And I never said I was supporting Lester Ray and I certainly wasn't in that courtroom as his friend. I never said I believed he was innocent—I definitely never said that, especially after that Academy Award–winning performance he put on for me in the prison, did I tell you about that?"

Before Mitch could respond, Regan went on.

"Mitch, I never said I was definitely going to write that book."

"I hear you, babe. But I think you're going to have to have this conversation with Mr. Booth."

"The sooner, the better." She grabbed her bag from the desk and started searching for her wallet. "He gave me his business card, I put it in here someplace. I'm going to call him and—"

Her cell phone began to ring. She took it from her pocket and checked the number.

"Oh, great." She groaned. "It's my editor. Go ahead and order something for me from room service. I think this is going to take a while . . ."

She opened the phone and raised it to her ear.

"Nina, hi. Let me guess . . . you're watching the news . . ."

Nine

"Listen, Roland, we have to talk."

Regan sat across the table in the small luncheonette from Roland and Lester Ray on Friday afternoon. Mitch sat next to her, his arm around the back of the booth.

"Are you her boyfriend?" Lester Ray stared at Mitch.

"Yes." Mitch stared back levelly. "Yes, I am."

"Okay." Lester Ray nodded. "That's cool."

"Lester Ray," Regan said. "Listen to me very carefully. This involves you."

"Okay." He nodded again.

Roland rested his arms on the table, an apparent attempt to look nonchalant, but his eyes were darting around the room.

"I need to make this very clear to both of you," she said. "I've only begun to look into this case. I have made no decisions regarding this book. I have very little information to go on right now, understand?"

"Yes," Lester Ray said uncertainly, then, "No."

"I need more information before I can decide if I want to work on this project. Specifically, Lester Ray, I want to know more about you. If I decide to go forward with this book, I'll be working on it for months. I need to know that this case is something I'm going to want to spend a considerable amount of time on."

"What other information do you need?" Roland looked wary.

"I need to know about Lester Ray's background. His family, his upbringing, prior arrests." She looked at Lester Ray. "You were arrested before, right?"

"Yes." He nodded matter-of-factly, neither cocky nor ashamed. "Several times."

"Yes, but what does that have to do with this?" He frowned. "This book should be about justice for all. I was railroaded, almost executed, because someone lied in court. Because someone in a lab somewhere didn't have enough people at work for a couple of weeks so he got backed up. What happened to me could happen to anyone, and that's the story you have to write about."

"Your life story is part of that, Lester Ray." Regan chose to overlook his theatrics. "The book is going to tell the whole story, how you got from wherever it was you started, to being arrested for the murder of Carolyn Preston, to your conviction, to your incarceration. It's more than just what happened to you over the past few weeks—it's how you landed in prison and how you got out. It's everything that led you to it, do you understand?"

She watched his face for a moment, waiting for some sign he was following her.

"Lester Ray. Remember what I told you. This is not just about you. It's about Carolyn Preston and it's about Eugene Potts, and what led them to where they ended up as well. It's about decisions we make and it's about finding the truth, and it's about justice not just for you, but for Carolyn. It's her story as much as it is yours."

"Okay, we get it." Roland waved her off. "When do you want to start?"

"We start now," Lester Ray told them. "Or we don't start at all."

"Fine. Lester Ray, why don't you tell me about yourself? Where were you born?" She took a small recorder out of her bag and set it on the table. "Where'd you grow up?"

"What's that?" He looked at the recorder suspiciously.

"I need to record the conversation, so that I can focus on talking to you, rather than taking notes." She smiled at him. "Do you mind if I record this? Is it all right with you?"

"Oh, ah, sure. Sure."

"Lester Ray . . ." Roland eyed the recorder.

"It's okay, Roland," Lester Ray told him. "I don't mind. Regan's cool."

Roland sighed and leaned back against the booth. "This is just for you, though, right? I mean, it doesn't get sold or passed around or anything?"

"Of course not." Regan smiled again, then turned to Mitch. "Would you mind getting me some ice cream from the counter?"

"Sure. Cone or a dish?"

"A dish. Strawberry."

"I think I'll get one, too." Mitch stood. "Lester Ray?"

"Ahhh, sure. Thanks. Chocolate."

"Roland, looks like you're going to have to give me a hand here," Mitch told him. "Three dishes, two hands."

Roland followed Mitch to the counter with obvious reluctance.

"So, Lester Ray, you were going to tell me where you were born . . ." Regan reminded him.

"Oh, yeah. Yeah." He nodded with a slight jerk of his head. "I was born in Georgia. Calumet, just over the Florida line. Small town near the coast."

"Tell me about your parents."

"Don't know nothing about my father." He shrugged. "Don't even know his name. Don't remember my mother. She left me with her folks right after she had me. Don't know where she went or what she did or where she is now."

"So your grandparents raised you." Regan fought a smile. Hadn't he recently sworn on his mother's grave?

"Till I was eight or nine. Then my grandfather died and my grandma went to live with her sister in Tallahassee. But her sister didn't like kids, so they gave me to the state."

"You were a foster child?"

"Yeah." He paused for a moment, then asked, "What's that word, *foster*, mean, anyway?"

"It means to bring up or to care for in place of the parents."

"Don't remember much of that," he told her. "The caring for part. Don't remember that anyone cared all that much about me."

"How many foster homes were you in, Lester Ray?" Regan watched his face, watched his eyes, wondering if he was going to launch into more of his dramatics.

"I don't honestly remember. There were so many . . ." He looked away, unrest settling around him.

"Are there any in particular that stand out in your memory?"

"Oh, sure. Not many of them so good. But I did have one foster mom who was real nice." He smiled weakly, the memory of something good coming to life in his eyes.

There, Regan thought. Just that little bit, a tiny flash of something genuine, something human.

"Tell me something about her. Why does she stand out in your memory?" Regan asked.

"She had three or four of us she took in, she didn't have kids of her own. We all got along real good, that was important to her, that we be like a real family, like real brothers and sisters. She made us lunches to take to school every day. And she used to make us cookies on Sunday. We all had to go to church with her in the morning, then in the afternoon, she'd bake cookies. Oatmeal, with raisins. They're still my favorites."

"How long did you stay there?"

"Almost a year." His eyes grew sad, and the light began to fade. "She got sick. The state came and took us all away. I never saw any of those kids again."

"After that home, where did you go?"

"Someplace not as nice. Someplace not nice at all."

He shifted uneasily in his seat, his eyes taking on a haunted look, the little spark gone completely.

"I don't like to think about being in that place, with those people. I don't like to talk about it."

"Maybe when you get to know me better, you will," she said gently.

He shook his head. "Some things you're better off forgetting about. That's what the reverend who came to the prison said. Some things you should just leave in the past. I'm all right with that."

"Was that the worst of the foster homes?"

"The worst?" He seemed to give the question great thought. "What makes one bad place worse than another?" Finally, he shrugged. "Let's just say I don't have very many good memories of being a kid, and we'll leave it at that."

Regan made a mental note to see if she could track down someone who worked with Lester Ray in the foster care system, maybe some of his foster parents. She was almost afraid of what she'd find. Acknowledging that she might eventually discover that Lester Ray was in fact a murderer, she could not help but ache for the sad child he must have been—a child whose memory of the foster mother who sent him to school with lunch and baked his favorite cookies had been the only good thing he'd brought with him from his childhood. How different might his life have been, Regan wondered, had that time with that good and caring woman lasted for longer than one brief year?

This, she knew, was the beginning of the story. Cold-blooded killer or merely a sad man whose life had taken an unjust and frightening turn: everything that Lester Ray was, or could have been, began right there.

She was glad to see Mitch and Roland return to the table. Her heart was starting to hurt.

"You might want to watch what you say, Lester Ray." Roland motioned for him to slide over. "At least, until she decides whether or not she's going to write this book."

"I've already decided," she told him as she licked ice cream from her spoon. "I spoke with my editor before coming here; she assured me my publisher is interested in moving ahead with this if I decide to go forward. I want to do the book. I'll have to speak with my agent, Roland. She'll call you, and between the two of you and my publisher, I'm sure something can be worked out that will be to everyone's satisfaction. I'd like to work on this project with you, Lester Ray."

"Hey, that's terrific." Roland beamed. "What do you say to that, Lester Ray?"

Lester Ray put down his spoon, thought about it for a moment, looked up at Regan and asked, "Do you think in the book, you could call me Darren?"

Lester Ray and Roland left the luncheonette while Regan and Mitch were still finishing their ice cream. They were eager to get on with their day, Roland to get Lester Ray a cell phone into which he'd program his and Regan's numbers so they could all stay in touch over the next week. The lawyer couldn't wait to discuss business terms with Regan's agent.

Lester Ray couldn't wait to head for the beach and the first vacation he'd had in many, many years.

"I'm going to the Outer Banks," he'd told Regan. "That's up in North Carolina. I heard someone say they had real nice beaches on this real thin little strip of land. They said it wasn't near as hot as it is down here, but you can sit on the sand and watch the dolphins. That's what I'm gonna do. Roland here is going to lend me some money, 'cause when my lawsuits get filed, I'm gonna be rich."

"Good luck working with Lester Ray," Mitch said after the two had left. "He has the attention span of a gnat."

"True. I'll earn every penny of my advance on this one. Haven't decided yet how much is an act, and how much is the real Lester Ray. You buying that 'aw shucks' thing he's selling?"

"Not even if he's giving it away."

"That's what I thought. He's creepy in a quiet sort of way. One minute he seems very calculating, very melodramatic, turns on the tears and the hang-dog expressions like a pro. The next, he's like some poor lost soul who doesn't know which end is up. I'm not sure which is the real Lester Ray." She wiped the last trace of ice cream from her fingers. "Ready to go?"

"Yes." He stood and waited for her, then together they stepped from the cool restaurant into the heat of a bright June afternoon.

"And what's with the name change?" Mitch asked as they walked to his car.

"Lester Ray thinks his name makes him sound like a redneck," Regan explained to Mitch. "He thinks Darren sounds smoother."

"I think it's going to take more than a name change to put some polish on him, but maybe that's just me."

Mitch stopped in midstride and snapped his fingers. "Forgot something. Be right back."

Regan window-shopped at the little gift shop next door while Mitch dashed back into the luncheonette.

He returned in a minute, a napkin in his hand. "That was close. They were just cleaning the table."

"What's that?" She pointed to the napkin.

He unwrapped it to show her.

"A plastic spoon?"

"Lester Ray's plastic spoon." He nodded and rewrapped it. "Far as I know, no one else has a good sample of Lester Ray's DNA. You never know when something might turn up that you might want to compare."

"You're looking in Potts's lab for things that might have been mislabeled, aren't you." It was a statement, not a question.

"Sure."

"What would you do if you found something?"

"We'd send it to the FBI lab to retest." He unlocked the car door for her. "But beyond that, some of the cases Potts worked on had connections to cases the local office worked on. We just need to make sure the results were right the first time."

"You're going to have the saliva from that spoon tested at the FBI lab?"

"Yes," he said as he opened the driver's side door and got into the car.

"Why?"

"Just a feeling I have." He smiled and started the car. "Call me a cynic, but I just have the feeling we're going to be hearing from Lester Ray again. I just want to be ready for him."

"Would that be admissible?"

"Probably not, but it would give us a baseline."

"Just in case something shows up at Potts's lab."

"Right." He brought the car to a stop at the light.

"Did something show up?"

"Not yet. But you never know." The light turned green and he was smiling as he drove on. "What time is your flight?"

"Six. And don't change the subject."

"I'm not changing the subject. I just wanted to know how much time we had, and now I know. Not much. We'll have just enough time to pick up your things from the hotel and get you to the airport."

"You swear you're not holding back anything?"

"I swear. There's nothing else to tell. Nothing has turned up at the lab that I'm not telling you about. I just like to have a little insurance, just in case something does."

"Something like what?" she persisted. "What could turn up that you could positively attribute to him?"

"Clothes matching the description of the victims." He glanced over to find her staring at him. "And no, I swear, nothing has been found."

"You'd tell me, though, right, if you did? I mean, if I'm going to be writing a book about how this guy was railroaded through the justice system and came within weeks of being executed, I'd sure as hell hate to have him turn up guilty later." She tucked a strand of hair behind her ears. "My publicist has already been contacted by several talk shows wanting me to come on and talk about Lester Ray and my feelings on the case and that sort of thing. I'd hate to go on national TV and talk about how this guy was screwed over by the courts, only to find he was guilty all along."

"There's always that possibility," he reminded her.

"So, in other words, watch what I say."

"That's always good advice, don't you think? Besides, you don't want to give away too much, right? You want to walk that line right down the middle. Maybe, between now and the time you finish your research, the truth will come out, once and for all."

He pulled into the hotel parking lot and waited for the valet. He handed over the keys, saying, "Don't bury it. We'll be back out in thirty minutes."

Mitch and Regan got out of the car. He took her arm as the double doors opened and they walked into the cool of the lobby.

"Maybe," Mitch said, "by the time the book is finished, you'll know for certain if Lester Ray was shafted, or if he is, as Lederer still believes, a vicious murderer."

He stopped suddenly and looked at his watch.

"Regan, it's Friday." He frowned. "Why are you leaving when we could be spending an entire weekend together here?"

"I booked the flight before I knew you were going to be here this week." She grinned and added, "But now that you mention it, I could go for some fun in the sun. Last weekend we worked the whole time. Now, throw in a run on the beach at dusk, and I could be talked into changing my flight."

"Definitely a run on the beach. I was going to suggest that myself. After which we could come back here for a nice dinner . . . then, who knows?"

"Let's go up to the room, and I'll call the airline and switch my flight to Monday morning."

"We can head out early in the morning, hit the beach . . ." he was saying as they walked hand in hand to the elevator. "Lie on the sand, listen to the waves pounding the shore . . ."

"I didn't bring a suit."

"The hotel has a shop right near the restaurant," he reminded her.

"Oh, right." She brightened. "And yesterday they had the cutest little pink and green bikini in the window. I think I'll stop in right now while they're still open and see if they have it in my size."

"While you're doing that, I'll stop at the front desk and see if the package is here yet."

"What package?"

"The package containing a copy of the police file on the Barnes case."

"The DA did say he'd send me one. I thought he'd forgotten."

"Yeah, well, he needed a little reminder. I had Dorsey pick it up and drop it off for you."

"How can I ever thank you?"

"We'll think of something before the weekend's over, I imagine."

"Oh, I imagine we will."

He laughed and leaned down to whisper in her ear, "And if you're a really good girl, there just might be a copy of the trial notes in it for you, too . . ."

"Agent Peyton, you sure do know how to turn a girl's head . . ."

Ten

"Bliss, you're amazing." Regan scanned the database on the computer screen. "I can't believe you did all this while I was in Florida."

"It was easy. Organizing and rearranging the files isn't so difficult, when that's all you have to do. Plus, Robert is away for a few weeks. He's one of three seminarians who were invited to attend a workshop in Maine, so while he's gone, I have a lot of time on my hands."

"Looks like you've been spending most of it here. I hope you're keeping close track of your hours."

"I will."

"Somehow that sounded like, you will in the future but you haven't over the past week?" Regan raised an eyebrow. "What time did you get here yesterday?"

"I think it was around eight thirty."

"And you left when?"

"Around eight thirty," Bliss admitted. "I would have stayed later, but I don't like going into our apartment building too late at night when Robert isn't there. It's not the best neighborhood in town."

"You could sleep over tonight, if you like. Not that I want you to make a habit of twelve-hour days, but if you're uncomfortable alone in your apartment, there's no reason why you couldn't stay here at the farm."

"I wouldn't have just slept in your house."

"I understand that, and I appreciate it. But now you know you can if you want to. I do have a guest room, if you ever need to stay."

"Thanks for the offer."

Regan pushed the chair away from the desk and stood. "Why don't you work in here at the desk today, since you've got your notes all ready to go, and I'll take the laptop out onto the porch."

"Oh." Bliss appeared apologetic. "I'm sorry, I didn't know you were going to want the computer today. I can find something else to do."

"Are you kidding?" Regan laughed. "No way am I going to stand in the way of your forward motion. I'm just as happy taking the laptop outside, where I can sit in the fresh air and try to collect my thoughts and organize my notes."

"You're going to start working on that book, the one they were talking about on the news the other night?" Bliss asked. "That poor young man, locked in prison, waiting to die . . . knowing he's innocent . . ."

"Well, we're hoping he's innocent," Regan said dryly. "The jury is still out on that. Figuratively speaking."

"It was good of you to go to Florida to offer him your support."

"I didn't go to Florida to offer him support, Bliss, regardless of what you might have heard on TV," Regan told her. "I went down there to talk to him, to talk to his lawyer, feel the situation out a little before I made up my mind."

"It had the same effect. The state won't be killing him."

"That fact has absolutely nothing to do with me. The judge made the only decision he could make," Regan said. "I take it you don't believe in capital punishment."

"No, I don't. I don't believe any man has the right to pass judgment on any other, send them to their death. It's nothing more than legalized murder, as far as I can see."

"Well, regardless of what either of us believes, the law of the land is such that certain punishments have been determined for certain crimes. The crime for which Lester Ray was convicted demanded the death penalty." Regan recalled the district attorney's description of what had been done to Carolyn Preston and inwardly shivered.

"Do you believe the death penalty is morally right?" Bliss persisted.

"I'm not sure what I believe sometimes. Some crimes are so horrific, you can't even imagine a punishment that would fit."

Before Bliss could respond, Regan added, "And if there's any doubt in your mind as to just how horrific, there are some photos in those files that make the case better than I ever could."

Regan gathered her notes and made sure the recorder was in her bag. She wanted to listen again to the interview with Lester Ray.

"I'll be outside on the side porch," Regan told Bliss, "in case you need me. Otherwise, I'll see you at lunch. Maybe we could eat out on the patio."

"That would be nice." Bliss waited until Regan moved from behind the desk before placing her files next to the computer. "Oh, Regan, I almost forgot. I took a phone message for you yesterday."

Bliss produced a pink message slip. "A Dorothy Brown called. She said she was returning your call and that you'd know who she is, and that you had her number."

"Oh, I have Dolly Brown's number all right," Regan said wryly. "I'll bet you lunch at the Country House that she doesn't pick up when I call her back."

"I can't afford to buy us lunch if you lose."

"Trust me, there's not a snowball's chance you'd lose." Regan grinned and leaned across the desk to grab the phone. She turned it around and dialed. The phone rang several times before the answering machine picked up.

"You've reached the home of Dolly Brown. Please leave a message . . ."

"There's a menu from the Country House in the top right drawer of the desk." Still grinning, Regan replaced the receiver. "You might want to start thinking about what you want to order . . ."

• • •

Lester Ray pulled into the parking lot and parked the car Roland had leased for him. He still had his old Florida driver's license—now expired but he had always been a good driver. He didn't figure on being pulled over unless he did something stupid. Which he was not about to do.

He looked in the rearview mirror and admired his haircut, also on Roland's credit card. And the new clothes? Ditto. What the hell, they were going to have money soon enough. With Regan Landry being such a big-time writer and all the money Roland figured they'd get from the state of Florida and the lab, they were sure enough going to strike it rich. Besides, he was thinking about having Booth sue that lawyer who'd tried his case, too. If he'd done a better job, there wouldn't have been a conviction. A good lawyer would have known the lab guy was lying, wouldn't he? Yeah, by the time this was over, Lester Ray figured he'd be set for life between all the lawsuits and the book.

He got out of the car and smoothed the creases from his new jeans and tucked in the white shirt. He'd been so happy to be able to wear something other than those damned orange T-shirts that marked you as a condemned man and those baggy blue pants. He'd stood in the dressing room of the store Roland had taken him to and just stared at himself. He hadn't seen himself dressed in anything but death-row garb in a couple of years.

He didn't look half bad.

Lester Ray went through the heavy wooden door and stood inside, relishing the feeling of being free and having a few bucks in his pocket.

Over the bar was a big-screen TV—bigger than anything he'd ever seen—and the picture was in color, no more of that black-and-white shit in the prison cell. There was smoke in the air, the scent of beer and aftershave, and just below it all, yes, the scents of women. Perfume. Hairspray. Sweet sweat.

Hallelujah.

He walked up to the bar, like any other customer would, and ordered a Bud. None of that light stuff for him. Uh-uh. The bartender set it before him on the bar, and he gazed at the foamy head with something akin to lust. When he'd teased himself enough, he lifted it to his lips and drank, closing his eyes in sheer bliss, savoring the moment. He drained the glass and gestured for another, then repositioned himself so that he could see the TV better.

Hot damn. Baseball. The Braves—the hometown team, here in Georgia—were playing the Phillies. He sat on the stool and munched peanuts from the basket the guy next to him silently offered to share. Life was suddenly so good, he could have cried.

Tonight, he was a free man, and he savored the thought. He was on his way to North Carolina and could take his sweet old time getting there. There was big money on the way—Roland told him the state had just paid someone two million dollars for having been wrongly locked up!—and he'd be able to spend it however he wanted.

He ordered a cheeseburger and fries from the cute little waitress, and took another sip from his beer. That would have been his choice for his last meal, had he had to choose. A big juicy cheeseburger and a pile of hot, salty, greasy fries. He forced a deep breath, reminded himself that he never had to think those thoughts again. From this night on, he'd be living the life. He could eat and drink what he wanted, come and go when he pleased, wear what he felt like wearing. And before too long, he'd have his name on the front of a book. Could life get better than this?

Apparently it could, he realized as a pretty blonde in a tank top and short skirt sat down next to him.

"Is this seat taken?" she asked.

"It is now." He waved the bartender over and told him, "Give the lady whatever she wants."

"The usual, Lorraine?" the bartender asked.

She nodded and turned to Lester Ray.

"Thanks." She smiled prettily. "I haven't seen you here before."

"Darren." He introduced himself, making a monumental effort not to fall into her cleavage. "Yeah, this is my first time here."

"Well, I hope it won't be your last." She was flirting with him, and he hadn't even had to make the first move! "I'm Lorraine."

It was an effort to keep his breathing under control.

"So, you a trucker, Darren? You own your own rig?" she asked.

"No, I'm a . . ." He smiled broadly. "I'm a writer."

Well, it was almost true, right?

"No way!" She gasped softly. "A real writer? A book writer?"

"A book writer, that's right."

"I never met a writer before." She cozied up to him. "Don't that beat all, a real writer, right here in Bucky's Place . . ."

Three hours, another order of burgers and fries and a half dozen beers later, Lorraine was leaning on Lester Ray's shoulder and telling a hilarious story about something that happened to her in the fourth grade, something about hiding under the bed because she was afraid of the bogeyman, getting stuck under there and scaring the shit out of her sister. Lester Ray couldn't have cared less, but he laughed at the appropriate places and tried to give the impression that she was the most fascinating woman he'd ever met.

It apparently worked.

"Darren, I think you should come on back to my apartment with me and check under the bed for that ole bogeyman." She leaned forward and gave him a tantalizing peek down her front. "But you have to promise not to get stuck . . ."

She fell into peals of laughter.

"Don't you worry none about that." He smiled and helped her off the stool. "You just grab your bag there from the back of the stool . . ."

He reached for her handbag and, looking up, met the eyes of a man who was watching from one of the tables along the wall. Lester Ray stared back, thinking he must be hallucinating. When the man smiled and waved, Lester Ray broke into a wide grin.

"Lorraine, honey, I want you to wait right here for a minute, I'll be right back." He eased her back into her seat and called to the bartender. "Give her one more beer."

He made his way through the crowd to the table and put out his hand.

"Cappy, I swear I thought I was seeing things. What the hell are you doing here?" Lester Ray grinned.

"Just stopped for a beer, Lester Ray." Erwin Capshaw grinned back.

"Now, what are the chances you and me would end up in the same bar in the same little town in Georgia?" Lester Ray pumped Cappy's hand. "You're looking real good, Cappy."

"That's what a few weeks of real food will do for you, eh?" Cappy gestured to the empty chair across from him. "Have a seat, Lester Ray. We'll talk about old times."

"I got a lady waiting for me, otherwise, I'd love to buy you a beer," Lester Ray told him. "But I don't want nothing to do with those old times. Uh-uh. Just bring on the new times. Bring on the new life. I ain't about to be looking back, bro."

"Well, things are looking real good for you right about now, aren't they?" Cappy nodded. "Got yourself a book deal and everything. I saw it on TV, that pretty writer from up north there someplace."

"Regan Landry, yeah, she's a real smart lady. She and I are gonna write a bestseller, Cappy, you wait and see." Lester Ray patted Capshaw on the back. "And I have you to thank for everything. Say, I'll bet Regan would want to talk to you. You've got the real story, don't you think? You were the one to go to the courts and make them look at this lab stuff."

He leaned over so as not to be overheard.

"And it must feel real sweet, knowing you did what you did, and you were able to walk away from it after all." Lester Ray shook his head and looked admiringly at Capshaw. "You played that system so good, I swear, you made us all proud down on death row."

"Hey, thanks, Lester Ray. I'm betting you make us all proud, in your own way, by and by." Capshaw's eyes went past Lester Ray to the woman who was approaching him from behind.

"Darren." The woman slid into Lester Ray's arms. "Can we go now?"

"Sure, Lorraine, honey, we're leaving right now. I was just saying hello to an old friend of mine." He smacked Capshaw lightly on the back. "This here's my friend Cappy." Lester Ray pointed to Lorraine and told Capshaw, "This here's Lorraine."

"Are you a writer like Darren?" Lorraine asked Capshaw, who tried valiantly to hide a smirk.

"You could say that." Capshaw nodded. "You could say that, at times, we shared the same muse."

"Well, you're not sharing me," Lorraine said indignantly. She poked Lester Ray in the chest. "You might share her, but I'm not that kind of girl."

"I know you're not, honey. Cappy was just talking some literary talk there." He winked at Capshaw and tried to keep from laughing. Even *he* knew what a muse was. "Good seeing you, Cappy. Maybe we'll run in to each other again sometime."

Lester Ray started from the table.

"Maybe so, *Darren.*" Capshaw smiled. "Might want to think about a little collaboration sometime, you and me . . ."

Looking over his shoulder, Lester Ray smiled back. "Well, now, I've always worked alone, but that might be something for us to talk about. It just might be . . ."

Lester Ray guided Lorraine with one hand in the middle of her back, and with the other he pushed open the door. He paused just outside and inhaled sharply, soaking in every bit of the night. He looked up into the stars, then down at Lorraine. He took her hand and led her to his car. She was older than he liked, but he was in no position to go after the young stuff. Someone could be watching him. He wouldn't put anything past that bastard DA. Better to stay clean now.

And how about running into Cappy like that? What were the odds they'd both end up in the same Georgia bar? He wished they'd had more time to talk, find out what kind of collaboration Cappy had in mind, but right at that moment, there was only one kind of work on his mind.

Hit by the horn-ray, as they used to say on that old TV show. He tried to think of the name of it; he'd watched the reruns over and over in prison—it was right on the tip of his tongue—but here was Lorraine, all but falling out of her tank, so who the fuck cared about some old TV show?

He opened the car door, and she slid against him as she got in.

Yeah. Whatever Cappy was thinking was just going to have to wait.

Eleven

On Thursday morning, Regan was still reading through the box of records she'd received from Lederer. She figured it would take her a while to read everything, making lists of who she wanted to speak with directly, but she hoped that, with luck, she'd have the groundwork for this section of the book pretty much completed by the end of the following week.

She'd just settled onto the sofa in the study when the phone rang. She glanced at the caller ID and yelled a triumphant "HA!" before picking up the receiver.

"Well, well. Dolly Brown. To what do I owe this return call?"

"Nice to hear from you, too, Regan," Dolly replied in much the same tone.

"How was Florida?" Regan asked to make sure Dolly knew she'd been keeping track.

"Warm and buggy when I was there," Dolly told her. "I was just about to ask you the same."

"The weather was perfect last week, thank you for asking. I even came back with a little bit of a tan."

"So you took a little time off from talking to that killer."

"Ah, so you saw the news . . ."

"Yes, we saw the news," Dolly snapped, "and we're wondering what the hell you're thinking."

"Who is we?"

"Me and Stella, who do you think? And don't avoid the question."

"What was the question, Dolly?"

"What the hell are you doing, running around with that killer and his sleazy lawyer?"

"Dolly, Lester Ray's conviction was dismissed, and he—"

"Yeah, yeah, I know all that," Dolly interrupted. "But anyone can tell just by looking at him that he's not a nice man. So just watch yourself, you hear? Be careful around him. Don't let him come to your house when you're working on that book, hear me?"

"I hear you, Dolly, but what's brought on this—"

"Yeah, we saw all that coverage." Dolly talked right past Regan. "We thought it was just terrible, the way that woman screamed at you like she did. As if you'd had anything to do with all that terrible business. I don't know who she thought she was."

"She was the sister of a murder victim, Dolly," Regan reminded her. "The man she believed to be responsible for her sister's murder had just walked out of court a free man. She had every right to be upset. It was a terrible thing that happened to Carolyn Preston. I don't blame her family for being so angry."

"She didn't have the right to take it out on you, is all I'm saying," Dolly countered.

"I was there, a convenient target when she came out of the courthouse."

"Still wasn't right."

"Dolly, I have to tell you, I'm touched," Regan said, amused but confused by Dolly's indignation. "But I have to wonder, what brought this on? You've spent the past eight months ignoring my phone calls. Why, all of a sudden, are you so concerned about me?"

"Stella was worried."

"Stella was worried," Regan repeated.

"That's what I said." A slightly defensive note crept into her voice. "So I told her I'd give you a call, make sure everything was all right. Let you know Stella was thinking about you."

"Why didn't Stella call me herself?"

"Well, you know Stella, she's a little on the shy side . . ."

"Oh, baloney. There's nothing shy about Stella. I spent an afternoon with her week before last, and we had a lovely time."

"Yes, so I heard."

Regan thought she detected a touch of something—could it really be envy?—in Dolly's voice.

"It would have been even better if you'd been there," Regan told her softly. "Maybe next time you could—"

"Yeah, maybe," Dolly replied brusquely.

Regan smiled to herself. Now there was the Dolly Brown she'd grown so fond of.

"I'll be back out there soon enough. Could we get together, Dolly? Could we sit down and talk, or go out to dinner?"

"If I'm free."

"You let me know when you're free, and that's when I'll come."

"In the meantime, you just be careful. Stella's becoming real fond of you, and it would upset her no end if something happened to you. Especially after she just lost Carl. So you just watch out for that Lester Ray guy. There's something not right about him."

"I hear you, Dolly. I'll be careful . . ."

"You see that you do." And with that, Dolly hung up.

Regan stared at the phone before returning the receiver to the base.

"What the hell brought that on?" she said aloud.

"What?" Bliss came into the study.

"Oh, just an odd phone conversation." Regan shook her head as if to clear it. "How are you doing this morning?"

"I'm doing great." Bliss smiled happily. "Robert came back last night, so I wasn't as uneasy, and I got a better night's sleep."

"I'm glad to hear it. I'm sure you were happy to have him home."

"I am, but he did such a good job leading the workshop, they asked him to come back. But that won't be for a few weeks, so all is well for now."

"Don't forget what I told you about staying here."

"I might take you up on that when he goes away next time. There are kids in the next apartment who party a lot, and have all kinds of people hanging around at night. It makes me nervous when I'm alone and have to come into a dark apartment," Bliss admitted.

"Then you just plan on staying here. Whether I'm here or not. You have a key."

"Thanks, Regan."

"Don't mention it." Regan smiled. "Now, how are you doing with the files from the storage room?"

"I'm doing fine. I've pulled out everything that contains material that should have been in files you have set up in here." She pointed to the filing cabinets. "I'm discovering a lot of random items, though. I'm thinking of maybe setting up a miscellaneous drawer in the big filing cabinet here, and we'll just file them in alpha order. I don't know what else to do with them."

"Oh, maybe I should take a look. There are probably things that we can get rid of."

Bliss frowned. "I hate to toss things out before we get through all the files. What if the one thing you throw out turns out to be important to something you find later? The way your father kept things, there's no telling what might turn out to be important."

"You're right, of course. Until we've gone through all of the boxes, we don't really know what is superfluous and what might turn out to be the key."

"Your father must have been quite the character," Bliss said. "He saved some of the oddest things."

She sat on the edge of an ottoman and picked up a stack of thin files. She held them, saying, "I started making separate files before I realized there were so many oddballs. If you'd like, I can put them all in one big file, maybe one of the ones that are closed on the sides so that the small bits of paper don't fall out."

"Small bits of paper?" Regan frowned.

"Scraps, in some cases. Here, see." Bliss held up a few small pieces of paper. "There's a phone number on this one, an address on this one, but no name on either. And here, here's a file of obituaries. Nothing to indicate why any of these people may have been important, there's just the obit."

"That was my dad." Regan sighed and held her hand out for the files. "There's always the chance that some of these might ring a bell with me, and we'll be able to file them with a master file. I'll take a quick look through later, after lunch."

But Regan became totally absorbed in Lester Ray's police file and forgot about lunch. It was late in the afternoon when Bliss poked her head in to let her know that Robert was on his way to pick her up.

"We're going out for dinner, and we're going to see a movie," Bliss told her excitedly. "Just like a date. We haven't had a night out in . . . oh, I can't remember the last time."

Tires crunching on the drive announced Robert's arrival, and Bliss peered out the window.

"Want to meet him?" she asked Regan.

"Of course. Introduce me to this wonderful man."

Regan followed Bliss out the door and into the drive, where Robert got out of the old sedan to shake Regan's hand and tell her how happy he was that Bliss had found a job she enjoyed so much. He was tall and thin and wore dark glasses and an earnest expression. There was a gentleness about him that Regan warmed to immediately.

"I'm the happy one," Regan assured him. "Bliss is making order out of the chaos that my dad left behind. I'm giddy at the thought of being able to actually find things in his office. I don't know what I'd do without her. I'm thinking about having a nursery built on to the back of the house so that she can work after the baby's born."

Bliss blushed, and Robert held the car door for her. He got in the driver's side, and both waved as they drove off for their date, their faces shining.

Regan looked after them until the old car disappeared at the end of the long drive, an unexpected hot shot of something that felt a lot like envy piercing her insides.

How lucky Bliss was to have that part of her life in order, Regan reflected. Married to a man she adored who clearly adored her in return, carrying their first child. What a special time that must be. Special and lovely.

She wondered wistfully if there'd be such a time for her someday.

She and Mitch never spoke of the future, or where their relationship was heading, though she wasn't sure why. Neither had ever
brought it up. It was only within the past few months that they'd put
a name for the feelings they had for each other. She been startled
when she realized how much she loved him, surprised at the depth of
her feelings, and had been greatly relieved to discover he felt the same
way. She missed him when he was away, delighted in his company
when they were together, didn't want to think about a time when he
wasn't in her life, but was almost afraid to think about what might
come next. She was thirty-six years old and had lived independently
for years. She'd worked with her father but she'd been a guest lec-
turer and taught at the university level as well. She'd traveled exten-
sively and owned her own home in Maryland. She had a black belt in
tae kwon do and had competed in triathlons. She'd done her own
thing, set her own agenda, accomplished things that had been important to her all of her life.

She walked back into the house and closed the door, suddenly
feeling very lonely. She wondered if Mitch was still in Florida, and if
so, if he was lonely, too.

She went into the study and sat down at her father's desk and
reached for the phone at the same time it began to ring. She glanced
at the ID before she picked up.

"I was just going to call you," she said. "I was just thinking
about you."

"Something good, I hope."

"I was thinking how great it would be if you were finished up in
Florida and could meet me in Maryland this weekend."

"There's nothing I'd love better, but I'm afraid I'm going to be in
Georgia for at least another day or so."

"What's in Georgia?"

"A dead woman." He hesitated before adding, "One whose
corpse bears a very striking resemblance to Carolyn Preston's."

"What?" The one word was all a shocked Regan could manage.

"Everything is exactly the same, right down to the smile painted
in blood and the flowers in her hands."

"You're thinking Lester Ray . . . ?"

"Oh, I'm thinking Lester Ray, all right." Regan could hear the frustration and anger in his voice. "We're all thinking Lester Ray. Bastard."

"Maybe it's not him, maybe it's someone else. A copy cat." Regan bit her bottom lip. "This must have been recent. I haven't seen this on the news."

"The body was found yesterday morning, but we were just brought into it this morning. We're still trying to trace the victim's steps over the past week. The story hasn't been released to the media; we're going to try to keep it quiet, not give this any press right away. We're thinking we'll have a better shot of bringing Lester Ray in if he thinks no one's found her, and therefore, no one's looking for him."

"You're probably right. If Lester Ray killed this woman, and if he thinks he's a suspect, he's likely to disappear." Her legs shaking, she sat on the corner of the desk.

"Obviously, we can't take a chance of that. We need to have him come to us."

"And that's where I come in, right?"

"You're getting very good at this, you know?" He sighed deeply. "As much as I'd like you to stay as far from this guy as possible, I do recognize that you are one of the few people who can draw him out. He likes you, he trusts you, and he believes you are going to make him even more famous than he already is."

"So I call him, I ask him to meet me to go over the book, he shows up, you nab him."

"That it would only go that smoothly," Mitch muttered. "Nothing ever does. But yeah, that's the idea. We're going to want to make him come to you, but first we need to know where he is. You still have his cell phone number?"

"Sure. I guess you contacted Booth already? To see if he's heard from Lester Ray?"

"Funny thing about Roland Booth. He seems to have disappeared."

"What do you mean, disappeared?" Regan frowned.

"I mean, no one has seen him since Saturday when he dropped some files at his new office."

"Hey, he's just coming off a big case. Maybe he went off to relax. He's probably sunning himself on a beach someplace." She thought it over for a minute. "I'll bet he's working on those lawsuits he can't wait to file. He's planning on a big-time score, you know."

"If he is, he didn't bother to tell anyone he was going." Mitch paused, then asked, "Do you think there's a chance he's with Lester Ray?"

"I think Lester Ray couldn't wait to ditch his lawyer and take off on his own."

"I guess now we know why."

"Mitch, if it turns out that Lester Ray really killed this woman in Georgia, I will never forgive myself for getting involved in this."

"You had no way of knowing . . ."

"If he did this, I'm going to be questioning my decision for the rest of my life. Maybe I should have considered that he might be guilty, instead of focusing on the conviction and Potts's testimony."

"But that's the story, babe. That was the big deal. Someone lied under oath and as a result, a man was convicted of murder and sentenced to death. Telling the story is still important, regardless of whether or not Lester Ray is guilty."

"But if he's guilty, then the conviction was right on."

"Not if the system was corrupted. You know that."

"But at least he was behind bars," Regan countered, "where he couldn't hurt anyone."

"If Lester Ray was guilty of killing Carolyn Preston, maybe we'll find a way to prove that eventually. In the meantime, we have another young woman dead, and if Lester Ray is responsible, I promise you, we will get a conviction without having to resort to lies on the witness stand."

"You're right," she said quietly. "Let's focus on this latest victim."

"That's exactly what we need to do. If Booth gets in touch with you, let me know."

"Of course. And in the meantime, I'll call Lester Ray and find out where he is, what he's doing, when he wants to get together. I'll call you right back."

"Don't let him know you know about the woman in Georgia, and don't let him know you're home alone, Regan. Just find out where he is and where he's going, see if you can arrange to meet."

"Don't worry about me. We know he's got a beach in his sights, not New Jersey farmland."

"Even so . . ."

"Mitch, what if I can't get in touch with him?"

"Then we release the story and put out an APB and we hunt him down."

"I'll call you right back." She hung up and looked for her wallet and the card Roland Booth had given her the week before.

She dialed Lester Ray's cell phone.

The number rang and rang, then went to voice mail.

"Hey, Lester Ray, it's Regan Landry. Please give me a call so that we can set up a time to get together to talk about our book. I had a long chat with my editor today, and they'd really like the book to focus more on you, and they'd like to publish it as soon as possible, to cash in on all the good publicity you've gotten. So here's my number, I'll look forward to hearing from you and getting together."

She repeated her cell phone number twice, then hung up, debating how long to wait for a return call before she called Mitch back. She tucked the phone into her pants pocket, wondering where Lester Ray was, and what he was doing.

Was he, at that very moment, stalking another young girl?

She glanced at her watch. It was ten fifteen. How long was long enough to wait? Fifteen minutes, she decided. Fifteen minutes before she'd call Mitch, and after that, Lester Ray would be on his own against the FBI.

Twelve

Lester Ray pulled off the interstate, running low on gas, but wanting one of those gas stations that had a little market attached to it so he could get a snack. It was early evening, and he was hungry and tired and had no idea how much farther north he'd have to drive before he found the Outer Banks. He drove cautiously, as he had since he left Florida, trying to avoid calling attention to himself. While he liked the idea of being a bit of a celebrity, he was hoping to keep his head down long enough to live it up just a little.

He found a station with an A-Plus Mart and stopped at the first available pump. After filling up the tank, he went inside to pay the cashier. He looked around casually, smiled at a pleasant-looking woman in her fifties who was looking over the premade sandwiches in the refrigerated case.

See, he said to himself, the smile still on his face, *I can be just like everyone else. I could be anyone, any guy on his way home from work. Normal. I could just be any normal guy with a family and a job.*

A man in a business suit came in and bought a newspaper. Lester Ray watched him, studied his nonchalance, and once the man left, he mimicked it. Strolled over to pick up the paper, glancing at the front page, above and below the fold, just like that man had done.

See, I can be just like anyone . . .

He searched the cold case for a few things to eat, then paid for his selections and the gas, and left with the newspaper under his arm. On his way back to the interstate, he passed a small motel that had a restaurant attached and a bar directly across the street.

Why not, he thought. No need to be driving till the sun goes down. No reason why he couldn't take his time getting where he was going. No reason at all.

He parked in front of the motel office and went in to book a room.

"One night?" the clerk asked.

"Yeah. Unless I find something local that makes me want to stick around."

"That'd be up to you." The man behind the desk was in his mid-forties and apparently humorless.

"How's that bar across there, Casey's?" Lester Ray handed over the credit card.

"Okay, as bars go." The man shrugged.

"Food any good?"

"Good as any." He handed Lester Ray a key. "Have a pleasant stay."

"Thanks." Lester Ray decided the desk clerk wasn't worth his making any further effort at conversation, so he took the key and went through the lobby in search of his room.

After a shower and a change of clothes, he headed toward Casey's. He wanted a good meal and a warm companion, in that order. Funny, he thought as he walked across the road, how quickly you can become accustomed to living like a human being again. It had taken him no time at all to get used to three good meals every day and, thanks to Lorraine, good sex. She had been a regular all-night girl. Lester Ray would never forget her.

He was whistling when he walked into Casey's, and walked up to the bar with a smile on his face. He ordered his dinner right there at the bar, and put away his fried chicken and French fries in short order. He watched the baseball game, pleased with himself for having read the sports page so he recognized the names of some of the players. He watched the other bar patrons, studying the way they casually tossed their money onto the bar and occasionally checked their cell phones for messages. He cheered when they cheered and groaned when they groaned. He got into a conversation with a man two stools down who told him the best way to get to the Outer Banks.

"You can make it from here in about six hours," he'd told Lester Ray, "unless you're going up the north end of the islands. That'll take longer, since you can't drive a car some places on the southern end."

"How do you get there, then?" Lester Ray asked. "Those places where you can't drive a car?"

"Ferry. Good fishing down around Hatteras, Buxton, if you like to fish."

Lester Ray had never been fishing.

"I want a beach, and some nice place to stay, not too crowded," Lester Ray told him. "I just want to relax."

"Oh, you're looking for a real vacation. Tell you what I'd do, then." The man motioned for the bartender to serve him and Lester Ray each another beer. "I'd go up the north end, all the way up to Corolla. Sit on the beach and maybe see them wild horses."

"They got wild horses up there?" Lester Ray put down his beer.

"Yeah. Couple hundred. They go right up on the beach. It's really something to see."

The man got off his stool and walked over to Lester Ray. "Got a piece of paper handy, I'll give you some directions."

Lester Ray searched his pockets, found neither pen nor paper. The bartender, who'd been listening, handed him one of each.

"You're going to want to take the interstate. Now, the roads up along the coast are real pretty, but it'll take you twice as long to get there, and you're still going to have to go north far enough so's you can drive onto the islands. Taking I-95 makes more sense to me, but I guess it depends on how much of a hurry you are in to get there," the man told him in his soft drawl as he wrote out the directions. When he was finished, he handed over the paper to Lester Ray. "Lots of pretty towns between here and there, though, once you get off the highway and start heading east for the coast."

"Thanks, man." Lester Ray pocketed the directions. "That's real nice of you. Next beer's on me, pal . . ."

Lester Ray drank with his new friend until the man's son showed up to drive him home.

"Nice fella," Lester Ray said to the bartender after the man left.

"Oh, yeah, Sherman's all right." The bartender nodded.

Feeling at home and comfortable, Lester Ray leaned on the bar and watched the game, feeling more content than he'd imagined possible. There was only one thing missing from the picture, he told himself. All he needed to make his night complete was the love of a good woman.

Five minutes later, the door opened, and three young ladies spilled in.

Hallelujah. Lester Ray smiled at them as they approached the bar.

"Girls, you behaving yourselves tonight?" the bartender asked.

"Julie and me are." The girl in the middle laughed. "But Pam is just on a regular old tear tonight. I swear, she has just been up to no good all night long."

"Then Pam should come sit next to me." Lester Ray boldly patted the red leather bar stool next to his.

Pam looked Lester Ray over, head to toe, then smiled prettily.

"I think I just might do that." She came closer and Lester Ray could see that she was young, maybe twenty-two or twenty-three. She wore a denim skirt that hit the upper part of her thigh and a red halter top. Her dark blond hair was piled high upon her head, and her silver earrings hung to her shoulders. "I don't remember seein' you here before. What's your name?"

"Darren," Lester Ray told her. "My name is Darren."

"Well, Darren, what brings you to Morrisey, North Carolina, on a Thursday night?"

"On my way to the Outer Banks for a little fun in the sun."

"Oooh, I love the Outer Banks. We used to go every summer, when I was a little girl." She pouted. "I haven't been in two summers."

"Well, maybe you can tell me about your favorite spots," Lester said as he put another twenty on the bar and gestured for the bartender's attention. "You know, bars, restaurants, that sort of thing."

"Sure. What part of the Banks you going to?"

"Corolla." He remembered what his buddy, Sherman, had told him.

"Oooh, wild horse country," Pam cooed.

"That's what they tell me." He reached in his pocket and pulled out his cell phone, pretending to check for calls the way he'd seen some of the other men do. To his surprise, he had a message waiting for him.

He stared at the phone, trying to figure out how to retrieve it.

"Something wrong, Darren?" Pam asked.

"Oh, this here's a brand new phone and I'm trying to remember how I get the messages off it." He frowned.

"Give it here, sugar, let me take a look." She took it from his hands. "This one is just like mine. Here, all you do is this . . ."

She went through the steps for him, and handed him the phone.

"What do I do now?" he asked.

"Now you just listen."

He listened once, then a second time to write down the number.

"Sorry, Pam, I'm gonna have to return this call. I'll be right back."

"That the wife calling to check up on you?"

"Wife? Oh, no, no wife." He laughed. "It's my . . . uh, my collaborator."

"Your what?"

"My collaborator. On a book I'm working on." What the hell, it had worked on Lorraine, hadn't it?

"You're a writer?"

"Uh-huh. Now, I'll just be a minute, so . . ."

"For real? You write books?"

"Uh, yeah. You just wait right here . . ." Lester Ray patted her bare back and walked outside to make his call.

"Did you hear that, girls?" Pam leaned down the bar as he walked away. "Darren here's a writer! Is this my lucky night or what?"

• • •

"Regan, hey, it's Les . . . uh, Darren. I got your call."

She had picked up the phone on the first ring.

"Thanks for calling me back. Listen, I was wondering when we could get together to talk about the book. I've had some really good ideas over the past few days, and wanted to run them past you before I started working. Where are you?"

"I'm headed for the Outer Banks, like I told you."

"Well, tell me where you are, and I'll meet you there tomorrow."

He hesitated. Through the window, he could see Pam at the bar, chatting with her girlfriends. If he played his cards right, he'd have that red halter top on the floor of his motel room before last call. If Pam was as good as she looked, he might even spend another night there in Morrissey. The last thing he wanted was Regan Landry leaning over his shoulder.

"Well, now, that's not going to be convenient for me, Regan."

"What do you mean?"

"I mean, tomorrow is no good. How 'bout we plan on maybe sometime next week, when I get to Corolla?"

"Corolla? Is that where you're planning on staying?"

"Yeah." He watched Pam slide off her bar stool and start to dance with one of her friends.

"Where? Do you have a room booked yet?"

"Why do you want to know?" Damn, that girl had some moves . . .

"I'm thinking it would be good if we stayed in the same place, make it easier to work together," Regan was saying.

"Oh, yeah. Right. But I don't know where I'm going to stay yet."

"But you think you won't get there until next week?"

"Maybe tomorrow or the day after." His mouth was getting dry, watching Pam gyrate to the music from the jukebox. "Why all the questions?"

"I just wanted to know when I should plan on driving down there. I'm excited about the book, and I can't wait to start working on it."

"You can drive down whenever you want. Call me when you get

there. Or I'll call you, when I get there." Pam was shaking her booty in his direction. "Right now, I gotta go."

He hung up the phone and returned it to his pants pocket. The book he would work on with Regan might make him rich and famous, but right now, Pam was hot. He walked back into the bar with a smile on his face. Tonight had all the makings of one very fine night.

Thirteen

"I'm really sorry," Regan told Mitch when she called back. "I tried to get him to tell me where he was, but he wouldn't. I was going to ask him if he knew where Booth was, but he cut the conversation short, like he was distracted. Mitch, I'm sorry."

"Don't be sorry. You did just fine. You got us information we didn't have before you made the call," he reassured her. "I'm having the call to your cell phone traced, so we may be able to home in on his location. We know he's still heading north, that he's within a day's driving distance of the Outer Banks, and we know he's headed to Corolla."

"Maybe if you knew what he was driving . . ." She tapped her fingers on the kitchen table. "How do you suppose he got the car? You don't suppose he borrowed one from Booth?"

"Booth's car is in his carport."

"So wherever he went, he went by train or plane."

"Or someone picked him up," Mitch added.

"Maybe Lester Ray has a rental car." She frowned. "How could he afford to rent a car?"

"Booth may have done that for him. We're checking on that."

"I'd asked Lester Ray if he'd called ahead someplace to reserve a room for himself in Corolla, thinking he'd have had to use a credit card, but he hadn't made arrangements yet. I thought if we knew he had a card . . ." She paused. "But he couldn't have gotten a card in his own name. He must be using one of Booth's."

"Right. We already have someone tracking down Booth's credit cards."

"Then you can see if he rented a car . . ." she thought aloud.

"Yeah, it would help a lot if we knew what he was driving," Mitch agreed. "In the meantime, we're trying to figure out where Lorraine Mason would have met Lester Ray. Her roommate said she frequented several bars in the area. We're checking those to see if anyone recognizes Lester Ray from his picture."

"When do you figure you'll get to Corolla?" she asked.

"I'm thinking Saturday, at the latest."

"I'll go online and see if I can find a hotel with a vacancy. It might be tight, this being June and the beginning of the tourist season. What do you think, three nights?"

"Uh, no, Regan. I don't want you anywhere near this guy."

"Face it, Mitch. He'll come out of the woodwork to meet with me. But he's going to be leery of anyone else. Especially if he killed that woman in Georgia. He's going to be looking over his shoulder." She let her words sink in. "Besides, you'll be there, you can be my bodyguard."

When he failed to respond, Regan said, "Mitch? You there?"

"I'm here."

"You know I'm right."

"Knowing it and liking it are two different things."

"I'll let you know where we'll be staying. I'd like to get there before he does, so maybe I'll try to leave tomorrow, Saturday morning at the latest. I'd like a little time to acclimate myself to the area."

"You'll keep in touch with me the whole time, and you will not let him know where you are, and you will not arrange to meet him until I am in your back pocket."

"Of course. He won't even think it's strange if you're with me, since he's already met you. I'm going to hang up now and see what kind of accommodations are still available for the weekend. I'll call you as soon as I find something."

"Regan . . ."

"What?" She'd been just about to hang up.

"See if you can find something with a Jacuzzi," he said, and she could hear the weariness in his voice. "For two."

Two nights later, Regan stood on the covered porch that ran past the room she'd rented and watched the sun set over the Currituck Sound. The night air was gentle and sweet, and across the water a pair of swans ushered their babies into the small cove where they'd made their nest.

The inn she found online had everything she'd looked for and more. Gorgeous water views, a sitting room where she and Mitch could work, a bedroom with a gas fireplace, and a whirlpool for two in a luxuriously appointed bathroom. She sighed. Everything was perfect. It was all here.

The only thing missing was Mitch.

Oh, well, she sighed, hopefully the only thing he'll miss tonight will be the sunset.

She dialed his cell and was disappointed when he failed to pick up. Not a good sign, she knew. It usually meant he was involved in something important. She left a brief message.

"Hi. Just wondering how close you are. The sunset is spectacular. They rent kayaks here, we can paddle all around the little estuaries here and see the wildlife. Once we've wrapped up Lester Ray, anyway. Call me soon."

Her rumbling stomach reminded her that she hadn't eaten since early afternoon, and it was now past eight. She changed her flip flops for leather flats, brushed her hair and pulled it into a ponytail, exchanged her tank top for a short-sleeved cardigan and her shorts for a short skirt. She buttoned up the sweater, tucked her phone into her bag, and left the room for the restaurant she'd noticed when she'd arrived an hour ago. Mitch could always join her, but in the meantime, she was starving. Chances are, he'd eaten by now anyway.

She was shown to a small table overlooking the water and ordered a glass of wine, the seafood of the day, and a large salad. Sipping her wine, she relaxed for the first time since she'd gotten the call from Mitch. She still didn't know if she believed that Lester Ray was a killer. A sleazy guy, yeah, sure, no debate there. An opportunistic ass, yes, that too. But a killer? She didn't know. She hoped he was just an ass. The thought that she could have in any way assisted a killer to go free was more than she could bear.

She ordered a second glass of wine when her fish arrived, and was halfway through her meal when her phone rang.

"Hey, where are you?" she asked softly so as not to disturb the couple at the next table.

"I'm in a place called Morrisey, a little town south of Greenville, North Carolina."

"Think you'll make it here tonight?"

"Not a chance." Mitch exhaled a long tired breath. "Regan, they've found another body. Same as the last one."

"Oh, my God, no." The couple at the next table turned to her in alarm. She mouthed an apology for having disturbed them as she grabbed her bag and headed for the French doors that led to the porch that ran along the entire length of the building, including the wing in which Regan's room was located.

Mitch continued talking in the detached voice that took over whenever he was discussing a particularly ugly crime.

"Local girl, didn't make it home last night, which her roommates said wasn't especially unusual. She's been known to stay out all night, so they didn't think anything of it."

"Until . . . ?" Regan prompted him to continue.

"Until her body was found on a path down near the river this morning by a jogger who tripped over her, literally. He called the sheriff's department, one of the deputies recognized the girl as a roommate of his ex-girlfriend. He called the ex to come down to identify the body."

"Oh, God, that poor girl. That must have been horrible for her."

"Yeah, well, I guess the roommate's counting her blessings right about now."

"What do you mean?" She leaned back against the porch rail.

"Seems last night, all three of the roommates—our vic, Pam Hobbs, included—were at Casey's, a bar not too far off the highway. There was a guy in there—nice looking, they said, well dressed—said the vic was all over this guy, left with him." He cleared his throat. "The roommates said that a little after ten, Pam told them the guy had gone outside to return a phone call from someone he identified as his 'collaborator.' "

"Collaborator?" Regan frowned.

"Yes. He told Pam he was working on a book with this collaborator."

She fell silent, dread creeping through her. Finally, she said, "Lester Ray returned my call around ten thirty."

"I know. The call from Lester Ray to your phone originated from Morrisey."

He let that sink in.

"That son of a bitch." She fought to keep her voice under control. She walked off the porch and along the path that led to the dock. "He called me, then killed a girl . . . ?"

"Looks that way. The roommates said they stayed at the bar till one, left Pam with the guy. Want to take a wild guess what the guy's name was?"

"Darren," she said curtly. "When he called me, he identified himself as Darren."

"Well, we've got him this time. I'm on my way to the sheriff's office right now. I want to put Lester Ray's picture into a photo lineup. While there's no doubt in my mind that he's the guy, I want to cross the t's and dot the i's. There will be no screwups this time." His voice lowered. "Sorry, babe. I was hoping to get there by midnight."

"I'll still be here tomorrow. And the next day."

"How's the hotel?" he asked, and she knew it was more to force a sense of normalcy into the conversation than any concern on his part over the room. Mitch wasn't overly fussy about where he stayed.

"Perfect. We have a large sitting room we can use as an office, a king-size bed, a fireplace in the room. A porch that overlooks the sound. Fine dining in the restaurant . . ."

"Stop, you're killing me," he groaned.

"I'll see how long I can extend the stay. We need at least an overnight or two together here. It's one of the prettiest places I've ever been." She glanced at the far end of the dock, her eyes following the string of tiny white lights that stretched from the sand to several hundreds of feet into the sound. "I watched a pair of swans with their babies tonight right across from our room. Everything is so peaceful here."

"I'll try to wrap this up here as soon as I can so that I can join you. In the meantime, the sheriff wants to put out an APB for Lester Ray. I really hoped we could track him down without having to resort to that."

"Because it'll be easier to bring him in, if he comes to you, rather than for you to have to chase him."

"Right."

"Maybe I can still get him to come to us, Mitch. See if you can buy another day."

"I'll speak to the sheriff, but you have to understand that we're going to have to take into consideration that the longer he stays on the loose, the greater the chance he'll go after someone else."

"If he disappears completely, it'll take you longer to find him, and who knows how many women he could kill between now and the time someone spots him."

"I'm not disagreeing. I'm just telling you, there's going to be a jurisdictional cluster-fuck between the local sheriff, the state police, and the feds. I don't know that I'll be able to talk them out of releasing Lester Ray's picture to the media. I'd like at least forty-eight hours to try to locate him."

"Do the best you can. Get your boss to pull some strings at a higher level. In the meantime, I'll put another call in to Lester Ray and see if I can get him to tell me where he is. He was really vague when I spoke with him on Thursday night. Now I know why."

"You're not going to let him know you're already in Corolla, though, right?"

"Right. I'll give you a call, after I hear from him." She amended that to, "If I hear from him."

"Okay." Mitch paused, then said, "I'm really sorry that I have to make this detour. I really thought I'd be there by now."

"I'll save a place for you in the Jacuzzi."

She hung up and searched for Lester Ray's number on the call log, then hit redial. The number rang and rang. Finally, he answered.

"Hello?" he said sleepily.

"Lester Ray, it's Regan."

"Huh?" He coughed quietly. "Oh. Regan."

"Did I wake you?"

"Yeah."

"Oh, sorry. I figured you'd still be up and out, this being Saturday night."

"I drove a lot today and yesterday, and I was up late the night before."

No kidding. Bastard.

"What did you want?"

"I was wondering if you've spoken with Roland."

"Roland?"

"Roland Booth. Your attorney."

"I know who you meant. No, I haven't talked to him. Was I supposed to?"

"I know he was going to be speaking with the people in New York. About your contract for the book."

"Like how much they're going to pay me?"

"Among other things."

"I didn't hear from him," Lester Ray said, awake now. "Maybe I should give him a call."

"Will you let me know if you catch up with him?"

"Sure."

"Why don't you call me back, either way."

"Okay."

"By the way, when do you figure you'll get to Corolla?" she asked casually. "That's where you said you wanted to meet up, right?"

"I'm there." He yawned into the phone.

"You're in Corolla?"

"Yeah. Got here this afternoon."

"Tell me where you are. We can get together."

"Can't tonight. I got plans. I'll call you back, after I talk to Roland."

"Lester Ray . . ."

He'd already hung up.

She quickly dialed Mitch.

"He's here," she told him when he picked up, "here in Corolla. But I couldn't get him to tell me where."

"Terrific. You're amazing. I'll get them to hold off on releasing the photo." Mitch sounded pumped. "You didn't give him any hint of where you're staying, did you?"

"I didn't even tell him I was on the island. For all he knows, I'm still in New Jersey."

"Good. Let's keep it that way." He paused, then added, "I love you."

"I love you, too, Mitch."

"I'll see you soon."

"Good." She hung up and slipped the phone into her pocket.

She walked to the end of the dock, smiling a greeting to the other inn patrons as she passed them, her mind on far less pleasant subjects than the beauty of the evening. Still, it was a lovely spot, serene and unspoiled, with lots of native trees and shrubs left on their own. She wished she could enjoy it all for what it was.

Finding out that Lester Ray was already here, in Corolla, had jarred her more than she'd admitted to Mitch. She walked back to the inn along a path that was dark and lined with azaleas on either side.

What, am I nuts? she asked herself. *For all I know, Lester Ray could be staying here. He could be crouched behind one of those shrubs, right at this minute, just waiting for me to do something dumb, like walk around the grounds alone in the dark.*

"It's not all that dark," she said under her breath. "And there are lights up there on the porch. Besides, I'm probably the only woman on the island who's safe. He needs me for that damned book."

Still, she took note of everyone she passed, and though she wouldn't have admitted it, she breathed easier after she walked back through the double doors and into the dining room where the young man who'd waited on her hovered around her table.

"Oh." He appeared relieved to see her. "We weren't certain if you were coming back."

"Sorry." She smiled a tight smile.

"Is everything all right?"

"Yes. Fine. I just had to take a call, and the reception was poor."

"Oh? It's usually pretty good here."

"Must be my phone."

He held her chair out for her, and she hesitated.

"Actually," she said, "I think I'm finished. If you'd just bring me the check . . ."

"Was the fish not to your liking?" He frowned at her half-eaten meal.

"It was fine. Delicious. I guess I just don't have much of an appetite tonight."

"If you're sure there's nothing wrong with the meal . . ."

"Positive."

"Could I send dessert and coffee to your room?"

She started to decline, then smiled. "You know, I'd love that. I already looked at the dessert selections, and I'd be happy with any one of them. Surprise me. And make the coffee decaf."

"You got it." He smiled back and handed her the check.

She added on a nice tip for his thoughtfulness and headed back to her room, thinking it might not be a bad idea to take all her meals in the room, at least until Mitch arrived. She kicked off her shoes and opened the drapes and leaned on the windowsill, watching the lights from a boat move silently far out on the sound.

Somewhere in this peaceful place, there was a killer. Somehow, it just didn't seem right that such a creature should be moving among the happy couples, the families with their children, who came here to relax and enjoy each other.

She checked her watch for the time. It had been almost a half hour since she'd spoken with Lester Ray, plenty of time for him to have called Booth and called Regan back. She redialed his number and listened as his phone rang and rang. When the prompt came on to leave a message, she hung up.

What had Lester Ray said, he couldn't talk about the book tonight because he had plans? She shivered, praying that his plans didn't include another unsuspecting young woman.

Fourteen

Mitch knocked on the medical examiner's door and waited to be admitted. This was, he knew, a courtesy on his part. He could have walked in and announced himself, but he didn't like to start off a new case by pushing his federal credentials down anyone's throat.

To his mind, Sheriff Herbert Dempsey was just asking for a little federal push and shove. Mitch had a feeling that before the weekend was over, Dempsey would get at least one, and from someone much higher up than Mitch.

The ME's assistant came to the door, and admitted Mitch as soon as he held up his ID.

"We're still working on her," the assistant told him. "Come on in."

"Who is it, Mary?" the ME asked without looking up from her work.

"Special Agent Mitchell Peyton," Mitch told her.

She glanced up and looked behind Mitch.

"The sheriff didn't come with you?" she asked.

"Was he supposed to?"

She grinned. "He never has in the past, but I was wondering if maybe he wouldn't want it to look like the FBI was showing him up."

She held up her gloved hands.

"Sorry, can't shake. I'm Virginia Moffitt."

"Nice to meet you, Doctor Moffitt." He walked closer, close

enough to see that the late Pamela Hobbs had had her throat slashed from ear to ear.

"The mouth that's painted on." He pointed to the victim's face, where a clownlike mouth grinned at them ghoulishly.

"Blood. Hers, I'm thinking. The lab reports should be back in before the end of the day, but I'd bet the Porsche it's hers." Dr. Moffitt's focus was back on her work.

"You have a Porsche you're willing to bet?" he asked.

"Vintage 911, 1989." She smiled without looking up. "And since my daddy always told me not to bet anything I can't afford to lose, I only bet on sure things."

"So what can you tell me about our young lady?" Mitch asked.

"She's in her early twenties, well developed, well nourished, but doesn't appear to have worked out much the way so many young girls do today. She's soft, poor muscle tone. Could have used some dental work, but it's too late to worry about that. Stomach contents, mostly alcohol. BAL was two point one, so she'd been partying with someone until shortly before her death."

"Drugs?"

"Drug screen has been run but like I said, the results on the blood work won't be in until later today."

"Official cause of death?"

"Exsanguination from a slash wound to the throat," she said without expression.

"Any other wounds?"

"None. That one was enough to do the job."

"Any sign of sexual assault?"

"There's evidence she had intercourse before she died, but no signs of a struggle." The doctor looked at Mitch over the girl's body. "I'd say she knew her killer well enough to have sex with him."

"But not well enough to know he was a killer."

"Right. There's no sign that she struggled, though there is some sign that she may have been suffocated."

"Strangled?"

"No, there's no visible sign that she'd been strangled, no bruising to her neck, the hyoid bone is intact. But there are signs of petechial rash around the eyes, so she'd had her oxygen cut off at some point. Asphyxiation was not the cause of death, but she may have been rendered unconscious."

"Put her out before you slash her throat?" Mitch rubbed his chin. "Usually, the slasher wants his vic to watch, wants her to know what's coming."

"Hey, I don't pretend to understand what these guys think. I'm only telling you what I see."

"When you're finished, I want to show you some photos of another crime scene."

The doctor looked up. "Show me now." She pointed to the torso. "I haven't gone inside yet, so I'm going to be a while."

Mitch opened his briefcase and took out a file.

"You're going to have to hold them up," she said, "because I don't want to pull these gloves off."

"Fair enough." He slid the photos out of the file and held up the first one. She stared at it for a long moment, then nodded, so he went on to the next. When they'd gone through the entire pack without her comment, he said, "So?"

"So it's the same guy."

"You willing to bet the Porsche?"

She looked up at him.

"Yeah. Look at the slash across the neck. It's jagged, like he was sawing. He didn't use a very good tool." She frowned. "And the cut goes from left to right, so I'm thinking the killer is left-handed. Same as our girl here."

She pointed to the pile of pictures. "And the posing is the same, hands crossed over her chest, ankles crossed demurely. Pam was holding a couple of flowers in her hands, just like the victim in those photos. I'd say the evidence points to the same guy."

"Any trace on the body?"

"Semen on her leg, and a couple of male pubic hairs. Two on her leg, three on her stomach. That's about it."

"Fingerprints?"

"Now you're stretching." She shrugged. "I don't think the boys out in the field thought about pulling latents. They just picked her up and put her on the stretcher when they were done taking photos."

"Which means lots of fingerprints on the body."

"Right."

"Do you have a lab down here that can run DNA quickly?"

"Depends on how you define quickly."

"I need them yesterday."

"How about next month?"

"I could pull some strings at the FBI lab and have it processed inside the week," he told her, "if you'd get me the samples."

"Just tell me where to send them."

"Adrianne Jensen at Quantico."

"I'll send them out first thing in the morning."

"I'll let her know to expect them."

"Anything else I can do for you, Agent . . . ?"

"Peyton. And I think you've answered all my questions for now."

"Don't hesitate to call if you think of something."

She lifted a saw in her right hand.

"Will do. Thanks." He grabbed his briefcase and started toward the door, then turned back and asked, "Could I get a copy of the photos you took of the wound?"

"The photos all go to Sheriff Dempsey. You'll have to pry the extras from him."

"I just want to go on record as having said that I do not like this." Sheriff Herb Dempsey frowned, drawing his eyebrows dangerously close to each other so that they all but touched in the space between. "If I had my way, this bastard's picture would be plastered all up and down the East Coast. But you want to do this your way, Agent Peyton, the blood of this man's future victims is on your hands, you hear? You want to go over my head, that's fine. You want to have some big-shot FBI honcho pulling everyone's strings, that's fine, too. But I'm telling you right here and now, this son of a bitch is going to kill again, and the blood of those women will be on you."

"Sheriff, I appreciate your position. And I agree one hundred percent, this man will continue to kill until he's brought in," Mitch said levelly, trying to placate the local law machine. "I'm simply asking for forty-eight hours before any photos of Lester Ray Barnes are released to the press. Give us time to draw him out, make him come to us. If we can't get him to do that by Tuesday morning, you send that photo out to whomever and wherever you please."

"What makes you so sure you'll be able to get him to come to you?"

"We have something he wants."

"Yeah, what's that?"

"His ticket to fame and fortune."

"Do better than that for me, son."

"Lester Ray thinks he's going to work with Regan Landry on a book about his case. She's already met with him. He wants that, wants her to write that book."

"How do you know?"

"I was there when she met with him. Trust me, he's got big plans for himself, him and his attorney both."

"You think he'll go after her?"

"No. I think the book is too important to him."

"Good. Hate to see that happen. I was a big fan of her father's. Shame what happened to him." Dempsey leaned back in his chair. "So she'll get him to come to her, and you'll be waiting for him."

"Right."

"I hope you are because I'd hate to have another girl end up like this." He pointed to the stack of photos on the edge of his desk.

"So would I," Mitch agreed. "But there's no way he'd blow Regan off. He thinks this book is his golden ticket. He'll meet with Regan, there's no question in my mind."

"Well, then, you've got your forty-eight hours, not that I have much say in the matter." Dempsey looked him straight on. "Make 'em count."

• • •

Mitch's next stop was Casey's.

The parking lot was filled to capacity, so he was forced to park across the road in the grassy field next to a small motel. He crossed to the bar and went inside. The room was crowded, smoky, and buzzing with excited voices. Every scrap of conversation he overheard between the front door and the bar focused on the events of Thursday evening. Those who had been there that night were talking about how Pam had come on to the stranger, or how he had played up to her. Mitch shook his head as he made his way to the bartender. There'd be a different version of the story for everyone who told it, and by now the sheriff's deputies had taken a statement from each of them. The rest of it was mostly gossip, repeating one version or another.

He walked to the end of the bar and waited for the bartender's attention. When he approached, Mitch waved him closer, then slid his ID onto the bar, making sure the bartender noticed.

"You're here about Pammie." The bartender nodded, and it seemed to Mitch that he was already getting tired of repeating the story.

"Yes."

"Look, I already spoke with the sheriff, with two of his deputies, the State Bureau of Investigation . . ." He ran a hand through his hair. "I honest to God don't remember another damned thing."

"What's your name?" Mitch asked.

"Drake. Drake Sullivan."

Mitch withdrew the picture of Lester Ray from his pocket.

"Drake, does this look like the man who was in here the other night?"

Drake stared long and hard.

"I can't tell for sure, man. The guy who was here, he had different hair, he was dressed real nice, his expression was different. He was definitely having a good time. This picture . . . that prison shirt, the look on his face . . . it's real different from the guy I remember." He shook his head. "It could be the same guy, but I couldn't swear it was him."

"How long was he in here?"

"Couple of hours."

"And in all that time, you didn't look at him closely enough to be able to say if this is him or not?"

"Man, the bar was crowded, we were watching the game. I served him a couple of beers, he ordered some dinner, then the game went on. Not long after, the girls came in. And like I said, this guy looked like he didn't have a care in the world, he was dressed decent. Looked more like a regular joe than an ex-con."

"Thanks for your time." Mitch handed him one of his cards. "If you think of anything else, give me a call."

"Will do."

"Oh, by the way, how'd he pay? Did he use a credit card?" Mitch asked.

"Cash." Drake looked disappointed. "Sorry, man. Wish I could help. Pammie was a real nice kid. Messed up a little, not very bright, not very selective, either, when it came to guys. But she was a nice kid. I hope you catch this guy, I really do. She didn't deserve what happened to her."

"No one does."

Mitch left the bar and stood on the side of the road, waiting for traffic to clear so he could cross. He was halfway across the lot when he stopped, and turned back to the motel.

Surely the sheriff had checked the motel . . .

Mitch walked to the door marked OFFICE and pushed it open. A bell rang as he crossed the threshold. The lobby, if the small room could be so called, was square and dark, with two worn faux-leather love seats and a registration desk with a chipped Formica top.

A short balding man came from a room in the back to greet Mitch.

"Looking for a room, I guess," the man said.

"No, actually, looking for some information." Mitch held up his ID.

"Sure. What do you need?"

"I need to see your registration log for this past week."

"What are you looking for?" The desk clerk pointed to the large computer monitor that sat at the end of the desk. "Give me the name, I'll check."

"Lester Ray Barnes. Any time from, say, Wednesday through Saturday." Mitch paused. "Check for Darren Barnes, as well."

The clerk sat on a stool and clicked away at the keyboard.

"No, sorry. I don't see any of those names."

Mitch pulled out the picture of Lester Ray.

"Maybe if I showed you a photo . . ."

"Wouldn't help." The man shrugged. "I'm only here on the weekends."

"May I see the names of the people who registered here over the last few days?"

"We're not supposed to do that . . . ," the clerk said, "I could maybe get in trouble with the owner."

"Or, you could maybe get in trouble with the FBI." Mitch smiled. "Up to you, which could be more trouble, in the long run."

The clerk waved Mitch behind the desk and stepped out of his way. Mitch began to scroll down through the screens, then stopped on one.

"Oh, of course." He all but smacked himself in the forehead. "I'll need a copy of this."

The clerk leaned forward and hit the print icon. When the page printed out, he handed it to Mitch.

"This is the car he was driving, and the license plate number?" Mitch asked.

"That's what he told us. We wouldn't have gone out to check. We pretty much take people at their word."

"Thanks a million. You've been a huge help."

"This have anything to do with that girl that got picked up over there at Casey's and ended up dead?" the clerk asked as Mitch folded the paper and put it in his pocket.

"Yes, it does. And when we bring him in, you'll be able to tell everyone that the information you provided to the FBI helped solve the case."

Mitch pushed open the door and walked briskly to his car, his heart beating a little faster, knowing they were that much closer. He was speed dialing his office as he got into his car.

"John, it's Mitch. Sorry to call so late on a Sunday night," he said when John Mancini, the leader of their unit, answered. "I have an ID on the car Barnes was driving the night of the murder . . ."

He explained the circumstances to his boss.

"He registered at the motel as Roland Booth?" John asked.

"Yes, with one of Booth's credit cards."

"Stolen?"

"I think it's more likely that Booth loaned it to him. Remember, they both think they're going to make a fortune off this book. Not likely, from what Regan tells me, but that's what they believe. I think that Booth may have rented the car Lester Ray is using, and handed over both the keys and the credit card."

"Generous of him."

"I'm sure he's figuring on getting the money back when he cashes in on Lester Ray's newfound fame," Mitch said dryly.

"We need the license plate of the car," John said.

"Got it from the motel, but it could be phony," Mitch told John.

"We'll run a trace on it," John said. "Think Barnes was smart enough to dummy up the tags?"

Mitch thought it over for a moment, then said, "Not really. I think there's a damned good chance he just gave them what they asked for."

"Then let's go with it," John said.

"Get a pen, and I'll give you the info on the car and the credit card."

"Go."

When Mitch finished, John said, "I'll have the credit card number run and we'll see where it's been used. With luck, he's used the same card there in Corolla. The card should lead us directly to him."

"I've never been that lucky, to tell you the truth," Mitch said.

"Hey, it's happened before, no reason why it can't happen again. I'm thinking Barnes isn't smart enough to cover his tracks."

"I can't argue with that."

"I have three agents already in Corolla. I'll get this information to them right now. If your investigation there is finished, I want you to meet up with the others as soon as possible."

"Who and where?"

"Mia Shields, Adam Stark, and Tom Parrish."

"Think someone could keep an eye on Regan until I get there? I'm uneasy knowing that Barnes is already on the island and there's no one watching her back."

"Mia checked in to Windham House a couple of hours ago. Regan's back is already being watched."

"Great. Thank you."

"Give Mia a call, let her know you're on your way."

"Will do."

"Nice job, Peyton."

"Thanks, John. I'll be in touch."

Mitch disconnected the call and started the engine. He'd stop at the sheriff's department and make a copy of the motel registration for the sheriff, fax another in to the State Bureau of Investigation.

On the way he'd call Regan and tell her he'd be there in time for breakfast. He hesitated for a moment, knowing that at this hour, she'd most likely be asleep. Then he thought of the way her voice sounded when she'd just awakened, soft and drowsy and just a little slow.

He should give her Mia's number. Regan needed to know there was someone there for her, just in case, between now and the time Mitch arrived. He'd hated the thought of her being there alone, with no one he trusted on the scene. God knows, he didn't trust Lester Ray Barnes.

Then again, if John was right, chances are they'd have Lester Ray under wraps by morning.

He speed dialed Regan's cell phone. There just might be time for that Jacuzzi after all.

Fifteen

"Is he still in there?" Mitch asked when he arrived at the parking lot behind the White Sands Motel.

"We're assuming." Tom Parrish got out of the car he'd been sitting in with fellow agent Adam Stark. "We've been here since around two this morning. Mancini called with the location about an hour after he spoke with you, and we drove right over."

"Dumb shit is using the same credit card everywhere he goes. Guess he was pretty easy to track." Mitch shook his head. "You sure he's here?"

"No one's gone in or out, and the car is here," Tom said.

"Where's the car?" Mitch looked around the lot.

"The row closest to the side street. The third from the end." Adam pointed to the dark blue sedan with Florida plates.

Mitch walked across the lot, and walked around the car, peering in first the front then the back windows. The front passenger seat was piled with fast food wrappers and a few crumpled potato chip bags.

"Looks like a junk food junky," Adam said when he joined Mitch.

"Hope he isn't planning on using that as a defense." Mitch watched the rising sun spread its light, little by little, across the lot. "Did we get the warrant for the car?"

"Mancini's working on it."

"Well, let's hope we hear something soon." Mitch looked back toward the street, expecting to see a cruiser join them any second.

"You care?" Adam asked.

"Do I care if the locals are in on this?" Mitch shook his head. "I don't care who collars him, I don't give a damn who gets the credit. I just want it done."

"That's pretty much how I feel." Adam nodded.

Tom whistled from across the top of his car, and when Adam and Mitch turned, he waved to them.

"Something's up," Mitch said, and the two men jogged across the parking lot.

"Mancini just called. The county is sending in its special response team," Tom explained. "They should arrive in about fifteen minutes. In the meantime, we need to evacuate the rooms on either side of Barnes's."

"I'll do that." Adam took off for the office.

It took almost twenty minutes, but the rooms adjacent to the one in which Lester Ray slept were quietly emptied. Five minutes later, the special response team arrived and, just as quietly, lined up on both sides of the suspect's door.

"I assume you guys want to go in first?" the deputy sheriff had asked the three agents, a touch of disdain in his voice.

"Your guys have the power." Tom gestured to the assault rifle in the deputy's hands. "You lead. We'll follow."

"Think he's armed?" the deputy asked.

"I haven't known him to carry a gun, but that doesn't mean he doesn't have one. I'd work under the assumption he has something in there with him, but it's nothing that will stand up to what you're carrying," Mitch said.

Adam handed the deputy the key to Barnes's room. "This should make it even easier."

Looking pleased, the deputy took the key with a nod of thanks, then motioned to the other members of the team that it was time.

He slipped the key into the lock, turned the handle, shoved the door open, as the members of the team poured into the motel room. Mitch was the last one in.

The room was empty.

The sheriff's men looked under the bed, in the bathroom, in the closet, behind the drapes, and behind a chair.

An oversized gym bag was found on the bathroom floor and seized in accordance with the warrant, but there was no Lester Ray.

The deputy sheriff stared at Mitch.

"I thought you said he was here."

"We thought he was." Tom frowned. "His car is here, it's been here all night . . ."

"Well, we'll take a look in there," the deputy said. "Guess we'll have to wait for the SBI to send in their guys."

"I think some of them might be busy down in Morrissey," Mitch said.

"This is the guy who killed that girl down in Morrissey?" the deputy asked.

"We believe so, yes."

The deputy stared at the motel room for a long minute. "Last thing we need around here at the beginning of the season is a serial killer."

"Last thing you need any time of the year, deputy," Mitch said.

"Sorry." The deputy flushed slightly. "I sound like that guy in *Jaws*." He shook his head and walked toward the car.

"You want to wait for the SBI field ops, or do you want to call Mancini and have our own people brought in?" Mitch asked Adam.

"I think we should give SBI a little time to get on board," Adam replied. "We may be down here for a while. Let's not step on the local toes before we have to."

"I wouldn't give them beyond today," Mitch said.

"Neither would I. We need to nail this guy." Tom nodded.

"Yeah, but we don't know where he is, or who he's with. For all we know, he's sitting in the luncheonette over there, laughing his ass off." Mitch looked across the street. "Right now, let's concentrate our efforts on finding this guy, and finding him fast. Let the locals work the crime scene. It would take us a while to get a team down here, anyway. We want Lester Ray now, before he finds another victim."

He looked from Adam to Tom.

"Let's pray he hasn't already."

"So where do you go from here?" Regan looked around the table in her sitting room where Mitch and the others had gathered. "How are you going to find him?"

"The locals are really hot now to release his photo tonight," Mitch said. "Which I don't want to do yet, I still want to wait one more day."

"He's going to disappear," Mia said. "They always find some place to hole up."

"He won't get off the island now, even if he steals a boat," Tom pointed out. "The highway patrol has checkpoints set up at the bridges and the ferries."

"All the marinas are being watched and the Intercoastal Waterway has checkpoints as well," Adam added.

"My guess is that he's going to be hiding out somewhere until he can find a way out." Mitch was thinking out loud. "Maybe with someone he met, someone he picked up."

"Maybe that's why he wasn't at the motel," Regan suggested. "Maybe he picked up some unsuspecting woman, went home with her . . ."

"If she's lucky, she's still with him. Still alive." Mitch blew out a long breath. "But if he sees his photo on the news tonight . . . knows that half the state is looking for him . . ."

"He'll probably kill her." Adam finished the thought. "Especially if she sees the report."

"I've already spoken with Mancini," Mitch said. "We've agreed there's a good chance Lester Ray doesn't know about the search of his room. If they leave the car where it is for now, chances are he'll come back for it. They're keeping the motel and the car under surveillance."

"For how long?" Regan asked.

"I think the best I can do is maybe get them to hold off until five this afternoon."

"So how do we find him before that happens?" Mia asked.

"I call him and tell him I have to meet with him today." Regan stood and began to pace. "I tell him I just got off the phone with my editor, she's really excited about the book, we need to get together right away because . . ."

She paused, trying to think of something plausible.

"Because . . . ?" Mitch asked.

"Because . . . she's faxing me a contract, and the sooner he signs it, the sooner they'll send him some advance money," Regan told them.

"Would that really happen?" Mia asked.

"Not like that, but he won't know it." Regan shrugged. "Maybe we should sweeten the pot and tell him that Booth is going to be here, too, and he's got the papers already drawn up for Lester Ray's lawsuit against the lab and the state of Florida and the DA and whomever else it was he wanted to sue for his incarceration."

She looked at Mitch and asked, "Has anyone heard from Booth? He hasn't returned my call."

"He's probably still working on those lawsuits," Mitch said dryly. "I'll give Dorsey a call and have her track him down, but I wouldn't mention him to Barnes. You don't know if he and Booth have been in touch within the past few days."

"I hadn't thought of that," Regan admitted.

"You really think you can flush this guy out? You think he'll meet with you?" Tom asked.

Before Regan could respond, Mitch said, "You know, the more I think about this, the more I don't like it. I don't want this guy within a mile of you. I don't want him to know where you are."

"Thanks, Mitch, but unless you have a better idea, you've got nothing else that could draw him in," Regan reminded him.

"It's risky, letting him know how to find you," Mitch persisted.

"But he'll never even see her." Mia walked through the plan: "Regan will give him the room number, the three of us will be out there on the porch, sitting in those rocking chairs, enjoying the afternoon. If he shows up without calling, he'll knock on the door, Mitch opens it, and we'll take him down from behind."

"That's not bad," Adam said. "That could work."

"Tom?" Mia asked. "What do you think?"

"I agree. It could work."

"What if, in spite of all our efforts, he gets away?" Mitch still wasn't convinced. "He'll know Regan's in on this. He'll know her room number."

"Mia, what's the number of your room?" Adam asked.

"I'm in 107, two doors down," Mia told him.

"That's the number you give him. You tell him to meet you in room 107," Adam said. "Even if he decides to come by tonight, unexpected, we'll be waiting for him."

"Mitch?" Regan asked.

"I still don't like using you as bait."

"If you can come up with another plan, we'll go with it," Mia told him. "Got any other ideas?"

"No," he admitted, his face grim.

"And you're going to be with me, right?" Regan asked.

"Every minute."

"Then what could happen?" Regan reached out as if to touch his face, then remembered there were others—his coworkers—in the room, and touched his arm instead.

"Go ahead." He nodded. "Make the call."

Regan took her phone from her pocket and dialed Lester Ray's cell, while everyone waited expectantly.

"Got voice mail," she mouthed. "Lester Ray . . . Darren. It's Regan again. I'm here in Corolla and just checked into the Windham Inn. Give me a call back as soon as you get this message so we can get together today. I have news from New York about an exciting contract for our book, and I can't wait to tell you about it. I'm in room 107, by the way, if you want to stop over this afternoon. Hope to hear from you soon . . ."

She disconnected the phone and said, "There. That should get his attention."

"Do you think he's going to suspect something?" Tom asked.

"He has no reason not to trust me, Tom," Regan replied. "We've already discussed this book. I can't think of any reason why he wouldn't think that call was anything other than what it seemed to be."

"Let's hope you're right." Mitch went to the window and looked out. "There are a lot of people staying here this week. I'd hate to think we're putting any of them in jeopardy by inviting him to the party."

"They'll never even know he's been here. Besides, there are four of you, and one of him," Regan said confidently. "And just think, with luck, in a few hours, Lester Ray will be in custody and all this will be over."

Sixteen

He stood in the shadow of the azaleas that grew high around the end of the porch, and watched the door. He figured if he stood here long enough, he'd see her. He'd listened to her message several times. It hadn't taken a genius to figure out that something was not right.

He still wasn't sure what that something was.

There were several people on the porch tonight, two men and a woman. The woman and one of the men sat in the rocking chairs that faced the sound. The other man sat on the porch railing, facing them. From time to time he glanced over at the door to room 105 which was to his immediate left.

Weird.

Room service appeared with a cart and went straight to room 105, which a tall muscular man answered.

The man in the shadows leaned forward, as if closing another six inches or so of space would improve the view.

The door closed, room service disappeared at the end of the porch, and the threesome remained in conversation.

He glanced down toward the path. A boy of eight or ten was walking toward the dock, pulling leaves off the shrubs as he passed by, and tossing them onto the path.

Stupid kid. Stupid parents, letting a child walk alone at night. Oh, sure, you'd think the Windham Inn was a safe enough place. But you just never knew about anyone. The most normal looking face could hide a monster.

He should know.

He glanced at his watch. Almost eight. Time for a shower, a late dinner, then on to other places, other things. He had a game plan, and he was going to stick to it.

He glanced back at her door. She had a place in the plan, but it wasn't time for her just yet.

Besides, he figured she'd stick around for a while. And he knew where to find her.

It wasn't in room 107.

Seventeen

Mitch stood in the window looking out at the sound, thinking that if they were on the opposite side of this little spit of land, he'd be watching the sun rise over the ocean. He had an urge to see it, to watch that big orange ball edge up over the horizon. He was just about to wake Regan—what was sunrise over the ocean without your main squeeze?—when his cell rang.

"Peyton."

He listened for a few moments, then asked for directions.

"I'll be there in ten."

He dropped the phone on the table and went to Regan's side of the bed.

"Hey," he said softly. "You awake?"

"Uh-huh." She yawned and turned her face into the pillow.

"Regan, I need you to listen." He pulled on his jeans, searched for a shirt.

"Okay." She rolled over. "I'm awake."

"That was Adam on the phone. He just got a call from the sheriff. A couple of guys surf fishing this morning found a body on the dunes."

She sat straight up, fully alert now.

"Don't tell me . . ."

"Sounds like it. Slit throat, mouth painted on in blood . . ."

She jumped out of bed and headed for the bathroom.

"I can be ready in five minutes."

"Make it three." He found his watch on the table next to the bed and strapped it on. While he waited for her, he called his boss.

Regan came out of the bathroom dressed in khaki shorts and a blue shirt. She pulled her running shoes from her suitcase and sat on the edge of the bed to put them on.

"You aren't arguing about me coming with you," she said as she tied her shoes. "Why?"

"Because we don't know where he is, but he knows where to find you. I can't leave you here alone." He stood at the door waiting for her.

"I have seen dead bodies before, you know." She picked up her bag and slid it over her shoulder, then pointed to the door. "I'm ready."

"Let's go." He opened the door and waited for her to follow.

"The others . . ." Regan pointed to room 107.

"Already there. Adam got the call from the sheriff; he called me."

Regan almost had to run to keep up with him, but she managed, arriving at his car almost when he did. Within minutes, they were within a block of the crime scene. Due to the number of cars that had responded, they had to park halfway down the street and jog the rest of the way.

The yellow tape was already across the foot of the path leading up over the dunes. Mitch showed his badge to the officer on the scene and led Regan toward the path before anyone asked her for ID.

"The dunes are protected," the officer called to them. "You're going to have to go down there to your left around twenty feet. There's a boardwalk, take you right to the beach."

Mitch waved his thanks and took Regan's arm. Together they hurried to the wooden walkway and followed it across the sand.

"There's Mia," Regan said.

"And just about every other cop in the state of North Carolina," Mitch muttered. "Too many hands in this pot."

He took out his phone and made a call while Regan joined Mia, who stood about fifteen feet from the body. The woman lay just as

Lederer had described Barnes's other victims. On her back, as if in a coffin, hands together holding a flower, but with a harsh red stain across her face in a grotesque imitation of a smile.

"Jesus." Regan shook her head. "Jesus . . ."

Mia reached out and touched her arm. "You don't really need to see this. Why don't we . . . ?"

"I'm okay. I just can't believe this bastard." Tears of anger began to sting her eyes. "I can't believe what he's done to this girl. And all this time, he's been howling about how innocent he is. It makes me sick."

"It makes us all sick, but look, if you want, I'll take you back to the motel. I'm sure Mitch brought you along so that you weren't alone, but I'll stay with you."

"You're needed here," Mitch said as he joined them. "Just hang around. There's going to be a changing of the guard in a few minutes."

"What do you mean?" Regan frowned.

"FBI in, locals out."

"Mitch, what did you do?" Mia asked.

"I called Mancini, asked him to move us in ASAP, send in our own crime scene people, our own lab people." He shook his head. "Look at this place: you have how many sheriff's deputies, how many SBI? Running all over the beach, burying any evidence in the sand we might have been able to recover. I don't want anyone handling her except our people."

"That will win you points with the locals."

"Sorry, Mia, but this is the third victim in less than a week. I want that body processed by our people. I don't want a damned thing left to chance. The only way to ensure that it's all done the way we need it done is to do it ourselves."

"No argument here." Adam walked over. "But I hate that we're going to have to stand here and watch until the call gets through."

"You won't have to suffer much longer," Mitch told him. "And for what it's worth, I think everything that was going to be lost has been lost—probably already was within the first five minutes. It will just take our people a little longer to . . ." He stopped and looked across the beach. A young woman, with a police officer on either side, was trying to get to the body.

"Let me see her!" she was shouting and attempting to pull away from the two deputies, who were trying to keep her from getting any closer to the body. "I want to see her!"

Mia was across the sand in a flash. She showed her badge to the deputies who held the struggling girl.

"Hey, hey. I'm Mia. What's your name?"

"SuEllen. SuEllen Eakin." She continued to fight. "They said they had my sister. I have to see my sister."

"SuEllen," Mia said softly. "We'll let you see your sister in a few minutes. Right now, we need you to calm down. Can you do that? Can you take a deep breath and try to calm down? I know it's hard . . ."

The girl began to sob, and Mia put her arms around her.

"Come on over here and sit with me on the beach, SuEllen. Maybe you could help us by answering a few questions?" Mia led her away from the scene. "Tell me why you think that's your sister . . ."

"She didn't come home last night. We went out and she—"

"Slow down, SuEllen." Mia turned and called to Mitch. "Could someone get us some water?"

She turned back to the young woman shivering on the sand.

"Would you rather have coffee?" she asked. "Something to help warm you?"

"That would be good, yes." SuEllen nodded with a jerk of her head. "Thank you."

"Add a couple of coffees to that," Mia called. "And a blanket."

Regan watched from the sidelines as the swirl of activity on the beach intensified. There was a confrontation between Mitch and someone from the SBI, which the sheriff tried gamely to mediate. Someone carrying a large black bag approached the body, but merely stood over it. Regan wandered a little closer, wanting to see, yet not wanting to see, what Lester Ray had left behind in the sand.

The young woman had been nicely built, not model thin, just

well proportioned. Light brown hair fell to her shoulders, and several strands had been blown across her face by the morning breeze. The smear of blood across her face masked her features and made it impossible to tell if she'd been pretty, this poor young woman whose life had been cut short so brutally.

The medical examiner arrived and joined in the discussion over jurisdiction. Regan walked down to the shore hoping the sound of the waves hitting the sand would drown out the argument that ensued over who was going to process the body and whose lab would take custody of the traces removed from the body. She jammed her hands into the pockets of her jeans, and wished she'd never heard Lester Ray Barnes's name.

He stood at the end of the long dock and leaned over slightly to watch the small silvery fish that darted through the water. He straightened up and rubbed the middle of his back.

Damn, but that girl had fought like a demon. Pulled the shit out of his back.

Not that it hadn't been worth it.

He continued to rub along his waistband as he began a slow walk along the pier in the direction of the inn. Might slow him down for a day or so, but it wasn't going to put him out of commission altogether. Uh-uh. He'd waited for too damned long to let some little thing like an ornery back muscle keep him from having his fun. He'd just have to baby himself a little today, take it easy.

"Hey, Darren!"

A man and woman stood at the foot of the path, waving.

It took him a minute to realize they were calling him. As he drew near, he recognized them from the inn's cocktail lounge the night before.

"Hey, folks! Beautiful morning, isn't it?" he called back congenially.

"You still planning on going on that tour to see the wild horses?" the husband asked. "They're getting ready to load up the cars. They're leaving in about twenty minutes."

"Oh, hey, almost forgot." He wondered what a couple of hours in a Range Rover bumping over the sand dunes and racing along the beach would do to his achy back. Then again, he'd heard about the wild horses from just about everyone he'd met since he arrived. "Sure, I'll be along. Need to stop back in my room for a minute, though. You go on ahead."

"We'll save you a seat," the wife called.

"Great. Thanks!"

He went straight to his room and grabbed the bottle of Tylenol he'd left on the bedside table the night before. After fighting with the child-proof cap, he downed three pills and washed them down with water from the bathroom sink.

He removed the baseball cap he'd bought in the gift shop the day he arrived, and smoothed back his hair before putting the cap back on. He looked longingly in the mirror at the whirlpool tub behind him and sighed, thinking how great a half hour in that tub would feel on his poor back.

Later, he promised himself. Later he could indulge.

He grabbed his sunglasses from the desk as he passed by and left the room, pulling the door tight behind him and sliding the DO NOT DISTURB sign over the handle. There were a few details he needed to take care of from last night—nothing significant; he wasn't that stupid—just a little bit of cleanup yet to do, and he didn't want the maids to inadvertently come across something that was better off kept hidden.

He pushed that all from his mind for now. It was a beautiful day and he was going on an adventure. He glanced at his watch and wondered if he had enough time to stop in the gift shop and pick up one of those little disposable cameras. It would be fun to be able to take pictures, if they did come across some of those wild horses, and then he'd always have them to look back on as a reminder of this wonderful vacation.

Eighteen

"So what do we have, exactly?" Mitch sat at the table in the sitting room and looked from one face to the other. It was the end of a very long day, and everyone was pretty much worn out, physically and emotionally.

"Twenty-nine-year-old Caucasian female. Raped and murdered on the beach," Mia replied wearily. "The ME placed the time of death at about four this morning. Victim was identified by her sister as Sandra—Sandy—Eakin. They were here on vacation from Ohio with another woman, Barbara Kingston, who worked with SuEllen Eakin, the vic's sister. The three of them went to dinner last night at the Crab Shack, later partied at Casey's on the highway. SuEllen said Sandy spent a lot of time talking to a guy at the bar, but that she didn't leave with him. All three women left Casey's together around two this morning."

"So how'd he get to her?" Tom leaned back in his seat on the sofa, put his feet up on the coffee table, and pushed the empty pizza boxes off the edge. He swore softly as he leaned over and picked them up, then stacked them on the floor in a neat pile.

"Followed them back to their motel, most likely. It's anyone's guess how he got her outside," Mia said. "My personal theory is that she gave him the number of her cell, and he called. Hey, I'm right outside, can't you just sneak out for a few minutes?"

Regan nodded. "I can see that happening. She's spent hours talking to this guy, he was a perfect gentleman the whole time. So she's thinking, nice guy, what the hell. I'll just go out and talk for a while."

"He was in that bar for five hours," Mitch said. "Why didn't anyone recognize his picture? The sheriff had that press conference at five, by six Lester Ray's picture was on every TV news program."

"Dark bar, loud music, everyone's drinking, dancing, trying to score." Tom shrugged. "Couple the fact that no one ever thinks something bad will happen to them with the fact that most people just don't pay that close attention to the news, especially when they're on vacation, and I can see how no one paid attention to him."

"You'd think at the very least, one of the women in that bar would have recognized him. This is a big story. You'd think women going out at night around here would be a little more alert to news like that," Regan said, an edge to her voice.

"Maybe he was wearing a disguise of some sort," Tom ventured.

"The descriptions don't sound like someone who's wearing a disguise," Mia pointed out. "The guy was described as having short brown hair, regular height and build, regular looking guy. That sounds like Lester Ray, right? Nothing weird, no mustache or sideburns, no long hair, no dark glasses. He wasn't hiding."

"So why didn't anyone realize who he was?" Regan repeated the question.

"I don't know how he could make himself unrecognizable. I'm going to ask John to send down a sketch artist. Let's see what Lester Ray has done to alter his appearance," Mitch said. He pointed at Adam. "If you're lucky, they'll send your wife."

"Great." He brightened. "That means we'll get to see each other for, oh, maybe a full twenty-four hours."

Kendra Smith, Adam's wife, was one of the Bureau's most skilled facial compositors. "She's been teaching a class at the academy, and going into the field. We haven't had much time together lately."

"Okay, so we put sketch artist on our list of things to do."

"I like the idea." Adam stood. "I like it so much, I'm going to call and see if we can put this in motion."

He nodded to Mitch and the others and left the room.

Mia placed the photos they'd taken earlier of Sandy Eakin onto the table.

Mitch shoved Tom's feet off the table, then placed the pictures of the last two victims next to the photo of Sandy Eakin.

"This is Lorraine. This is Pam." He gave them a minute to study the pictures.

"Boy, he didn't deviate an inch, did he?" Mia leaned forward. "All the victims were left in exactly the same position, right down to the crossing of the feet." She pointed to the three photographs. "Right ankle over left in each one."

"The neck wounds are exact, as well," Regan pointed out. "They start at exactly the same place, under the ear, and extend along the same line to the same spot on the opposite side. Literally, ear to ear."

"The victim's clothes were all stacked neatly, the underwear folded inside the outerwear," Mia said. "What does that tell us?"

"That he's organized, he has some script he's following, every single time," Tom said.

"Can we get photos of the first victim? The one he killed in Florida? The one he went to trial for?" Mia asked.

"I have copies," Regan said. "I have a copy of the police file."

She left the room for several minutes, then returned with a file under her arm. She sat cross-legged on the floor and opened the file. "This is Carolyn Preston."

She held up several photos, then placed them on the table along with the others.

The three agents in the room studied the photos silently.

Finally, Mia said, "Interesting little differences. Like the flowers. Carolyn's are plastic. The other three are real."

"Can you tell what they are?" Mitch leaned forward.

"We need a closer shot." Regan shook her head. "I know flowers—some, anyway—but I can't tell what those are."

"We need to have the photos enlarged," Mia said.

"I can do that." Mitch gathered the photos. "Give me a minute to scan them into my laptop and we'll see what we've got."

"While Mitch is doing that, I'm getting some coffee," Regan said.

"Let's call room service and ask them to send some of that strawberry shortcake along with the coffee." Mia grinned.

"Good idea. Tom? Dessert?" Regan asked.

"None for me."

"That means you don't get to pick at mine," Mia told him.

He nodded. "Okay, order one for me."

Regan placed the call for four desserts and a large pot of coffee. She was just hanging up when Mitch returned with the photos.

"Look at the way Carolyn Preston's throat was slit." Mitch placed a photo on the table and pointed to the cut line. "Straight across, but hardly the length of the others. Even in the original pictures, you can see the cuts go all the way across."

"And the cut is more even"—Tom pointed to the photo on the table—"not jagged like those other three. He didn't use the same knife."

"He couldn't have used the same knife. The one he used on Preston was part of the evidence at his trial," Mitch reminded them. "Looks like he just used whatever he had handy on the others."

"We'll have to wait for the ME's report to find out if she—Sandy—was also smothered before her throat was slit," Mia said. "Lorraine and Pam were . . . how about Carolyn Preston?"

"I don't remember seeing any reference to that in the coroner's report," Regan told her, "but I can look that up easily enough."

"Now, here are the blow-ups of the flowers found in each of the vic's hands." Mitch placed them on the table side by side as he called their names. "Carolyn, Lorraine, Pam, Sandy."

"Let's take a look." Regan leaned forward to study them. "Carolyn's are clearly plastic. Daffodils. Lorraine's look like azalea. Pam's, those look like magnolia. Sandy . . . I don't know, some kind of wildflower."

"Maybe the locals could tell us what it is. He must have picked it someplace right around there where he killed her," Mia said.

Regan started to comment, then stopped, stared at Mitch for a moment, then asked, "What?"

"This guy is organized. He's got a script. So why doesn't he bring the flowers with him, like he did the first time, for Carolyn Preston?"

"So?" Mia asked.

"So, the scene is really tidy, really controlled. He'd thought of everything. Why deviate from that now? You can buy plastic flowers anywhere."

"We've all seen cases where killers change little details over time. Maybe that's what's happening here," Mia suggested.

"Maybe." Mitch rubbed his chin. "But something's not right."

"Maybe we should call Annie, see what she thinks," Mia said.

"That's not a bad idea." Mitch took his phone from his pocket and dialed Anne Marie McCall, the unit's profiler. When she answered, he gave her a quick rundown on the case, then put her on the speaker.

"I'm here with Mia, Tom Parrish, and Regan," Mitch said. "We have photos from the four crime scenes laid out in front of us. All are in the same position, feet crossed at the ankle, hands together as if in a coffin. All the vics have flowers in their hands."

"So what's the question?" Annie asked.

"The first vic is holding a couple of yellow plastic daffodils. The other three all are holding real flowers, maybe what he found near the scene."

"So you think the first was planned, the others were catch as catch can?" she murmured.

"That's how it looks," Mitch agreed. "We can check to see if these plants were in bloom near where the bodies were found, but in the meantime, I'm thinking there's something wrong with this picture. How important would the flowers be?"

"You field people really do like to put me on the spot, don't you?" Annie complained good-naturedly. "I'd like to see the photos, Mitch—could you e-mail them to me? Usually when a specific scene is played out like that, over and over, the killer is re-creating something that is important to him, whether it's fantasy or based in reality. Send them over, let me take a look, and I'll call you back."

"I'll do it right now." Mitch disconnected the call and got his laptop. Since the photos were already scanned into his computer, it was merely a matter of sending them off to Annie.

While he was on the computer, room service arrived with their order. By the time he'd finished sending the e-mail, coffee had been poured and desserts passed around.

His phone rang just as he was about to take the first bite.

"Okay, this is what I'm seeing," Annie said without bothering to identify herself. "I'm thinking he's definitely re-created something here, not just a fantasy, but maybe something that happened. Someone he cared about, probably. Notice that the eyes of the victims have been closed. I agree, the flowers seem to be important. But to know for sure, you're going to need to find out what prompted this, what put this into his head. And again, this is just a gut reaction, without seeing the file or knowing any background."

She paused, then asked, "Am I correct in thinking the smiles are painted on in the victims' blood?"

"Right."

"Not sure what to read into that," she said softly.

"What are the chances that we're looking at two different killers?" Mitch asked.

The others in the room looked from one to the other.

"Oh, I wouldn't rule that out. If the first scene is the one that's true to him—if he set out to re-create something that was meaningful to him, the death of someone he cared about, for example, he'd have come prepared." She paused for a moment, then said, "On the other hand, if the other three are copycat killings, the second killer wouldn't understand the significance of the flowers. He'd be content with anything he could find at or near the scene, whatever's convenient. So, yes, I'd be inclined to think there could be two killers here."

"Working together?" Mia asked.

"Tough to call." Annie hesitated. "If they're working together, the first killer might not want to share what he might consider intimate details of the killing scene with someone else, such as the importance of bringing a specific kind of flower. That might be too personal for him. He might not want someone else seeing the victim the way he sees her."

"Thanks, Annie. You've given us a lot to think about," Mitch said.

"Any time. Let me know if you need anything else."

"How 'bout I get back to you if we can find some event that might loop into this scene? See if you think it fits?"

"By all means. Keep me up to date. Bye, everyone." Annie clicked off.

Mitch reached over and turned off his phone.

"You think there's a copycat?" Mia frowned. "Or that Lester Ray has picked up a buddy?"

"I think we have to give consideration to both possibilities." Mitch picked up his plate of dessert and ate a forkful of cake. "That would explain why no one in the bar recognized Lester Ray's picture."

"Who else is there?" Tom frowned. "Who could he be working with?"

"That's what we're going to have to find out."

"This might be off the wall," Mia said, "but what about this lawyer? Roland Booth? What are the chances he's joined up with Lester Ray and he's turned to the dark side? Why aren't we taking a closer look at him?"

"That would be a surprise," Regan told her. "I don't think he's got the balls to kill anyone, but then again, I don't really know him. That could have all been an act." She thought it over for minute. "Christ, maybe it was. God knows, Lester Ray always seemed to be putting on an act, this poor little me, over the top, sob story over-dramatized . . ."

"To tell you truth, the only time I ever felt he wasn't acting was when he was talking about his childhood. I guess that was so bad, he didn't have to embellish it."

"Unless that was part of the act," Tom said.

"I don't think so. I think that was all real." Regan shook her head. "Annie said Lester Ray could have been re-creating the death scene of someone he cared about. When I spoke with him, he mentioned one foster mother who'd been very good to him, but he said she had to give up her foster kids when she became ill. Maybe she died. Maybe Lester Ray went to the funeral. Could have made a huge impression on him."

"This was in Florida?" Mitch asked.

Regan nodded.

"How long will it take you to track down Lester Ray's records through child services?" Mia asked.

"Might not have to." He took another bite, then put the fork down and picked up his phone and speed-dialed a number.

He took a swallow of coffee while he waited for his party to pick up.

"Dorsey? Mitch. Were you able to get those transcripts from the Barnes trial?" He paused to listen. "I know you're busy. But if you have them there, could you look up something for us? We need to know if Barnes was put on the stand, and if he was, did he go into his background . . . We're looking for the name of a foster mother he had when he was . . . how old, Regan?"

"Eight, ten, twelve, maybe . . ."

"Age eight to early teens . . . yes, the name of the foster mother. We think he may have been removed from the home when the mother got sick, and she may have died . . . Yeah, that'd be great. Appreciate it."

He dropped the phone back into his pocket and took another bite of his strawberry shortcake.

"Dorsey has the trial notes. She's going to see if she can find his testimony, assuming that he was put on the stand. She also said she has a source at the state that might be able to track down the foster mother but that might take some time."

"The lab reports from the first two murders should be available," Tom said. "The DNA results will tell us if it's Lester Ray or not."

"And we match it to what?" Mia reminded him. "As far as I know, Lester Ray's DNA was destroyed by the lab that started this whole mess."

Regan turned to Mitch. "The spoon . . ."

". . . is in the capable hands of the FBI lab."

"What spoon?" Mia asked.

"Mitch and I met with Lester Ray at a diner the day after he was released from prison. We all had ice cream. Mitch lifted the spoon Lester Ray used."

"Why?" Tom asked.

"Because it was there." Mitch grinned. "And because we didn't have his DNA and I thought there might come a time when we might need it."

"How admissible might that be?" Tom asked.

"It went straight to the lab. Chain of possession is pretty clear." Mitch shrugged. "But let's assume we catch this guy and this goes to trial, even if a really smart defense attorney managed to have it kicked, it still will tell us if the samples from the most recent killings can be matched back to Lester Ray."

"It's a good place to start," Tom agreed. "At least we'll know if we're on the right track."

"That's what I'm thinking." Mitch nodded. "So we need to get the DNA from all three victims to Adrianne at the lab, and see if it matches up to our spoon."

"And if it doesn't?" Regan asked.

"If it doesn't, we're in deep shit," Mitch said, "because right now, we don't have a whole lot."

"A second suspect would explain why Lester Ray isn't responding to Regan's phone calls," Tom noted.

"That still doesn't make sense. Even if he was working with someone else," Regan said. "He was so hot to trot on this book. I can't believe he decided to blow me off."

"And then Booth disappears," she said thoughtfully.

"Well, if he's not the second killer, you really couldn't blame him for going underground," Mia said. "After all this, he gets Barnes out of prison, and in a highly public way, with the entire country watching, and then to have him turn out to be guilty after all . . ."

"Not just guilty. But to go on a killing spree like this . . . not even change his fucking MO. I'd have wanted to crawl under a rock, too, if I were in Booth's shoes." Tom added, "Unless, of course, I was on a killing spree with him."

"Well, one way or another, we'll know by Thursday," Regan said. "We're both supposed to appear on TV with Owen Berger."

"*And Justice for All*?" Mia asked.

Regan nodded. "He wanted both of us on with Lester Ray. It might just be the two of us now."

"When did you set this up?" Mitch asked. "I don't remember hearing about this."

"Owen's people called my publicist on Friday and she called me while I was driving down here. Owen wanted me, Lester Ray, and Roland. I said sure, count me in. At the time, we had no idea Lester Ray would go on this killing spree. Then this morning, while we were all still at the crime scene, Owen called and asked if I'd still come on; said he hasn't heard back from Booth. I told him I'd be there if he still wanted me." She stretched her legs out in front of her. "I'd almost forgotten about it until just now."

"That should be some show," Mitch said. "You and Berger, Booth's and Lester Ray's empty chairs."

"We need to track Booth down now, see what he's been up to," Mitch said. "If we can't find him in Florida, we'll put a call into the Chicago office, get someone to work the case out there."

"I'll get the ball rolling on that." Mia nodded. "If he shows in Chicago, you're going to let him go ahead and do the show?"

"Sure. You never know what he might say in that context. Of course, as soon as he steps off the set, he'll be picked up for questioning."

"And if we find him in Florida, he's going to have to have a good story about where he's been for the past five days," Tom noted.

Mitch turned to Regan. "When will you be leaving?"

"Thursday morning. We're to do the show live in Chicago on Thursday night, then I'll fly back on Friday."

"Maybe you'll want to stay over an extra day, see if you can catch up with Dolly Brown," Mitch suggested.

"If I thought she'd talk to me, I would make the time before my plane on Friday."

"Who's Dolly Brown?" Tom asked.

"Long story." Regan shrugged it off. "Not very interesting. Not germane to Lester Ray and the case at hand."

"Maybe Lester Ray will catch the show and decide to give you a call after all," Mitch said.

"If he does, you'll be the first to know."

"Looks like we have our work cut out for us this week." Mia stood and stretched. "I'll call Florida as soon as I get back to my room, see if we can get someone to locate Booth."

"I should have asked Dorsey while I had her on the phone," Mitch said. "She knows the territory."

"I'll give her a call," Mia replied. "Adam's taking care of getting the sketch artist here. I'll also put in calls to the investigators in Atlanta and Greenville, see if we can find out if the flowers found on the bodies were taken from plants near the crime scene."

"If it's okay with you," Regan said, "I'd like to follow up with Dorsey on Lester Ray's foster mother. I really want to know what happened to her. If you could have seen Lester Ray's face when he was talking about her . . . it was obvious that she was a really special person. If we can find a relative, or someone who knew her, I'd like to speak with them."

"Fine by me," Mitch told her. "With the investigation just beginning here, we'd be hard pressed to find the time to follow that lead right now."

She smiled. She would have gone on her own anyway, and Mitch knew that. All her instincts told her that this unknown woman held the key to understanding the man Lester Ray had become. Regan wanted to be the one to find it.

Nineteen

"Thank you for seeing me, Mrs. Holman." Regan smiled at the woman who had answered the door and now stepped aside to invite her in.

"I'm still not sure I understand what you want to know about my sister, Miz Landry. Rosemary's been gone now for almost twenty-eight years."

Janelle Holman's drawl was thick as molasses and right at home among the live oaks that grew behind the red brick house.

"As I mentioned on the phone, I'm looking into the background of someone who had been a foster child of your sister's," Regan said as she followed the woman into the cool of the pleasant home.

"Oh, my, yes, Rosie had any number of them." Janelle gestured for Regan to have a seat in the small sitting room to the right of the foyer. "She never had children of her own, you know. Never married, never had any inclination to. She did right by those children on her own, though, and let me tell you, some of those kids, they were natural-born hellions."

She took a chair opposite Regan's and rolled her eyes to the heavens.

"How my sister ever put up with some of their shenanigans, I swear I do not know. But I can tell you this"—she leaned forward as if to offer a confidence—"any child lived beneath her roof got unconditional love. They might have been demons when she took them in, but they were sure enough changed when they left."

"She sounds like an exceptional woman," Regan said.

"That she was. Shame, her getting sick like that, just when everything was going so good for her." Janelle sighed. "My sister had been a bit of a hellion herself when she was younger. Just rebellious as all get-out there for a time. Left home at nineteen—we were never really sure what all she'd gotten herself into while she was away, and she never offered the details, so I can't comment on that time in her life. I do know that she was a changed person when she came back. She bought herself a little house down there in Gracie Point, in Florida, got herself a good job. A few years later, she took in a little girl from the state, bit later she got another one. Then for a time she had a couple of boys."

Mrs. Holman stared out the window for a minute, then said, "She did love those kids, Miz Landry. Every one of them."

"That's really why I'm here. I spoke with one of her foster sons about a week ago, and he was telling me how much she'd meant to him. How good she'd been to him. I had the feeling that the time he spent with her might have been the best time in his life."

"She was good to those kids, made a proper home for them," Janelle said. "The happiest I ever saw her was when she had those kids. She always had a smile on her face. Made you smile, too, just to be around her."

"The man I spoke with told me he'd stayed with her until she got sick."

Janelle nodded. "That would have been around 1978, '79. She kept the children as long as she could, but finally, she got so sick, she couldn't do much at all. The kids were taking care of each other after a time. The state got wind of that, took them back, and God only knows what happened to them after that."

"Do you remember the names of any of the children?"

"Little girl named Laurie Jean, she was a doll baby. I think she was sent back to her mama before Rosie got sick. She's the only one I have a clear recollection of."

"Mrs. Holman, do you remember if any of your sister's foster children attended her funeral?"

"Oh, yes. Several of them came. That social worker, Ms. Plunkett, rest her soul, was real sweet about that. She knew how close the kids were to Rosie, and she made sure they all knew when Rosie passed. Brought three or four of them to the funeral home. The family appreciated that. We thought it was real thoughtful of her. Especially since we buried Rosie here, in Georgia, and Ms. Plunkett was taking a chance, bringing those kids across the state line from Florida."

"Do you remember if any of the children in particular . . ." Regan tried to choose her words carefully. ". . . reacted strongly?"

"You mean made a scene at the church or something?" Janelle shook her head. "Not that I recall. They were all real nice, well mannered, the boys as well as the girls."

"This is awkward, Mrs. Holman, but when your sister was buried, was she holding anything in her hands?"

"She had a little bouquet," Janelle said suspiciously.

"May I ask what kind of flowers were in the bouquet?" Regan could see Janelle Holman beginning to bristle.

"Daffodils," she replied without smiling. "Daffy down dillies, she called them, like that poem? It always annoyed her so that she couldn't get them to grow down there in Florida. Miz Landry, I'd like to know what this is about."

"The man I spoke with last week, the man who'd been one of your sister's foster children, is suspected of murdering a woman in Florida."

"Why in the name of God . . ." Janelle Holman appeared stunned. "But what would that have to do with my sister?"

"The way he'd posed his victim, on her back, her hands folded, yellow plastic daffodils in her hands . . ."

"Like the way Rosie was laid out."

"Yes, ma'am. The FBI thinks he was re-creating something—most likely a scene from his childhood. We know that he cared deeply for your sister and was very upset at being taken from her home, and later by her death. Obviously, seeing her at the funeral left a huge impression on him."

"Oh my God." Janelle shook her head. "That is just horrible. Rosie must be rolling in her grave if that's true. Why in the name of God would he do such a thing?"

"I'm going to have to leave it to the experts to figure that out," Regan told her.

"Well, I hope you share that with me when you find out, because I sure do not understand that." She shook her head again. "I surely do not . . ."

"Mrs. Holman, I thank you for your time." Regan rose, and opened her bag to dig out a card, which she handed to her hostess. "This is my cell number. You can reach me there anytime if you think of anything you'd like to add."

The woman took the card, but said, "I can't think of another thing. I still can't believe that one of those little guys Rosie was raising grew up to be a killer."

Regan walked toward the front door, and Janelle followed her slowly, as if still thinking. "Rosie was so good for those kids, Miz Landry, I just can't help but wonder if maybe this boy'd have turned out different if he'd had a few more years with her."

"I've wondered the same thing myself, Mrs. Holman," Regan told her. "I think he would have."

"Sad, isn't it? Waste a life like that?"

"Very sad, Mrs. Holman. For everyone . . ."

Regan called Mitch the minute she got in the car and on the road. She couldn't wait to relay the gist of her conversation with Janelle Holman. "Clearly, Rosemary Jenkins's death made a huge impression on Lester Ray."

"I'd have to agree. I'll run that all past Annie," he said. "Let's see what she thinks. I'll give her a call as soon as we hang up."

"You sound rushed. Did I interrupt something?" she asked. "I probably shouldn't have launched into all that so quickly, but I was so excited."

"It's okay, but yeah, we've had some good news, and some bad news, as the expression goes," Mitch told her. "The good news is, we've found Booth. The bad news, we found him facedown in a drainage ditch. With all the heat they had down there in Florida this past week—well, let's just say it took them a while to positively identify him."

When she failed to react, he said, "Regan? You still there?"

"I'm in shock. I don't know what to say. I'm just stunned." She pulled the car over to the shoulder of the road and turned off the ignition. "He's been dead since last week?"

"The ME thinks since Friday a week ago."

"Mitch, that's when we met with him and Lester Ray."

"Correct."

"You think Lester Ray . . . ? But that would mean he must have killed him shortly after we left the deli that afternoon, then took off for the Outer Banks, stopping in Georgia long enough to pick up Lorraine and kill her . . ."

"That's the way it looks."

"You know, in the beginning, I really didn't know if he'd killed Carolyn Preston. I didn't want to be prejudiced by Lederer because I know he had a personal stake in that. I have great respect for him as a DA—I was impressed by him, frankly—but I know how it is, when a cop or a prosecutor invests a lot into an arrest and it later falls through. No one ever wants to admit they brought in the wrong person. I didn't have a feel for it either way, frankly, but Lederer had Lester Ray pegged all along."

"I just can't figure out his motive. How does killing Booth benefit Lester Ray? Booth had just gotten Lester Ray out of prison, he was filing lawsuits on Lester Ray's behalf, he was negotiating this book for him, he'd given him a credit card to use, probably some cash as well. Rented a car for him." Mitch paused as if reflecting on his own words. "Why would he kill him? I can't think of one good reason, Regan."

"Maybe there was an argument of some kind. Maybe it was a spur of the moment thing, an accident of some kind. Lester Ray didn't strike me as the most mature person, and over the past few years probably hasn't spent much time thinking about anger management or his conflict resolution skills," she said dryly. "Maybe Booth pissed him off somehow, maybe said he wanted a higher percentage of the lawsuits, for example, and Lester Ray got pissed off and just took a swing at him or something."

"Maybe. We'll have a better idea when the ME comes up with the cause of death. Dorsey's trying to keep on top of that."

"I spoke with Dorsey a few hours ago, and she didn't mention this."

"I don't think she knew. She called me less than a half hour ago."

"Will you call me when you find out what killed him?"

"Sure. Where are you going to be?"

"I was thinking I might just fly directly from here to Chicago for Owen's show on Friday night. I suppose I should give him a call, give him a heads-up on Booth's death. Tell him that out of the three guests he thought he had lined up, he's down to one." She paused. "I should call him right now. If he wants to cancel out all together, he might still have time to schedule another guest."

"No chance. He's going to want to bring you on. You've been in the midst of this thing with Booth and Barnes since it started, and it's a huge story that just seems to get bigger and bigger." He paused, then said, "As a matter of fact, you're the only one he can talk to about this whole mess. Booth orchestrated Lester Ray's release, but you gave him some of the ammo he took into court. Lester Ray is God knows where planning God knows what. Trust me. Owen will be dancing in the streets, he'll be so happy to have you on his show. Especially since you haven't been on any of the other talk shows or the morning shows."

"Well, I did get a call to appear on *This Morning, USA,* with Heather Cannon tomorrow, but I wasn't sure how long it was going to take me to find Janelle Holman. If I'd known I'd have found her so quickly, I might have done the show. I like Heather. She's had me on several times to promote my books."

"If we don't get our hands on Lester Ray soon, you might want to take her up on that. It might be good to keep you out there, talking about this. If for no other reason than as a reminder that this guy is still on the loose."

"Has Kendra arrived yet to do that sketch? I'm thinking if she can get a good composite, I'd like to take it on Owen's show."

"She flew in last night to that airport down in Dare. She's meeting with SuEllen Eakin, the sister of the latest victim, this morning. After that, she'll be meeting with the other witness there, the friend who came on vacation with the Eakin girls. Then we'll see if we have a mystery man or whether it's Lester Ray with a new look."

"Well, we know he isn't Roland Booth." She tapped her fingers on the steering wheel. "Poor Roland. He was a bit of a jerk, but I think he was pretty harmless, all things considered. I had the feeling he was just someone who'd sort of plodded along his whole life, and was just crazy-happy at having an opportunity to *be somebody,* you know? Get the lawsuits going, get this book thing going . . . I'd be willing to bet he had ideas for a few books of his own. I think he saw big things in his future."

"Well, unfortunately, he didn't see Lester Ray for what he is."

"I don't think any of us did."

"What time is your flight?" Mitch asked.

"Four o'clock from Jacksonville. I'm thinking about calling Stella Kroll to invite her to have dinner with me."

"Good idea. You could probably use a night to decompress."

"I could. After the frenzy of the past few weeks, it would be nice to have normal conversation with a nice, normal lady. It would also give me an opportunity to think about what I'm going to do as far as my next book is concerned."

"You're not abandoning the Lester Ray book?"

"That's still an important story, maybe even more so now. It was big when it appeared that Lester Ray was innocent and had been railroaded by bad testimony, but that story would have had a happy ending. You know, innocent man set free, justice served in the end. But this story . . ." Her voice trailed off momentarily. "Man set free because of bad evidence, turns out to be guilty as sin. Kills again and again and again. The consequences of the bad conviction become even greater. It raises the stakes for everyone: the lab, the witnesses, the cops, the DA, the judges."

"That's going to be a totally different book."

"Totally different," she agreed. "I want to let my mind free-fall for a while, see what I come up with, what approach I want to take. I think I need some time to regroup on this project."

"Does that mean you aren't coming back?"

"I'll be back. I want to be there when you bring him in."

"Aren't you optimistic."

"Always. I have faith in you. You always get your man, Agent Peyton."

"We can't get this one soon enough. He's killed four times—that we know of—in less than two weeks. Not a good sign. And who knows if we've even found all his victims? This guy is just out of control now."

"That still baffles me," Regan admitted. "I never would have picked him to go off the deep end like that."

"It just goes to show, you never really know these guys. By the way, the lab results are back. The semen on Lorraine's leg was Lester Ray's, ditto Pam's. Interesting there was no semen found on Sandy, though. We figure she consented to have sex with him if he used a condom and since he was planning on killing her later, maybe he wanted her complacent during sex, who knows."

"So we don't know whether it was Lester Ray or this possible accomplice who murdered Sandy."

"There were five pubic hairs retrieved from her body. Two from her upper thigh, three from her stomach. We're still waiting for the DNA results to come back."

"If it's not Lester Ray's, you can run it through CODIS, see if there's a match."

"Right. So within another twenty-four hours, I expect we'll know if in fact Lester Ray had a partner. We have managed to determine that the flowers found on the latest victims were from plants that grew right around where the bodies were found."

"It still strikes me as off that he wouldn't have come prepared for that. That he'd have left the flowers to chance. What would he have done if there hadn't been anything in bloom nearby?"

"This time of year, there's something flowering everywhere you look. He wasn't in much danger of not finding something to use," Mitch pointed out.

"But the victims should have been holding plastic daffodils, like Carolyn Preston was. Rosemary's favorite flowers. Not whatever was accessible at the moment."

"I agree. I'll run it past Annie, see if she has any other thoughts on that."

She glanced at her watch, realized how late it was getting, and turned the key in the ignition. "I need to be getting to the airport. I have a bit of a drive yet."

"Drive carefully, babe."

"Will do. Talk to you soon . . ."

She closed the phone and placed it on the console. When she got to the airport, she'd call Stella and see about that dinner. She hadn't thought of it until almost right before the words came out of her mouth, but once she'd said them, it seemed like a great idea. There was something calming—comforting, even—about Stella. A few hours in her company would go a long way toward helping Regan shake off the sense of grief that had spread through her when she witnessed SuEllen Eakin's anguish at seeing her sister's lifeless body on the beach.

Mitch was right. She needed to decompress. Over the years, she'd witnessed a lot while working with her father. She was certainly no stranger to the horrors a man could devise to inflict pain upon another. But something about this case was affecting her in unexpected ways. That she'd begun to question his guilt even as others, far more experienced in such matters than she, questioned his innocence, nagged at her conscience. That she'd played a role, however small, in Lester Ray's release, haunted her.

She drove slowly along the rural roads that led to the highway that would take her back to Jacksonville, wishing her dad were still alive so that she could talk it all over with him. Wishing Lester Ray was already in custody and that she and Mitch could sneak off to some deserted island for a week. Or two.

Since none of that was possible, she'd settle for a nice dinner with a sweet little old lady in Sayreville, Illinois, and an early night. Tomorrow she'd work on an outline for her book; in the evening she'd do Owen's show; and first thing the next morning, she'd head for the Outer Banks, and Mitch. With luck, by the time they were together again, maybe—just maybe—the beast would be back in his cage and the nightmare would be over.

Twenty

Mitch sat on the steps outside the room he and Regan had shared at the inn and finished off the roast beef sandwich Mia had brought back for him from a little shop in Corolla proper. Adam and Tom were still at the ME's attending Sandy Eakin's autopsy, and Mia had just run inside her room to wash her hands.

"I need to wash up and I want to change, so I'll be a minute," she'd told him as she tossed him first a bottle of water then the sandwich in its white paper wrapping. "I don't expect you to wait for me."

"Good thing," he'd replied. He hadn't seen food since his seven-thirty breakfast, and that had been a breakfast sandwich from a fast food drive-through. Just thinking about it made his stomach ache all over again.

He polished off his sandwich, then opened the bottle of water and took a long drink. He leaned back against the newel post and closed his eyes. Most of the guests had gone into the dining room for a real meal, and at this hour, with the sun dropping over the sound, there was little foot traffic at this end of the porch. Just for a moment, there was peace. There was quiet.

There was the ringing of his cell phone.

Well, it had been a pleasant respite. All two minutes of it.

"Peyton."

"Mitch, it's Annie. Sorry I couldn't get back to you sooner. I listened to your message. Sounds as if you have Lester Ray pegged pretty accurately."

"In which way?"

"I agree that with his victims, he's reliving seeing his foster mother. There are a few things we need to talk about." As always, Annie was all business. "I think he actually felt some fondness for his victims, the first one, at any rate. Why he was compelled to kill, I don't have a handle on that. But by taking the time to lay them out, so to speak, put flowers in their hands, he's honoring them, showing them respect. I felt that strongly with the Preston woman. The others, not so much."

"That's interesting," Mitch said. "We were getting a different vibe, too. We were thinking the flowers should have been more important to him."

"I agree. Let's look at Carolyn Preston. He re-created his recollection of the way his foster mother had looked in death, right down to the daffodils in her hands. Not so the others. The flowers were an afterthought—he grabbed whatever was convenient. A small detail, but an important one. He never would have overlooked that."

"So you think we're looking at a copycat."

"No. Here's the important thing I'm getting from all this. A copycat would get it right," she said firmly. "Whoever is doing this doesn't know Lester Ray, doesn't understand the importance of the daffodils. He wants you to think it's Lester Ray, but he lacks the sophistication to understand that the flowers are part of the statement."

"What do you think about Lester Ray killing his lawyer?"

"I don't see him for that," she said thoughtfully. "I think he needed Booth. Booth was almost like a surrogate father. He provided for him, you said? A car, a credit card, cash? Got him out of prison. Why would he kill him?"

"That's what we all thought, too."

"It just makes no sense to me. Now, because you have heard me say it a million times, you know that profiling isn't an exact science."

Before Annie could continue, Mia stepped outside and waved a hand to get Mitch's attention.

"Hold on a sec, Annie." He lowered the phone. "What's up, Mia?"

"The lab just called. Those pubic hairs found on the victims? They were Lester Ray's."

Mitch frowned. "Are they sure? All three samples?"

"That's what they said."

"Okay. Okay. Thanks." He nodded and put the phone back to his ear. "Annie, Mia just got a call from the lab. The pubic hairs found on all three bodies were a match to Lester Ray."

"All three?" Annie asked, and Mitch could almost see her frown.

"All of them."

"Well, that certainly proves what I just told you about this not being a perfect science. I would have sworn . . ." She took a breath, exhaled it. "Well, it doesn't matter now. Let's just say that I'm surprised."

"Me too," Mitch said. "Listen, thanks, Annie."

"Any time."

He hung up the phone and set it next to him on the step while he drained the water bottle. He stared out across the sound and watched the sun begin to set. A great blue heron, its wingspread an easy six feet across, lifted majestically from the marsh across from the pier and glided past Mitch's field of vision, a dark silhouette against the coral and turquoise sky. He wished Regan had been there to see it, to share that moment of tranquility. He watched it until it disappeared somewhere over the quiet water.

He wondered how Kendra was doing with that sketch she was working on, if, after speaking with witnesses all day, the face that was emerging was Lester Ray's, or someone else's.

There was one way to find out.

He opened his phone and scrolled through the directory to find her number. As he started to dial, the door to room 107 opened, and Mia stepped out. Even before she spoke, he knew from the look on her face that his tranquil moments had come to an end.

"Mitch, they found another one . . ."

Twenty-one

Dinner with Stella had been the only thing on Regan's agenda that had gone smoothly since she'd arrived at O'Hare. Her flight had been late, and while her plane had made it to Chicago, her luggage had not. Her rental car had not been waiting for her, and the only vehicle they had available was a subcompact that smelled heavily of cigarette smoke.

She'd been more than a half hour late to pick up Stella, but she'd called on her way and Stella had been most gracious about the delay. When Regan finally got to the Kroll house, she found Elena, Stella's daughter, chatting with her mother in the kitchen. She'd felt obligated to include the young woman in their plans, and reluctantly did so. She wasn't sure why, but she'd been disappointed not to have Stella's attention all to herself.

Silly. She'd shrugged it off as they left for the restaurant, with Elena insisting on driving because she knew the way and besides, hers was the bigger car. From the backseat, Regan had studied Elena. The woman was younger than Regan, maybe mid- to late twenties, as opposed to Regan's mid-thirties, and she had a mass of strawberry blond curls and green eyes. Her profile was much like Stella's and, like her mother, Elena was warm and friendly. Like mother, like daughter, Regan had mused.

Stella had called ahead to the small neighborhood restaurant and reserved a table. The greeting they'd received from the owner, a long-time friend of Carl's and Stella's, had been warm and welcoming.

"Stella, we're so happy to see you!" Amelia, the owner, had embraced her. "We've missed you. And Carl, God rest his soul, we miss him, too. Elena, thank you for getting your mother out of the house, and bringing her here where we can dote on her."

"I can't take the credit," Elena had told her. "Thank Regan."

"Amelia, this is Regan Landry. From New Jersey. She's a friend of the family." Stella had patted Regan on the arm fondly, and that small gesture had made Regan's throat catch.

Must be a reaction to all the violence this week, she'd told herself. *Stella's gentleness is such a contrast to Lester Ray's uncontrolled rage.*

Amelia had brought them wine and bruschetta and made suggestions for their dinners, and throughout the evening, the conversation had flowed as easily as the wine. More than once, Regan had found herself observing the easy and obviously loving relationship between Stella and Elena. To Regan, who had not been particularly close to her own mother, the give and take between the two had a bit of a novel, almost exotic flavor. Mother and daughter were a solid force of one, and it had come as a surprise to Regan to learn that she and Elena had been equally curious about each other.

"I've heard so much about you," Elena had said when Stella had momentarily table-hopped to chat with an old friend from her church. "My mom and my aunt Dolly both talk about you so much."

"You're kidding!" Regan had been taken aback. "Why?"

"Oh, they were both big fans of your dad's," Elena had said. "They read all his books. I understand you're a writer, too, like he was."

"I am."

"And you're working on that story down in North Carolina. The serial killer who got out of prison because the lab screwed up the DNA."

"Yes."

"What's it like, interviewing a killer?" Elena had rested her arms on the table and stared intently at Regan.

"When I interviewed him, I didn't know if he was a killer or not. It was like interviewing anyone else, I suppose. You chat, you ask questions, you get answers."

"Are you annoyed that I came with you and my mom tonight?" The question had come out of the blue.

"What?" Regan frowned. "Why would I be annoyed?"

"I just have the feeling you'd rather it was just you and Mom." When Regan had started to protest, Elena held up her hand. "It's okay. Everyone always wants to be with Mom and just bask in her glow. She's such a . . . a *positive force*. I always feel better when I'm around her. Everyone always does. Knowing where you've been this week, I could understand if you felt the need to spend a little time with her. She just has a way of soothing you when your edges feel rough."

Regan had put down her wineglass.

"I couldn't have put that into any better words, Elena. That's exactly . . . perfect."

"I imagine your edges are a bit rough right now," Elena had said gently.

Regan nodded. For the second time that night, for no apparent reason, her throat felt tight.

Before she could respond, Stella had returned to the table with a story she'd just heard from her friend, and the conversation had taken many other quick twists and turns as the night progressed. There had been lots of friendly chatter, mostly about family and friends, with Stella occasionally supplying family lore, such as the fact Carl's cousin Bud had gone over Niagara Falls in a barrel when he was eighteen and drowned, and that his aunt Cecilia had entered the convent when she was thirty-seven. By the end of the evening, Regan knew more about the Kroll clan than she'd ever wanted to know.

Except the ever elusive Eddie, of course. The one time Regan had brought up his name, Stella had shaken her head and told her, "Like

I've said before, I never really knew Eddie. By the time I married into the family, Eddie was long gone."

Not that Regan had expected to learn anything new from her. She'd stopped looking to Stella as a source of information as far as Eddie was concerned, and sought her company merely because she enjoyed it.

"What are your plans for tomorrow?" Stella had asked when they'd returned to her house and Regan was preparing to drive to her hotel.

"Well, if my luggage doesn't arrive, I'm going to have to run out and pick up something to wear tomorrow night. I don't think I want to go on national television wearing the same thing I've been wearing almost all day today."

"There's a mall just a mile or so from your hotel, and there are some nice stores there," Elena told her.

"I'm sure I'll find something," Regan had nodded.

"You call me if you need anything." Stella had given her a brisk hug. "Elena, did you give Regan your number? Maybe she should call you if she has any shopping questions. You're closer to her age."

"I'd be happy to help." Elena had pulled a card with her work number on it from her wallet and handed it to her. For just a second, Regan thought Elena, too, was going to hug her.

She thanked them both, then got into her car, and headed for her hotel, where she showered and got into bed. Not even bothering with the television, she pulled the covers up to her chin. She fell asleep envying the easy camaraderie between Stella and Elena, and wondered, if her mother had lived, whether they'd have shared that same kind of bond.

"So, how was the dinner with Stella?" Mitch asked when he called right around sunup the next morning.

"It was fun. I had a good time," she told him. "Stella's daughter Elena joined us."

"What's she like?"

"Nice. A lot like her mother, actually. I liked her a lot."

"Good. I'm glad you were able to take a little time off to enjoy yourself," Mitch said.

In his voice, Regan heard distraction, loud and clear.

"So, what's going on?" She sat up in bed and stacked the pillows behind her. "Did you speak with Annie?"

"Yes. She agrees with everything you and I said about Lester Ray and his foster mother, and the fact that the last-minute flowers were the odd note. As a matter of fact, we were both thinking that there has to be another killer when . . ."

"When . . . ?"

"When I got a call from Mia telling me the DNA from the hairs found on all three bodies matched Lester Ray's profile."

"Even this last one?" She frowned.

"Ah, the last one being Justina Waters. They found her yesterday."

"Another victim? Same thing? Same wounds, same flowers . . . ?"

"At first glance, same everything. I'm going to meet with the ME in about a half hour, which is why I called so early. See what showed up at the autopsy."

"It's okay." She ran her hand through her hair and held it back off her face. "So now there are four. The first three are positively Lester Ray's, this last one most likely as well."

"So it would seem."

"What about the second man? How's Kendra doing with the sketch?"

"She said she thought she'd have something ready today. We'll see what she's come up with. If there is a second man, he's been following so closely in Lester Ray's footsteps we'd have missed him completely if not for the flowers."

"Did Annie have any thoughts on why Lester Ray might have killed Booth?"

"She doesn't see it as his. She doesn't see motive. I'm still waiting to hear back from Dorsey on cause of death."

"So we're back to our mystery man."

"Maybe." He sighed wearily.

"You sound tired, sweetie."

"I am," he admitted.

"Anything I can do?"

"Pray for a miracle," Mitch said. "Pray we find him before he kills someone else."

"I will," she told him. "Be careful, Mitch. I'll see you soon. Love you."

"Love you, too."

The coffee she'd ordered from room service the night before was delivered just then, and Regan poured herself a cup, adding cream from a small ice-cold pitcher while she checked with the airport for her luggage, only to find it had been sent, inexplicably, to Omaha. She asked that it be rerouted to her New Jersey address and got dressed to go shopping. She checked in with Bliss, and found that the organization of the Landry home was actually ahead of schedule.

"I have all the files from your dad's office back in the cabinets, in order," Bliss had told her happily, "and I've started on the boxes in the basement."

"Well, find something else to do until I get home," Regan had told her. "I don't want you lifting heavy things."

"I'm fine. Really. I won't pick up anything that's too heavy for me. If there's anything that's too bulky, I'll leave it for Robert. He'll be back from Bible camp tomorrow evening, so he can bring the heavy boxes up for me."

"As long as you don't do it yourself," Regan said.

"When do you think you'll be back?"

"I'll be going back to North Carolina from here," she said. "Unless you need me for something?"

"No. Everything's fine here."

"You don't mind being there by yourself all day, every day?"

"Not at all. I like the peace and quiet here."

"I should be back there sometime next week. And you have my cell number, if you need anything."

"I can't think of anything, but thanks."

"See you then. Have a good weekend."

She ended the call and set out for some shopping, which she wasn't in the mood to do. She'd hoped to have time to work on her book, and to think over what she wanted to say later that night when she appeared on *And Justice for All.*

Well, she'd have the afternoon for that, she thought as she set out to find the mall Elena had mentioned the night before. While on her way, she called Mitch, and was disappointed when she had to settle for voice mail. She knew he'd be busy, but felt confident that if there'd been any breakthroughs, he'd have let her know. She left her phone on and tucked it into her pocket, where she'd be sure to hear it ring.

The work she'd left undone weighed heavily on her conscience, so she made her selections in record time. She found a linen suit in a natural shade, a silk tank in the same color, matching shoes, and on her way out of the store, she picked up a necklace made of multi-strands of turquoise beads to give her outfit some punch. She liked the color so much that she went back and bought earrings and a wide silver and turquoise bracelet.

Now I'm ready for prime time, she told herself as she headed back to the hotel. *And now I can focus on tonight.*

She went over the sequence of events in her head as she drove, ticking off each step from the night she'd tuned in Owen's show to hear Roland Booth describe his client's predicament, her meetings with Lederer and Booth and Lester Ray, through the scene in the courtroom and her one-on-one with Lester Ray, right down to the discovery of the latest victim Mitch had just told her about. By the time she'd mentally run through it all, she was at the hotel and slipping the key into the door.

She kicked off her shoes on her way into the room, then turned down the air conditioning a bit. She hung up her purchases, scanned the menu for room service, called in an order, and tossed her brief-case onto the desk. She took out a notebook and began to jot down her thoughts on the case.

Her lunch was delivered, and she ate her salad absentmindedly.

She was almost finished when there was a quiet knock on her door. Still chewing, she walked toward it and called, "Who is it?"

"Dolly Brown."

Regan's eyebrows shot up nearly to her hairline. She opened the door, looked out, then slid the safety chain off.

"Well, well, well." Regan grinned. "To what do I owe this surprise?"

"Can I come in?" Dolly asked uncertainly.

"Of course, please." Still grinning, Regan made a sweeping gesture.

"I won't keep you long," Dolly said.

"Have a seat." Regan offered her visitor one of the armchairs, while she herself sat at the desk. "I was just finishing lunch, but if you'd like something, I can call room service."

"No, thank you. I'm not staying." Dolly sat stiffly on the chair, her hands in her lap, and, Regan noted, appeared nervous.

Dolly Brown, nervous?

"So what's up, Dolly?" Regan asked.

"Stella says you're going on that television show tonight."

"*And Justice for All.*" Regan nodded.

"And that you're going to talk about that killer you hooked up with. The one you thought was innocent, who is anything but." A bit of the old Dolly started to creep back. "And that you're going to go back to North Carolina where this killer is running loose."

"Yes." Regan sat back in the seat, wondering where this was leading.

"Well, we don't think you should do this."

"Who is *we,* and what don't you think I should do?"

"*We* is me and Stella, and we don't think you should keep after this killer." Dolly looked her square in the face. "He's a dangerous man. He could come after you."

Regan stared at the woman for what seemed to be a long time.

"Well, I hardly know what to say." She was both puzzled and amused. "I'm touched that you're concerned about me."

"Stella's worried."

"Right. Stella. Stella's the one who always worries about me. Now, why is that?" Regan stood, her hands on her hips. "And you know, it's funny, but Stella didn't voice any of this concern last night."

"I'm sure she wanted to, but . . ."

"What's really going on here, Dolly?" Regan's eyes narrowed. "You have barely given me the time of day in the past six months. You're never available when I want to talk, and when I do finally manage to collar you, you don't tell me jack shit. So why all of a sudden are you so damned concerned about my welfare? You don't give a crap about me, Dolly, so what's really at the bottom of this?"

"That's not true. That I don't give a . . ." Her lips began to quiver.

"What the hell is going on, Dolly?"

Dolly stared at the floor, then sighed heavily as she pushed herself out of her chair.

"I guess . . ." She wet her lips. "I guess you're going to have to come with me."

"I think you're going to have to do better than that." Regan stood her ground. "I'm pretty busy right now, so if you have something to say, just say it."

"I can't," Dolly said softly.

"Why?"

"I don't know how." She shook her head.

"You don't know how, *here,* but you'd know *how* if we were someplace else," Regan stated flatly.

"Yes."

The two women stared at each other, then Regan shrugged and grabbed her bag off the back of the desk chair.

"Okay, Dolly. You win. Let's go." She pointed to the door. "But this had better be good, and it had better be important . . ."

Twenty-two

Mitch stood in the cool of the autopsy room and watched the transfer of Justina Waters's body from one cold metal table to another and thought that in life she'd probably been a very pretty girl. In death, however, her skin was mottled and there were dried patches of blood on her torso and head and in her hair from the gash that connected one ear to the other. Now a victim, every part of her physical self was subject to the most intimate scrutiny.

He blew air from his lungs in a steady stream, reminding himself that finding the killer was only part of the obligation owed to the dead. Somehow, leaving a young woman alone with only the ME, to be cut and weighed and analyzed, dissected and sawn apart, had struck Mitch as just plain wrong. He never wanted the victim to feel deserted, as if she were nothing more than a specimen in a lab. From a rational standpoint, he knew the dead felt nothing. On another level, he hoped there might be some small comfort to the deceased to know that she was not alone for this final indignity, this last invasion of her privacy.

"Cause of death, exsanguination," the ME said without looking up from his work, "but you probably guessed that."

"Yes." Mitch stood with his hands in his pocket. "Any sign of petechiae?"

The doctor inspected the victim's eyelids and inside her mouth.

"None," he told Mitch. "But there's some bruising on her wrists, and what I'm thinking is a defensive cut here on her right forearm."

He stepped back for Mitch to see.

"We'll compare this one with the one on her throat, but I expect to find they were made with the same weapon," the doctor continued.

"She tried to fight him," Mitch said under his breath.

"Yes, she did," the ME said. "You any closer to finding this guy?"

"No."

The ME, a man in his mid-sixties, shook his head. "I've been here for going on ten years. Never seen anything like what I've seen in the past few days. I thought I'd left all this behind when I left L.A."

Mitch stayed until the autopsy had been completed, until the doctor finished his dictation and had carefully returned the body of Justina Waters to the refrigerated compartment where she'd wait until her body was claimed. When Mitch walked outside, he blinked against the bright sunshine and felt in his pockets for his sunglasses. Autopsies always left him feeling unsettled, and this one even more so. To Mitch's mind, this was a death that should not have occurred. Lester Ray should be in custody. They should have identified his cohort, should have been able to save this young woman's life, and her family from the agony they were now going through.

"Should have had him by now," Mitch muttered under his breath as he got into his rented car. "Lester Ray, you bastard, where in hell are you?"

Regan looked out the window of Dolly's sedan and watched the scenery morph from the commercial strip malls of the highway to the quiet small-town streets of Sayreville. She was surprised when Dolly passed her own street, but she hadn't commented. Regan had felt certain that the Brown home was their destination, but when they passed Stella's street as well, Regan grew even more curious. There'd been no conversation since they'd left the hotel, which in itself was odd, but Dolly was apparently intent on a bit of mystery. Regan would let her have her little drama. While she was certain it would in the end turn out to be much ado about nothing, Dolly was evidently into it. Regan chose to let it play out, whatever *it* might turn out to be.

Six miles outside of town, Dolly put on her turn signal and made a right through the tall iron gates of Holy Sepulcher Cemetery. She slowed as she maneuvered along the narrow paved road that was barely wide enough for one car. Ever more curious, Regan quietly watched the uneven rows upon rows of headstones file past the window as the car followed the winding road. Finally Dolly pulled onto a grassy section and stopped the car.

Without glancing at her passenger, Dolly opened her door and said, "Come with me."

Regan followed Dolly several hundred feet along a path that led between the markers. Finally, Dolly stopped.

"My father, Edward Kroll, Senior." She pointed first to a tall headstone, then to the stones on either side. "My mother, Margaret, and my sister, Catherine."

Dolly drew in a long sharp breath, then said, "They all passed on while Eddie was away. When he came home, his parents were gone, his little sister, too . . ."

"That must have been terribly hard for him," Regan said. "Especially if he'd been close to his family."

"Before . . . well, before he got mixed up with those two that got him in trouble, Eddie'd been our golden boy. You have to understand, try to see him the way he was before all the trouble. He was the smartest, the best looking, the best athlete, he could do anything, could have been anything. My father doted on him. My mother adored him. We all did." She shook her head, tears forming in both eyes. "Then he somehow got talked into taking part in what those other two told him was going to be a robbery. Eddie swore to us they told him all they wanted to do was rob the kid, and he'd get an equal share of the money. Why he even agreed to do that much, we'll never know, but he did it. And once they got this boy alone, it was all over. Afterward, Eddie said he didn't know what took over him. They handed him a bat and told him to swing and he did."

Dolly was crying, the tears fat and swollen and rolling down her cheeks like raindrops.

"But you know all that. You know what happened, you know what Eddie did and why he got sent away. What you wanted to know all along is what happened to him when he got out." She searched in her pockets for a tissue, found one and blew her nose. "You sure you want to know?"

Regan nodded.

Inside her pocket, her phone began to ring. Her fingers found the *off* button. Regan sensed that Dolly was on the verge of finally telling her what she wanted to know. There was no way she'd interrupt the woman now. Whoever was calling could wait.

"This way, then." Dolly waved Regan to follow her. They walked along the path to a point farther back in the cemetery, Dolly talking all the way. "The first thing Eddie did when he got out was to come here. I brought him, just like I brought you. He stood there in front of those graves and sobbed like a baby. All he could say was, 'I'm sorry. I'm sorry. I'm sorry . . .' "

Dolly fell silent for several steps, then said, "Finally, he just took off, right down this path we're walking on, and he ran till he got to the fence back here and there was nowhere else to run. 'I have no right to carry their name,' he was crying. He looked like an animal trapped in a cage, walking back and forth in front of that fence right over there. 'There's nothing for me here. My life is over.'

"Well, I told him, that's nonsense, you paid your debt, you can't change the past."

Dolly jammed her hands in her pocket. "And Eddie said, no, he couldn't change the past, but he could change the future."

She walked to a headstone that sat alone near the fence and pointed to it.

"Read it," she told Regan. "Read the name."

Regan came close enough to see the letters that had worn with age.

"Joshua Stuart . . ." She stopped, her jaw nearly dropping to the ground. "Joshua Stuart Landry, 1872 to 1935."

She turned to Dolly. "I don't understand. Is this man my grand-father? I'm confused."

"No," Dolly said gently. "We just left your grandfather's grave. Your grandfather, and your grandmother, and your aunt."

"My . . ." Regan's knees began to shake, and she went hot all over, and something pounded inside her head. "But that would mean . . ."

"Eddie Kroll was your father," Dolly said simply. "He was twenty-one years old the day I brought him here. I didn't see him again for almost seventeen years. By then, he'd put himself through school, sold some of his work—he'd become a whole new man, liter-ally. He'd become Josh Landry. By the time we saw him again, Eddie Kroll was long gone."

Regan's shakes finally got the best of her and she lowered herself to the ground.

"But that's not possible. My father and I were very close." She began to cry. "He never would have kept a secret like that from me. He wouldn't have. He would have told me . . ."

"Honey, I'm just as sorry as can be, but I swear to you, it's the God's honest truth." Dolly fought to get her own emotions under control. "He never wanted you to know the truth about him, never wanted you to know that your father had killed a boy for the stupid-est, the most inexcusable of reasons. Stella and Carl and I, we all tried to talk to him, we told him that it wasn't right, him not telling you the truth. But he wouldn't hear it. He loved you so much, honey. He just couldn't bear the thought that you wouldn't love him if you knew who he really was and what he'd done."

"But that's crazy, how could he have thought that I'd . . ." Regan cried. "How could he have kept this from me?"

She covered her face with her hands and sobbed. Dolly sat down next to her and put her arms around her niece.

"When you put that ad in the paper, looking for someone who knew something about Eddie Kroll, I showed it to Stella and I said, she's looking for us, looking for her family. He told her the truth after all." Dolly rocked Regan gently. "Then when you came out here and we talked, I realized that it wasn't your family you were looking for, but just the answer to a puzzle that you'd stumbled over."

"Eddie's report cards from grade school. I couldn't figure out why my father had them, and I was curious. I thought I'd just return them to him or his family. But then everything was so mysterious. No one would tell me what happened to Eddie once he'd served his time. And then I found out you lied to me, that you hadn't been Eddie's neighbor growing up. You were his sister." The words poured out of Regan so quickly, she was short of breath. She stopped and inhaled deeply. "That makes you my aunt . . ."

"Yes. It does."

"And Stella . . . Elena . . ." Regan whispered.

"Your aunt by marriage. And your cousin." Dolly nodded. "You have quite a few cousins."

"They know about me?"

"Only Elena and her sister Julie. They know."

"I can't believe this is happening."

"I'm sorry, honey, I really am. Stella and I talked it over, and decided it was time you knew. Especially with both your parents gone, we thought you needed to know you have family. That you're not alone."

Regan tried to speak, but her throat closed. She swallowed hard to force the lump away, then asked, "Did my mother know?"

Dolly hesitated for a moment too long.

"She did," Regan said. "He told her?"

"I don't think she took it well." Dolly made an attempt at diplomacy. "Stella said you'd told her that there came a time when your mother was spending more and more time away from home, that she'd go back to England to be with her people."

"This is why? Because of what he'd done?" Regan frowned.

"That's why he was afraid to tell you. He was afraid you'd want to leave him, just like your mother did."

"I had no idea. I thought she was just homesick. And then her mother was sick." Regan appeared dazed. "I thought they were happy. I thought they loved each other."

"At one time, I'm sure they did."

"I need to go." Regan fumbled to her feet. "I need to go . . ."

On unsteady legs she hurried down the path, Dolly hustling behind her. When they got to the car, Regan got into the passenger seat and slammed the door. When Dolly got behind the wheel, Regan said, "Please take me back to my hotel."

Dolly nodded and started the engine, and began the quiet ride back.

Mitch lay exhausted across the bed and closed his eyes. He'd ordered a steak and salad from room service, and it had been a struggle, but he'd somehow managed to stay awake long enough to eat it. He was pretty sure he hadn't had a real meal since before Regan left, but couldn't remember exactly how long ago that had been. Two days? Three? More? However many, to his mind, she'd already been gone too long. He knew she had a life of her own and respected her for that, knew she had work to do that mattered to her, and he applauded her success. But knowing those things did not make him miss her less.

He knew his reputation was that of computer geek, and part of him found that amusing. Secretly, he thought of himself as more of the caveman type, and there were times he wished he could just whisk Regan away to some secluded spot where they could be together, away from all the doom and gloom and the ugliness they both dealt with every day.

When this is over, he told himself as he drifted off, *we're going to take a vacation.* Drive up the coast of New England, all the way to Maine, and spend some time with his family like they'd planned on doing last Thanksgiving. They'd been all set to go—had plane tickets, a rental car on order, plans for the entire week. And then a graduate student down in Tennessee had gone on a rampage, killing six people in less than twenty-four hours, and Mitch had ended up spending his holiday week chasing Christopher Coughlin across the Great Smoky Mountains.

This time we're going, he promised himself. He'd been wanting to take Regan home to his family for months. Now would be the time.

He rolled over and checked to make sure he'd set the alarm on his watch. *And Justice for All* went on at ten and he didn't want to miss a minute. He knew Regan would be great. She always handled everything with such style. He was awestruck sometimes by how cool and professional she could be.

As he'd told her a dozen times, she'd have made one hell of an FBI agent.

He'd called her several times throughout the day and left messages for her to call him back. He figured she must have left for the studio early; maybe she was going to meet with Owen Berger before the show. She and the host had known each other for years, so maybe they'd made arrangements to have dinner. He couldn't think of one other reason why she'd have ignored his calls.

Half asleep, he leaned over and grabbed his jacket from the chair where he'd tossed it earlier. He reached into the pocket, took out his cell phone, and laid it next to him on the bed. She'd probably listen to her messages right before the show. He wanted to make sure he didn't miss her call.

It was the last thought he had as he turned over and fell into a deep and dreamless sleep.

Twenty-three

Hours later as she dressed for the show, Regan's head was still pounding and her hands had yet to stop trembling. She tried to refocus her attention on the case, tried to redirect her thoughts to Lester Ray and his victims, but her mind kept returning to the cemetery. Inside her head, voices bounced back and forth between denial of Dolly's news—*she has to be lying, my father would have told me*—to anger—*how dare he not tell me?*

The story she'd heard that afternoon had shaken her very foundation.

How could it possibly be true?

But . . . why would Dolly make up such a thing if it wasn't?

Regan cursed with frustration as she poked a thumbnail through her pantyhose and a run rapidly spread down the entire length of her leg. She pulled the stockings off and tossed them across the room. She tried again with a new pair she'd bought on her outing earlier. She slipped the top over her head and stepped into the skirt. Her fingers fumbled with the button and she had trouble getting her earrings on. She tried putting on makeup but her hands still had a bit of tremor and she smudged mascara on her eyelid.

Hell with it all. She took a deep breath, pinned her hair back, and washed her face. The canvas once again blank, she took control and started over. When she finished reapplying all her makeup—without smudges—she studied her reflection in the bathroom mirror. To her own eye, her skin remained pale beneath the powder, her eyes uncertain behind the mascaraed lashes.

"Best I can do," she said to her reflection, then snapped off the light. "The rest I leave to the station's makeup artist."

If there'd been a way out of this show tonight, she'd have taken it. The buzz in her head had been relentless all afternoon and she was having trouble thinking. She'd glanced at herself in the mirror and barely recognized herself.

She put on her jacket and shoes, found her purse, and was halfway out the door when she remembered she'd left her phone on the desk. The battery was down to next to nothing so she didn't bother to go back for it. Besides, there was no one she wanted to talk to. Mitch had called several times but she just wasn't ready to return his calls. What could she say?

Oh, hey, honey, you're not going to believe the day I've had . . .

For the first time in her life, she wasn't sure she knew who she was. Regan Landry? Or Regan Kroll? She didn't think she could face anyone until she knew.

Of all nights to have to appear on national television.

Then again, she reminded herself, it will be so anonymous. People see you, but they don't know you, can't touch you, don't know your secrets.

Mitch would need to know, but she wasn't ready to share.

The call came to announce that the car the station had sent for her had arrived. She tucked her room key into her pocket and headed out the door. For the next several hours, she was going to have to put Eddie Kroll—and Josh Landry—out of her mind. She hoped she could.

The room was dark and silent, except for the ringing in his head, and for one long minute Mitch had no idea where he was. It took several seconds before he realized the ringing was the alarm on his watch, which was on the arm under his pillow. He turned off the alarm, turned on the light, and checked the time: nine fifty-one. He ran a hand over his face and sat up, remembering why he'd wanted to be awakened. He went into the bathroom and splashed cold water on his face, hoping to clear the drowsy fog from his brain.

Better, he thought as he came back into the bedroom and turned on the television. Five minutes to show time.

The phone rang, and he smiled. Just as he'd thought. Did he know his girl?

"Hey, babe," he said.

"Hey yourself, big guy." Tom's normally deep voice replied in falsetto.

"Shit, Tom. What's up?"

"Nothing you're going to like hearing."

"Christ, not another one . . ." Mitch sat down on the edge of the bed.

"Yeah, another body, but not what you're thinking." Tom cleared his throat. "You'll never guess who was pulled out of the marsh up there near the wildlife reserve."

"I have no idea."

"Lester Ray Barnes."

The theme music for *And Justice for All* began to play.

"Mitch? You there?" Tom asked.

"Yeah. Yeah, I'm here. When and how?"

"How, one clean shot through the back of the head. But the when is just gonna kill you." Tom paused. "The body was found a few hours ago by someone working for the reserve who'd gone out to check on one of the new foals, one of those wild horses? Found the body in one of those marshy areas. The ME says he's been dead for almost two weeks."

"Can't be him," Mitch said flatly. "After two weeks in a marsh, the body has to be badly decomposed, especially in the heat we've been having. What makes them so sure it's Lester Ray?"

"His wallet was in his back pocket."

"How can that be, Tom? We've been told the DNA from the hairs found on the bodies is a match to Lester Ray." Mitch's eyes were on the TV, where Owen Berger was just introducing his lone guest.

"Hey, I can't explain it."

"Maybe the wallet was a plant," Mitch thought out loud. "Maybe it's someone else, someone Lester Ray killed and dumped with his ID, to throw us off."

He thought back to the photographs and the placement of those hairs. "Or maybe someone planted the hairs."

"You got any thoughts on how you'd go about getting some other guy's pubic hairs, Mitch?"

"Ahhh, no."

"Me, either," Tom said. "Oh, almost forgot. This body's in real bad shape, but there's a little bit of a tattoo on his upper right shoulder. What's left of his right shoulder, anyway. Two numbers, looks like a six and a one. One of the Carolina state guys says it looks like the kind of tattoo guys get in prison, you know? Handmade, not professional."

"Someone's following up with the Florida Department of Corrections, I'm assuming. If the body is Lester Ray's, he'd have gotten the tattoo on their watch."

"Right. I already sent digital photos of the tattoo via computer to the warden. He should know if it matches the style of the ones his boys give each other."

"They're going to need to send some tissue samples to our lab to run the DNA profile," Mitch said.

"We'll be sending samples first thing in the morning," Tom told him. "Oh, and one other thing. Kendra finished her sketch. She's uploading it now and will be sending it to you within the next twenty minutes or so."

"Anyone we know?" Mitch asked, distracted. He moved closer to the screen and Regan's image. He studied her face. Something was wrong.

"No one I've seen before, but chances are, once we get the sketch out there, someone's going to know him."

Mitch hung up and raised the volume on the television. He was almost face-to-face with Regan's image on the screen. She was pale, paler than he'd ever seen her. And her eyes weren't right. They seemed unable to focus or to stay focused on any one thing. She appeared nervous, jumpy. Distracted.

Something was very wrong. Mitch was certain of it.

He dialed her number one more time.

"What's wrong, baby?" he said softly after the beep. "Call me, please, Regan. Tell me what's wrong . . . whatever it is, let me help . . ."

He closed his phone and dropped it into the pocket of his jeans, his eyes still on the screen.

"Tell us how you became involved with Lester Ray Barnes in the first place," Owen was saying to Regan.

"Actually, I first heard about him while watching your show, the night Roland Booth was on talking about Lester Ray's trial, subsequent incarceration, and death sentence."

"We have so much to talk about tonight, I hope we can fit it all in." Owen glanced at the note cards on the table. "First of all, Roland Booth has been a victim of foul play himself recently, yes?"

"Yes." Regan nodded. "But as far as I know, there are no suspects in custody at this time."

"That was such a big shock to me, I have to tell you, Regan. The man had been sitting right where you're sitting . . . well, as you said, you saw him." Owen gestured toward the chair. "Now, do you think Lester Ray is responsible for Roland's death . . . ?"

"Personally, I don't. And it's my understanding that the FBI profiler didn't think Lester Ray killed him, either. There'd be no benefit to Lester Ray to murder his lawyer."

"You saw Booth on my show. What happened next?"

Regan walked Owen through her contacts with Booth, with the district attorney, and with Barnes.

"So you were trying to look at this case from every angle?"

"I was." Regan nodded. "I needed to know if it was something I was willing to invest a good deal of my time on."

"And you'd decided to write the book . . . Why?"

"Well, you have a very compelling story here: the nightmare of the innocent man having been convicted of a crime—not because the

evidence proved his guilt, but because others with an agenda pre-
sented bad testimony, testimony that could only have led to a guilty
verdict. That sort of thing goes against everything we say we stand
for. And then of course if Lester Ray was innocent, that would mean
that Carolyn Preston's killer had gotten away with murder. That, too,
goes against our sense of fair play."

"Truth, justice, and the American way?"

"Something like that," Regan told him. "But also, after I spent
some time speaking with Lester Ray, I realized that he was one of
those people who'd had it all stacked against him from the very beginning." She counted off on her fingers. "He'd been abandoned by
his mother—never knew his father's name—and later was placed into
the foster system by his grandparents. He went through a series of
foster homes, finally landed in a very good and loving home, but that
only lasted a year. His foster mother fell ill; he and the other kids in
the home were removed and sent elsewhere. Later, the woman died.
Again, abandonment. Then, he's arrested for this murder, put on
trial, and convicted for all the wrong reasons."

"Do you think he killed her? The woman he was convicted of
killing?" Owen asked.

Regan hesitated, then said, "You know, Owen, I never really was
sure about that either way. Now, I think maybe there's a good chance
he did."

"And of course, since his release, he's suspected of killing four
women, that we know of. Do you now regret your involvement with
him? Do you feel any guilt, feel as if you helped put this monster back
on the streets?"

The question appeared to catch her off guard.

"You should have seen that coming, babe," Mitch said under his
breath.

"Lester Ray was put back on the streets because people lied at his
trial. If the lab owner had testified honestly, if the witness hadn't been
coerced, there'd have been nothing for Roland Booth to have taken
back to the courts. So to answer your question, I don't believe the

fact that I was interested in writing this book had anything to do with his release. The judge had no choice but to let him go."

"Are you still planning on writing that book?"

"Probably not. I think I'm too close to the story now. Besides I haven't been able to get in touch with Lester Ray for the past several weeks."

"Since the killings started again."

"I spoke with him after the first two victims were found, the first in Georgia and the second in North Carolina, right after he arrived in the Outer Banks. Shortly after, Sandy Eakin's body was found, and I've been unable to reach him since."

"You think maybe he decided that killing helpless women is more interesting than collaborating on a book with you?"

In his room at the inn, Mitch winced. Regan chose to sail right by the salacious remark.

"It's hard to know what's going through his mind, Owen. I honestly don't know. But I never in a million years would have guessed that he'd have gone on this killing spree."

"Why's that?"

"I just didn't see that viciousness in him."

"But you do now?"

"The facts speak for themselves." She took a sip of water.

"What's this we're hearing about a second killer?" Owen leaned closer.

"I think you're going to need to speak with the FBI about that." She shrugged. "I don't know what that situation is right now, and I don't want to give wrong information."

Owen turned to face the camera.

"Maybe someone from the FBI can call us at the number on the bottom of the screen and give us the right info." Owen smiled. "We'll be back after the break . . ."

There was a *ding* sound from the next room, signaling that e-mail had arrived. He went into the sitting room, turned on the light, and leaned over his laptop.

E-mail from Kendra with an attachment. He pulled out a chair, sat, opened the attachment, and watched the face appear.

Light brown hair, slightly thinning. Wide-set brown eyes. A broad forehead, ears close to his head, narrow nose and thin lips.

Mitch stared at the face for almost a full minute. It was a face he'd never seen before.

Mitch debated his next move. He opened his phone, punched in numbers, and listened to it ring for what seemed like a long time. He was very disappointed to have to leave voice mail.

"Annie, it's Mitch. Something's come up and I—"

"Mitch, sorry. I couldn't find the phone." Annie sounded out of breath. "What's going on?"

"Are you near a television?"

"Yes. What do I want to watch?" she asked.

"*And Justice for All.* I don't know what channel you get it on there."

"I have it, hold on . . . okay, there it is. What's tonight's show about?"

"Regan's on, talking about the book she was going to do with Lester Ray. There have been a number of developments that she doesn't know about. I wanted to run a few things past you if you have a minute."

"Go on," she said.

Mitch filled her in on the information he'd gotten earlier from Tom.

When he finished, she said, "Let me get this straight. There's been trace found on the bodies of the last victims that definitely came from Lester Ray."

"Right."

"But Lester Ray has been dead for almost two weeks."

"If in fact that's Lester Ray they pulled out of the marsh."

"And you have a facial composite of the man who was seen in the bar with your last two victims."

"Right."

"Okay, so we want to connect those dots." Annie's breath in the phone was steady and even.

"The sooner the better."

"Okay, this is what I'm seeing. Let's start with the body. Obviously you need a positive ID on that. Could be Lester Ray, could be this other guy."

"If it's Lester Ray, why would he plant his own hair on his victims?" Mitch wondered.

"Could be his way of bragging. He'd be figuring you know it's him anyway. Why not stick it in your face?"

"I could buy that."

"And if the killer is this second guy, he'd be doing it to keep the kills in Lester Ray's column. Keep the heat on Lester Ray, no one's looking for him."

"Think they could have been working together?" Mitch asked. "Lester Ray and this second guy? They maybe planted another body to throw us off, make us think Lester Ray is out of the picture . . ."

"While the two of them continue to play their game? I wouldn't rule out anything right now."

"Then maybe we should turn the heat up on our UNSUB," Mitch said. "Let him know we're on to him. Put out the story about finding Lester Ray's body, make Kendra's composite public."

"It will be interesting to see how he reacts, once the spotlight is turned on him. All this time, he's been hiding behind Lester Ray," Annie mused. "Which is a sure way to have Lester Ray blamed for the murders."

"Why?" Mitch asked. "What would be the motive?"

"Well, there's the obvious, so that he can have all the fun of the kill with none of the pressure of being hunted. If he's working with Lester Ray, it's a good way to confuse everyone."

"Does that seem very simplistic to you? Maybe a little too convenient, too coincidental?"

"Sure does," Annie agreed. "And you know, I don't believe much in coincidence."

She fell silent for a moment, and Mitch wasn't sure she was still on the line.

"Annie?" he asked.

"I'm still here. I'm just thinking of other reasons why you'd want to blame someone else for murders they didn't commit."

"You'd have to be pretty angry with that someone," Mitch noted.

"That's what I'm thinking, too."

"Carolyn Preston's sister and brothers were really angry when Lester Ray was released from prison," Mitch told her.

"I remember, they'd confronted Regan after she left the courthouse," Annie said. "I could maybe see motive there for one of them to have killed Lester Ray, but not the girls. They wouldn't have killed the girls."

"Not even if that would send him back to prison for good?"

"Absolutely not. There's no way they'd want any other family to go through what they went through. Besides, you have a composite there. Does it look like either of the brothers?"

Mitch walked back to the laptop and stared at the screen. "No. They're younger than this guy is. Darker hair . . . uh-uh. This isn't either of them. Of course, they could have hired someone."

"Mitch, I don't see it, but certainly, check them out."

"Lester Ray's been behind bars for years now. Maybe he pissed someone off while he was in prison, and they're getting even now."

"Which means they'd be out now, too, though. Maybe the warden in Florida could help you there," Annie suggested.

"We'll look into that. Thanks for the tip."

"You're welcome. Now, what are you thinking about doing with that sketch?"

"I'm thinking of faxing it in to Owen Berger right now and asking him to put it up on the screen."

"Excellent idea. Go ahead and toss that bait out there, see what you catch," she said. "Good luck."

"Thanks. I'll be in touch." He hung up as he walked back into the bedroom. He stood in front of the television screen, his phone in his hand.

Regan was going to be blindsided if he faxed the sketch in without any explanation, he thought, and she has no idea what's been going on, doesn't know about the body that may or may not be Lester Ray's.

This was one of those times he was going to have to lead with his chin, he told himself. The show was running out of time. He'd act now, get the okay later. He hoped his boss would understand.

He dialed the phone number on the screen.

"You've reached *And Justice for All*," the recorded message played in his ear. "Please hold, and your call will be answered by the first available operator . . ."

Mitch sat on hold for a full minute before the call was picked up.

"Special Agent Mitchell Peyton," he told the woman who answered. "Mr. Berger requested that an agent close to the Barnes investigation call in."

"I'll put you through."

"Wait. Can you give me a fax number?"

"Certainly." She read off a number and he copied it down, then clicked the keys to put his computer into fax mode.

"Anything else, Agent?"

"Just put me through to Owen, please." Mitch sent the fax.

"Please hold."

A moment later, Owen was on the line.

"Agent . . . ?"

"Peyton. Mitchell Peyton." He watched the screen, and saw the faintest hint of a smile touch Regan's lips. The smile barely touched her eyes, and that worried him.

"Agent Peyton, are you actively involved with the Barnes case?" Owen was asking.

"Yes." Mitch's eyes never left Regan's face.

"What are you able to tell us?"

"I can tell you that, based on the evidence we now have, Lester Ray Barnes did not murder Sandra Eakin or Justina Waters."

"That's news." Owen looked into the camera as if addressing Mitch directly. "The FBI has proof of this?"

"The body of Lester Ray Barnes was found in the marsh above Duck a few hours ago. The medical examiner thinks he's been dead for as long as two weeks. Clearly, he could not have committed either of these murders."

Regan appeared to have been struck dumb.

"Is there a suspect?" Owen was obviously delighted to have this revealed—live—on his show.

"We have a composite sketch of a person of interest that will be released in the morning. But we wanted to make this new information public as soon as possible. Up until now, everyone's been focused on looking for Lester Ray. I'm faxing the composite to your studio right now, and I'm going to ask you to show the picture."

"You're sending it here, now?" Owen's eyes were wide and he looked behind him, off the set. "Yes, they're telling me a fax is coming through. We should be able to show it on the screen in just another minute or so."

Owen got out of his chair and reached off stage. When he turned back to the camera, he held up the faxed picture.

"This is the man you believe to be the killer, Agent . . ."

"Peyton. We believe he has a connection to Lester Ray Barnes and to the case we're currently investigating."

"So, if anyone recognizes this face, they should do what?"

"Call my office." Mitch gave the number. "Give whatever information you have. If you think you've seen him before, or you think you know him, call as soon as possible."

"Agent Peyton." Regan addressed him for the first time.

"Yes, Ms. Landry?" Mitch smiled. In his ear, he heard the call-waiting signal. Probably his boss, wanting to know what the hell he was doing. He'd call John as soon as the show concluded.

"If I recall, there was evidence removed from the bodies of the victims that contained Lester Ray's DNA."

"That's correct."

"How is that possible, if he was already dead when these killings took place?"

"We're still trying to figure that out."

"Let me get this straight." Owen's eyes were glowing now. "The FBI has documented that Barnes's DNA was found on the victims, but he'd already been dead for days when they were killed?"

"That's correct."

"Well, I'd say the FBI has quite the mystery on their hands." Owen was rubbing his chin thoughtfully. "Stay with us, everyone, I'm being told we have to take a break now. We'll be right back with Regan Landry and Special Agent Peyton . . ." Owen told his audience.

Mitch heard the call waiting signal again, and ignored it. A few seconds later it clicked again. Seconds later, yet again. He looked at his phone and saw the message on the screen: 1 NEW VOICE MAIL.

He disconnected the call to Berger's show and accessed his voice mail, then cursed himself for not having taken the call when it first came through.

"Mitch, it's Dorsey Collins. Call me the minute you get this message. I know who your mystery man is . . ."

Twenty-four

Mitch returned Dorsey's call within seconds. "I'm all ears."

"The man you're looking for is Erwin Capshaw. Convicted of raping and torturing a woman to the extent that she's been institutionalized since the attack."

"Why isn't he behind bars?"

"He was, for several years, but he was the first of the inmates released following Eugene Potts's admission of having played with the lab results."

"Played how?"

"He misplaced the samples from both the victim and from Capshaw. Instead of admitting it and asking for new samples, he lied on the stand. Said there was a definite match."

"So there wasn't even anything left to test . . ."

"*Nada.* He couldn't even find the clothing the victim had been wearing the night she was attacked." Dorsey swore softly under her breath. "Dumb shit screwed up, and that bastard got to walk."

"You sound as if you believe he was guilty."

"I tracked him for weeks, Mitch. I brought him in. There's no doubt in my mind that he was guilty."

"How long has he been out?"

"He got out right before Barnes did. His was the first case to be dismissed because of Potts's fuck-up."

"What do you know about this guy?"

"He's a sadistic little coward," she said flatly.

"You think he'd have worked with Lester Ray on this? Maybe as second man?"

"No. Cappy doesn't play well with others."

"Do you know if he and Lester Ray knew each other? If he'd have had any reason to have it in for Barnes?"

"They were both in the same prison, both in the max unit; their paths must have crossed at some point. But they wouldn't have been friends. Capshaw had no friends. He's strictly a loner." Dorsey fell silent, then said, "But I'm betting there was no love lost there, as far as Cappy was concerned."

"What do you mean?"

"Capshaw was the first man let out after the lab story broke, like I said. Booth filed the brief for Barnes shortly thereafter."

"How come I never heard of this guy?" Mitch frowned.

"Capshaw was a lifer. Barnes was on death row with only a few weeks left to live. Both get out of prison around the same time, but which story has more pop?"

"The guy on death row," Mitch replied without hesitation.

"Right. And Booth played up that innocent man snatched from the jaws of death thing in a really big way. He came on like gang-busters, Mitch. You couldn't turn on the television down here but Booth was there. I'll give him this, he got great coverage for his client."

"And pushed Capshaw right out of the picture."

"Hey, Capshaw was yesterday's paper, once Booth got hold of the media. Lester Ray was less than two weeks away from his date with the death chamber when Booth went to court and started talking up Lester Ray's predicament."

"And Capshaw fell into obscurity."

"The real nowhere man of the story," Dorsey agreed. "There's no question in my mind but that Capshaw was mightily pissed off."

"Think he was pissed enough to kill Roland Booth?" Mitch asked.

"Oh, yeah," Dorsey told him. "I think he was pissed off enough to kill anyone who had a hand in snatching his fifteen minutes right out from under his nose."

"Capshaw had to sit there and watch Barnes get all the media attention. All the hoopla he thought should have been his."

"Newspapers, magazines, television," Dorsey said. "Not to mention a book deal."

"Oh, shit." A chill went up Mitch's spine. "Regan . . ."

Twenty-five

The car dropped Regan off in front of her hotel less than an hour after the show had gone off the air. She'd begged off Owen's suggestion that they go out for a drink, pleading a killer headache, which was the absolute truth. She was halfway across the lobby when she heard someone calling her name.

She turned to find Stella and Dolly coming toward her.

"We watched you on the show," Dolly was saying. "You looked so pale and tired, I said to Stella, we have to go get her. She should not be staying in a hotel all by herself after . . . well, after today."

"And I said, of course she should not." Stella reached Regan first and put an arm around her. To Regan, it offered all the comfort of a soft shawl. "And I told her, Dolly, you should have prepared her a little better. You just don't tell someone something like that without a little bit of, you know, foreplaying."

Regan smiled in spite of herself.

"Stella, you mean forewarning," Dolly corrected her.

"Look, I appreciate you both coming here. And I appreciate that you're concerned about me," Regan told them, "but really, I'm all right. I just want to get some sleep."

"I know how upset you must be, and I'm not sure that I agree with what Dolly did today, or the way she did it, but I really do believe you have the right to know. It was time, honey. I really think your father would have wanted you to know."

"Then why didn't he tell me himself?"

"I'm not sure that he wouldn't have," Stella said gently. "He just didn't expect to die when he did. The last time we saw him—"

"Wait a minute. You saw him? You met with him?"

"Oh, of course. Every time he came to the Midwest, we got together," Dolly told her.

"You never mentioned that." Regan stared at Stella accusingly. "You told me you didn't know him."

"I think what I told you was that I didn't know him when he was a child, before he went away," Stella replied.

"He may have changed his name, he may have put his past behind him, but he never stopped needing his family," Dolly told Regan. "He realized that after we showed up at his book signing the first time he was on tour out here. Carl saw his picture in the paper and thought it looked an awful lot like Eddie, so of course, Carl, Stella, me and Frank, my husband—he was still alive then—we all had to go and see if it was really him. It had been almost seventeen years since we'd seen each other. He was sitting at a table, signing books, and when Carl walked up to him, I thought he was going to burst into tears." Dolly sighed, remembering. "I did burst into tears. We had one grand reunion that night, and we never lost touch from that day until the day before he died."

"I think if he'd known how and when he was going to leave us," Stella said, "he'd have made sure you'd know where to find us."

"I don't know what to do about all this, I don't know how I feel and I don't know what to say to either of you." Regan felt her throat tighten. "And I'm not sure I understand why the two of you drove all the way up here."

"We didn't think you should be staying alone tonight," Stella said simply. "We know you must have questions you need to ask."

"So you thought you'd bunk in with me here tonight?"

"No, we thought we'd take you back to Sayreville with us. Dolly made up her guest room for you, so you'd have a place to stay."

"I don't think I . . ." Regan began to shake her head.

"Same room your dad stayed in when he was here," Dolly said. "We were thinking maybe it was time you did, too."

Regan looked from Dolly to Stella. Maybe they were right, these two unlikely aunts of hers. Maybe it was time.

"All right." Regan nodded. "Let's go up to my room and get my things . . ."

He lounged on the bed and waited until the credits had finished rolling before turning off the television.

"Looks like it's time to get out of Dodge."

That FBI fella with Regan must be smarter than he looks, he thought as he started to empty the clothes from the closet into the suitcase he'd picked up only last week. Good thing he'd done all that shopping while he could; by morning his picture was going to be everywhere.

Won't that be a big shock to all those nice folks he's been hanging around with here? He chuckled as he tossed his razor and toiletries in with his clothes. He could just hear the conversation in the coffee bar the next day.

"Why, we went sailing with him over the weekend!"

"We had dinner with him just last night!"

Oh, yes, you did, Sheila Letterman. You and your sister Kelly Ann had dinner with a serial killer, even had our picture taken together. Now, that's what I call a souvenir. Yes, sir, beats those Outer Banks coffee mugs and T-shirts any day!

Those old biddies will be talking about that for the rest of their lives.

He was still laughing when he checked the dresser, looked under the bed, and took one more look in the bathroom. He'd packed it all.

He snapped off the light, then opened the door. He turned back to look at the room. He really wished he didn't have to leave. He'd liked it here. He'd wanted to stay a few more weeks at the very least. Damn that agent calling in when he did. Now he not only had to leave, he'd have to leave the island while he still could. He knew there'd been a checkpoint out there on route 12 earlier in the week, but since they'd found Lester Ray's body, he figured they'd closed that down. No point looking in cars for a man they already had in the morgue, right? But any minute now, someone would figure he'd be primed to move on, and they'd be right. Only difference was, he'd already have gone. He just wasn't sure where.

He closed the door and went right to the parking lot. Sooner or later, they'd realize he'd slipped out on the bill. They had the credit card information, though, and they'd just bill the charges to it.

He'd like to see them try to collect. As far as he knew, dead men didn't write checks.

He smiled as he opened the trunk of the car and put his suitcase inside. He got into the car and drove from the parking lot onto the road that followed the sound for a half mile or so before feeding onto the highway. He rolled down his window when he stopped at the stop sign. From off in the distant darkness, a night creature screamed. A howl of terror, or a cry of triumph; he couldn't tell for sure. He thought of how the sounds were so similar, how over the course of his life, he'd known both intimately.

Now there was a story, he thought, a story that should have been told. Would have been told, if that asshole Roland Booth hadn't jumped in there with both feet. Why couldn't he have waited a week or two? What would it have mattered, in the long run? No way the state wasn't going to let Lester Ray go.

But no. He had to charge ahead, pushing everyone out of his way. And that dumb shit representing me just let him do it.

What's the difference, Erwin? They let you out of prison, didn't they? Who cares if he's getting all the publicity?

"I care, you dumb dick. I care."

Funny thing was, up until then, he hadn't even thought about selling his story, but once the seed was planted, once he saw how Lester Ray was being treated, it just burned the hell out of him that no one was beating a path to his door. No one gave a shit about how he felt, no one bothered to ask him what it was like for him those years he spent in prison.

No television for him, no interviews. No book deal.

Well, there wasn't going to be a book deal for Lester Ray now, either, was there? Teach him to get in my way. Bastard.

He drove for over an hour without a destination. He wasn't getting tired. He could drive all night if he had to. He only wished he knew where he was going. He turned on the radio for company, but when he started through the Great Dismal Swamp and heard mostly static, he got tired of jumping from one station to another, trying to find one with a strong signal. To kill time, he started thinking about how his own story might sound, if it was written down the way Lester Ray's would have been.

At eight-thirty the next morning, he drove into the parking lot of a donut and coffee place. Twenty minutes later, after having purchased his breakfast and used the men's room, he headed off for the public library.

He had a plan and a destination. All he needed now were directions.

Twenty-six

"What do you mean, she's not there?" Mitch snapped at the Chicago agent who'd had the misfortune to call his counterpart in North Carolina with news he didn't want to hear.

"Hey, Peyton, don't yell at me. You called me at ten thirty, I was here, at her hotel, by eleven fifteen. She'd already checked out."

"Sorry, Chuck. I don't suppose the desk clerk knows where she went."

"The desk clerk came on at eleven. He wasn't even here when she left."

"Thanks. I owe you." Mitch hung up and blew out a long hot breath of frustration.

Where the hell was Regan? Why wasn't she returning his calls?

Mitch walked outside and leaned on the porch rail. He'd checked the airlines only to find that she'd cancelled her ticket to Norfolk, and the car she'd had waiting for her as well. Where would she have gone?

And why wasn't she telling him?

He opened his phone again to check for messages, but his voice mail box was still empty.

Why would she have cancelled her ticket out of Chicago?

Maybe, it occurred to him, because she wasn't leaving Chicago this morning. Maybe she'd decided to call on Dolly Brown after all.

He went back into his room and sat at his computer, determined to find the right Brown if it took him all afternoon.

It pretty much had. By the time he'd found Dolly and explained who he was, Regan had already left for the airport. But at least he knew where she was going. She was flying into Philly, and from there had a charter to Princeton Airport.

"Do you know why she changed her mind?" Mitch had asked Dolly.

"I'm afraid you'll have to ask her that," Dolly had responded.

"Did she have a good visit?"

"You'll have to ask her that, too," Dolly had said, right before she hung up.

I can see where the woman gets on Regan's nerves, he thought as he dialed the number for the Landry farm. At best, he thought, Bliss would still be there and could take a message. At worst, he could leave a message for Regan on her answering machine.

He'd almost given up on hearing a live voice when the phone was picked up.

"Hello?"

"Hello, is this Bliss?" he asked.

"Yes."

"This is Mitch Peyton, I'm a friend of Regan's. Is she there?"

"No, she isn't."

"Well, do you know what time she'll be there?"

"No. I'm sorry."

"Well, you do know that she's going home today, right? Have you spoken with her today?"

"No, I'm sorry."

"Well, would you tell her to call me right away, as soon as she gets there? She has the number. Tell her it's very important."

"Sure. Okay."

"Thanks." Mitch hung up, wondering why Regan was so high on her assistant. The woman had all the personality of a shoe.

He took a bottle of water from the bag he'd brought back from the drugstore earlier that morning, opened it, and took a long swig. He pulled up a map of the United States on his computer screen and stared at it. If he were Erwin Capshaw, where would he be?

Ten minutes later, he was still asking himself that same question. Finally, he had to admit he'd never have the answer. He didn't know Capshaw, didn't know how he thought. There was only one person he knew who did. He called her back.

"Any chance you could join us on this job?" he asked Dorsey when she picked up. "I don't know this guy. None of us do. I'm thinking we'll find him sooner if you're in."

"If you can clear it, I'm there," she told him.

"I can clear it," he told her. "How soon can you get here?"

"I can be there by tomorrow morning."

"Not soon enough. I need to know where he is, what he's thinking."

"Hey, I don't need to travel out of state to help you there. He's thinking he wants what he wants. He'll go wherever he has to go to get it."

"Thanks, Dorsey. I have no idea what that means."

"You think he wants to talk to Regan? He'll go where she is."

"How will he know where to find her?"

"You're kidding, right?" She made a *tsk* sound. "He'll go to a library or a bookstore and he'll look up her books. He'll read her bio and every damned thing he can find out about her until he figures out where she lives. It may take him a while, but trust me, if he's determined to find her, he will."

"Thanks, Dorce. That's what I needed to know. Talk to you soon."

His next call was to the Plainsville police.

"You did real good, hon."

Bliss's unexpected visitor patted her on the back and she visibly cringed.

He laughed. "Don't worry, I'm not going to hurt you. I told you. You help me, I'll help you."

He pointed to a chair in the study where'd he chased her when he'd arrived at the Landry farm around noon.

"I want you to sit there, and I want you to stay there."

She sat, never taking her eyes off him.

When he approached her with the length of rope, she opened her mouth to scream. He slapped a hand over her mouth and whispered in her ear, "That kind of behavior isn't good for your baby."

He wrapped the rope around her ankles.

"Both hands behind your back. And if you don't make me tell you again, I won't tie your wrists as tightly as your ankles."

He looped the rope around her hands and pulled. Before she could protest, he tied a scarf he'd taken from Regan's dresser upstairs over her mouth.

"Now, I'm going to do a little more exploring," he told her, "and you're going to wait patiently for me to come back. If you're a good girl, I might even let you have a few sips of water later."

He ruffled her hair and pretended not to notice that she'd drawn back from him again.

Well, what do you expect, he told himself as he went up the main stairwell. *You blow in here, you scream in her face, interrogate her, tie her up, make her answer the phone at gunpoint. Oh, and yeah. You shoot her husband when he comes to pick her up. That would make any woman a bit touchy.*

He poked from room to room, studying the way people lived in this house. From the master bedroom, which looked as if it hadn't been used in a long time, with its empty closets and dresser drawers, to two connected rooms that were probably used as guest rooms, since there was nothing personal in either of them. No books, no photos. Nothing that your average person would normally keep in their rooms.

Not that he'd know firsthand what normal people did, or kept in their private spaces. He'd seen magazines, though, and movies. Neither of these rooms appeared to be anyone's private space. Then there was Regan's room.

It was high-ceilinged and looked out across the fields to the pond.

The furniture was painted white and had some kind of vines painted on it. This room had framed photographs, lots of them. He stared at each one, and followed Regan through her childhood to her teen years, then into young adulthood. Photos of friends, her parents, several with dogs.

He studied the images without emotion.

See, he told himself. *That's what I'm talking about. Normal people. Normal rooms.*

From her window he could see some kind of flowering tree that dropped large white petals on the ground, and behind that, grapevines grew over an arbor. He opened a window and let in the scent of wild roses and honeysuckle. He closed his eyes and breathed in deeply, the scent sending him somewhere back a long way in time.

Well, no surprise there. Today he'd spent more time looking back than he had in years. It was painful, mostly. Most of his memories hurt. But it was okay. He'd have to face it, all of it, since he'd need to remember those things if he was going to share it with Regan. She was going to need it for the book.

He went back downstairs and wandered, sitting first on the camelback sofa in the formal living room—which he found too stiff for his taste—and then on the well-worn slip-covered sofa in the family room, which was a little too soft. He started back to the study, where the leather sofa had been just right.

Just like the those bears, he chuckled.

"And here's Goldilocks," he said as he came through the door.

Bliss had tears running down her face and she was beginning to shake.

"Now, listen," he told her. "You like that baby of yours, right? You want that baby to be born, right?"

She nodded her head up and down, sobbing.

"Then you are just going to have to get hold of yourself, hear me? Don't piss me off." He sat on the sofa opposite her. "Crying pisses me off. You know what my old man used to do when my old lady cried?"

He lifted his feet and rested them on the hassock.

"He'd smack her. 'You want to cry, I'll give you something to cry about.' And he did." He looked at Bliss, whose wide eyes seemed even larger. "Do not make me give you something to cry about, okay? You're a nice girl, I can tell you are. Don't piss me off."

He rested his head against the back of the sofa and closed his eyes. After a time, Bliss's sobs had softened into sniffles, and then, eventually, stopped. He was really glad she had quit. He couldn't have taken five more minutes of that choking crying she was doing. At least now she was settling down, which was a good thing. The last thing he wanted was for Regan to come in and think he'd been abusing her assistant.

Shame he'd had to shoot her husband, but damn it, the guy wouldn't go away. He kept banging on the door, over and over. And of course, once he'd shot the husband, the wife proceeded to wail for an hour. Only threats of harm to that baby she carried were keeping her in line.

He was standing in the window looking out toward the road when he first saw the headlights. There was no missing the light bar on the roof, even though the lights were turned off.

"We have company, missy."

He turned back to Bliss and said, "We're going to need an award-winning performance from you, you understand? That's the police out there. If you don't say what you need to say to make them go away happy, I will blow your head off. At that point, I will have nothing to lose, so if you die, your baby dies. I won't give a shit, you hear me?"

He was untying her hands and feet as fast as he could. He pulled her to her feet and pushed her to the side door.

"I asked you if you understood?"

"Yes. I understand."

"Then open the door. And do not forget for one second that I am only one step behind you."

Bliss did as she was told.

"Hi," the young police officer said when she opened the door. "You Miss Landry?"

"No. I'm her assistant. She's out of town."

"Know when she'll be back?"

"I spoke with her earlier in the day, but she wasn't sure when she'd be home. Something about connecting flights."

"That your car there in the drive?" He shined the light on it.

"Yes."

"Have you been here all day?"

"Yes. Since around eight this morning."

"Notice anything unusual?"

"No. Nothing."

"Are you here alone?"

"Yes. What's this about?"

"It's just a precaution. We got a call from the FBI, seems there's a fugitive who might be headed here. It could be an overreaction on their part, but it's probably not a good idea for you to be out here alone."

"Actually, officer, I was just getting ready to leave. I just need to check the doors and set the alarm."

"Would you like me to wait for you?"

"Oh, no. That's not necessary. I won't be a minute."

"Well, if you're sure . . ."

"I'm positive. Thanks anyway."

"Close the door slowly," Capshaw whispered in Bliss's ear.

She did as she was told.

"You're really a very good liar, you know that?" He slid the bolt to lock the door. "I'll bet you lied a lot as a kid."

He watched out the window, the gun to the back of Bliss's head, until the patrolman got into his car and started the engine. Capshaw watched the taillights disappear back down the drive.

"Now, back into the study with you."

"May I have some water?" Bliss asked, her voice shaky. She'd been sweating heavily since he'd raised the gun to her head.

"Oh, I suppose so. You were a good girl."

He followed her into the kitchen, where she took a bottle of water from the pantry and opened it, and drank it half down.

"You want to slow down with that," he told her, gesturing with his gun in the direction of the hall that led back to the study. "You drink that too fast, you're going to get sick."

Back in the study, he retied her ankles and hands.

"I'll leave the gag out if you promise to be quiet," he told her.

"I'll be quiet," she whispered.

"That means no crying either."

"I promise."

He settled back into the soft leather. This really was the life. He'd thought the Windham Inn was a pretty sporty place, but this place, this was where it was at as far as he was concerned.

From across the room, he could see the shelves upon which Josh Landry's books were displayed. The guy sure had written a lot of books. Of course, Capshaw'd heard of him. Everyone knew who Josh Landry was. He wrote all those books about killers. He must have sold a lot of books, to afford a place like this.

Well, who's to say I can't do the same? I know lots of killers. I could write me up a couple of books, buy myself a crib like this . . .

Who am I kidding? I got a dead guy in the backyard and before the night is over, I'll probably have a dead woman in here.

He looked back over his shoulder at Bliss, whose eyes followed his every move.

There's no way I can talk my way out of all this, he told himself. The best I can hope for is that I get my story told, and then maybe disappear.

He was just thinking of places he could go where maybe he could hide for a while, places where maybe the FBI wouldn't look for him, when lights reflected onto the window. He looked out and saw the white sedan driving up the long dark lane. He watched as the car came to a stop near the back porch. Regan got out and slammed the door, then walked directly toward the side door.

"You will be quiet, hear? Don't make a sound. If you try to warn her, it will be very bad for you and your baby."

He went quietly through the hall and flattened himself against the wall. The kitchen light turned on, and he heard something thud as it hit the floor. Her bags, he thought. She stepped into the hall and called Bliss's name. When there was no answer, she walked around the corner and came face-to-face with the man Kendra had sketched.

"Welcome home, Miss Landry," he said. "We've been waiting for you."

Twenty-seven

Regan's first thought was that Kendra's sketch had been incredibly accurate.

"Where's Bliss?" Her heart was in her throat, pounding so loudly she was certain he could hear. "Her car's outside."

"Waiting for you in the study."

Regan tried to push past him, but he grabbed her arms and pushed her into the wall.

"You have to ask permission," he told her.

"I'd like to see Bliss." She fought the rising panic.

"Please." He leaned closer to her face. "I'd like to see Bliss, please."

"I'd like to see Bliss, please." She stared into his eyes. There was nothing there.

"That's better. That was nice." He stepped out of the way to permit her to pass.

She all but ran into the study, and was sickened to see Bliss tied up.

"You have to untie her." She turned to Capshaw. "She's pregnant, this isn't good for her."

"I don't think you're in any position to ask me for favors, do you?" He held up a handgun.

"What do you want?" she asked, her insides cold. She knew who this man was and had a damned good idea what he'd done. She'd done enough research and enough reading and more than enough interviews to know she had to play this exactly right, if she and Bliss were going to survive.

"Oh, I have what I want." He grinned. "Now I have everything I want."

"What do you want?" she repeated levelly, not permitting a hint of tension to show through her voice.

"I want you to do for me what you were doing for Lester Ray," he told her. "I want you to write my book."

"Write your book . . . ?" Had she heard correctly? "You want me to write a book . . . ?"

"Not a book." He waved the gun around and she held her breath. "*My* book. My story. You were all hot to trot to write Lester Ray's book, but let me tell you, that piece of shit had nothing on me."

"Ahhhh . . . well." She cleared her throat to mask her surprise. This man was a psychopath. She'd expected robbery or rape or torture or all three.

"What, you don't think I have a story?" His face began to redden and his eyes went a few shades darker.

"I'm sure you do, Mr.—I'm sorry, I don't know your name."

"What did you call Barnes?" he asked, as if it mattered.

"I called him Lester Ray."

"Then you'll call me Erwin."

"Erwin. Do you have a last name?" She took a deep breath and exhaled slowly, willing her voice to remain calm and low. She knew she could not afford to permit him to sense how terrified she was.

Once she'd asked her father how he was able to sit across the table from a man he knew was a vicious murderer and get that man to open up to him.

"Keep him talking. Listen carefully to what he says," her father had told her. "Find the key. Find his trigger. Never give up control, but let him think the stage is his. And never, as the saying goes, never let him see you sweat."

Easier to do, Dad, when you're sitting in a locked room with an armed guard and the guy you're interviewing is shackled. Not so easy to pull off when he's the one who's armed and you're on your own.

"Capshaw," he said. "Erwin Capshaw."

"Erwin Capshaw," she repeated. "I know that name from someplace."

"First man released by the state of Florida because of Eugene Potts's fuck-up," he told her. Was that a touch of pride in his voice? "You would have heard a lot more about me if that dickhead lawyer of Lester Ray's hadn't jumped right in there the way he did. Pushed me right off the front page."

"He stole your limelight," she said. "He got all the publicity that should have been yours."

She'd read once that many psychopathic personalities are narcissistic. *Copy that,* she thought.

"Dumb-ass Booth was everywhere, on TV, in the newspapers, everywhere I looked, pedaling that sob story about how poor Lester Ray was on death row, how he was just weeks away from death . . . well, that turned out to be true, didn't it?" He smirked. "I mean, that's what they said on the news. Somehow he got dead."

"Somehow." She nodded, studying his face.

"So, since you're not going to be writing his story, you can write mine."

"I'll consider it," she told him, testing the waters. How badly did he want this book written?

"You'll consider it?" He laughed. "You don't have much choice."

"Writing a book isn't a paint by numbers process," she told him without emotion. The less he saw of hers, the better. "It's a lot of work. It takes focus. It's a serious endeavor."

He appeared to like the sound of that. "Sure. I figured that."

"I can't focus while Bliss is tied up like this. You have to untie her." Regan moved to behind Bliss's chair. "She needs to keep her circulation moving. She needs to get up and walk around. If nothing else, at least let the poor woman go to the bathroom."

"Don't push it, Miss Landry." His eyes narrowed.

"What do you have to lose by letting the woman go to the bathroom?" She looked him in the eye with far more bravado than she felt. "You're the one in control. You've got the gun."

He considered this.

"All right. But you stay where you are until I have her untied."

Capshaw pulled the rope from her wrists and her ankles. She immediately began to sob.

"Shut up." He grabbed her by the collar and pulled her out of her chair. He looked up at Regan. "Make her shut up."

"Bliss, honey, pull it together." Regan came around to the front of the chair and took Bliss by the hands. "You need to stop. You're making him angry. Let's not do that."

"He shot Robert." Bliss rocked back and forth, sobbing. "He shot him, in the driveway."

"I'm sorry honey, I'm so sorry," Regan whispered, a cold rush running through her. Robert dead? Oh God . . .

"Shut her up, I'm warning you," Capshaw yelled.

"Bliss, you have to stop." Regan tried to help her up from the chair. "Come on, now, honey. I'm going to help you to the bathroom. Can you walk?"

Bliss continued to cry softly.

"That's better, honey. Come on. We don't want to make him mad," Regan told her.

"You are every bit as smart as you look," he said.

"Thanks." Regan started to lead Bliss from the room.

"Wait a minute, where do you think you're going?"

"I'm taking her to the bathroom," Regan told him.

"She's a big girl, big enough to get herself knocked up. She should be big enough to go to the bathroom without help from you."

"She would be, if her legs weren't so weak from sitting with her ankles tied together for so long. Isn't that right, Bliss?"

Bliss nodded vigorously.

"I can't take the chance that she'll fall." Regan continued to lead Bliss by the hand. Taking her cue from Regan, Bliss slowed down and walked on stiff legs.

"Don't think you're going to try to outsmart me here. You think you're gonna go out the window or something." He waved the gun around again.

"There's no window in the powder room off the kitchen," Regan told him. "No escape route there. Come on, Erwin. Don't make a big deal out of this."

"Okay, you can take her, but I'm right behind you."

The threesome made their way down the hall toward the kitchen. When they arrived at the powder room, Regan turned on the light and stepped inside, holding Bliss by the arm as if she were an invalid.

"May I please close the door, Erwin?" Regan asked.

"You can close it over, but not all the way," he said.

"Fine."

Regan pulled the door ninety percent closed, and he pushed it open another ten.

"Can this woman have a little privacy, please?" Regan asked through the door.

"She's got all the privacy she's gonna get." He leaned back against the wall.

Regan stood inside the door and blocked his view as much as she could. She had one weapon, and this might be her only time to use it.

She slipped her left hand into her pants pocket and took out her cell phone, hoping she had enough battery power left for one call. She entered the number for Mitch's cell, and silently held it up to Bliss. With her thumb, she showed Bliss how to make the call, then tilted her head in the direction of the sink.

Bliss got it. Make the call for help, turn on the water while she spoke with whoever answered so that Capshaw couldn't hear. Pray he wouldn't hear.

Regan passed the phone to Bliss under the guise of helping her to the toilet.

"You can take it from here," Regan told her, loud enough for their captor to hear. "I'll be right outside with Erwin."

She pushed through the door, then closed it over almost all the way, and stepped into the hall.

"Any chance we could get something cold to drink?" she asked him. "I'm really thirsty after all the travel I've done today."

"When your girlfriend is done." He didn't appear likely to move.

"She's okay now. Can I get you something?" She took a few steps toward the kitchen.

"How 'bout a cold beer."

"I'm sure I have one. Come on."

"I already looked. You're out." He still didn't move.

Regan heard the toilet flush, and a few seconds later, the faucet was turned on. Bliss couldn't be expected to wash her hands forever.

"Are you sure?" Regan frowned. "Did you look all the way in the back on the top shelf?"

She started toward the kitchen. "I'm sure there's beer in here . . ."

"You're real gutsy for someone who's being held at gunpoint." He let her walk past him into the kitchen.

"You want your story written, you're not likely to shoot me until it's done." She shrugged and tried to appear casual. If he knew how sweaty her palms were, it would be all over.

"Maybe I could get someone else to write it." He narrowed his eyes, challenging her. "Maybe you're not the only writer around."

"Maybe. But you want your book to be a bestseller, right? That's what Lester Ray wanted, that's why he wanted me to write his book. Because I write books about crime, and a lot of people buy them because my name is on the cover. You want a bestseller, you go with a proven winner. You know any other bestselling authors of true crime, Erwin?"

She boldly returned the challenge.

To her great relief, he laughed out loud. "You're something, you know that? You got real balls."

She forced a smile, tried to make it appear genuine.

"Thank you."

She heard Bliss in the hall and called to her. "We're in here, Bliss. Would you like some water or some tea?"

"Just get the beer." He motioned to her with the gun, the laughter gone.

Regan opened the refrigerator and peered inside.

"Oh, hey, you were right. There's no beer left." She turned and said, "I could make iced tea if you like."

"Tea time's over." He closed in on her in a flash, and stood toe to toe. He reached around her and grabbed a bottle of water from the door. "You can take one for you and one for her."

Regan did as she was told.

"Back to the room with the desk." He held the bottle in one hand, the gun in the other.

Regan took Bliss's arm and patted it to comfort her. "Everything all right?"

She hoped Bliss understood she wasn't asking about the woman's health.

"I don't know." Bliss looked straight down the hall, as if afraid to make eye contact, and shook her head. "I don't know . . ."

Regan patted Bliss on the shoulder and led her back into Josh's study.

How ironic that he'd chosen this room, Regan thought as she helped Bliss into her seat, where her father worked every day for so many years, piecing together the lives of so many men just like Capshaw in an attempt to understand them, to find their truths.

Especially ironic, she reminded herself, when she was still learning the truth about her father.

One of Josh Landry's truths was that he loved his guns. She was pretty certain he'd kept more than one here in his study, but couldn't recall if she'd put them all away after her father died and she closed up the house. But there was at least one in here someplace. One of the filing cabinet drawers, maybe? Or maybe in that trunk where he kept those wooly throws he liked to toss over him on those chilly mornings?

"Well, shall we start?" she asked Capshaw when he came into the room. "Shall we begin working on your book?"

"Sure, sure." He set the water bottle on the edge of the desk.

"I'll need my bag," she told him. "I left it in the kitchen."

"Why?"

"I need my recorder."

"What recorder?"

"I always record my interviews. That way, if I have questions later,

I don't have to rely upon my memory. And besides, you wouldn't want to be misquoted."

He hesitated.

"Could you get it for me, please? I'm not going to go anywhere," she told him solemnly. "I'd never leave my friend. And besides, I'm intrigued by writing this book. It could be my biggest bestseller."

"Just remember, she can't run very fast. And it would only take one bullet."

"I promise. I will not leave this room." Regan made the cross sign over her heart.

He left the room but she knew he'd be back in a matter of seconds.

"Did you get Mitch?" she whispered to Bliss.

"I don't know. There was so much static. I think someone answered but I don't know if he understood what I was saying."

Regan heard Capshaw's footsteps in the hall. She turned and opened the chest that sat next to the sofa.

"What are you doing?" he demanded.

"I'm trying to find a light blanket for Bliss," she said without looking up. "My dad kept some . . . here we go, this should be fine."

She pulled a light blue afghan from the chest, but not before she'd run her hand around the bottom and felt between the other throws for weight and, not finding any, realized the gun was not there.

She smiled at Bliss and said, "It's really late, almost eleven-thirty. You must be exhausted. You lay down over there on the sofa, and I'll cover you."

He screwed up his face in disgust.

"This ain't no sleep-over party." He pointed to her bag, which he'd tossed onto the desk.

Regan walked around the desk and sat in her father's chair. Capshaw's eyes narrowed as he watched her.

"I'm used to working here," she said as she started to open her bag. *Only one of us can sit in the seat of command, and it's going to be me.*

He slapped her hand away from the bag and emptied the contents onto the desk.

"See? Nothing but a wallet, a makeup case—you can see right through it, nothing in there but some powder and lip gloss—some gum, a candy bar—which reminds me, I'm starving, are you?"

"Later I'll let you make me something to eat."

"Fair enough." She shrugged and continued to look through the pile on her desk. "Here are some pens, my sunglasses, my recorder."

With her forearm, she slid all the items back into her purse except for her tiny tape recorder, which she sat on the desk.

"Sit down"—she pointed to one of the leather side chairs—"and let's get started."

"I don't think I like this." He remained standing near the corner of the desk.

"What don't you like, Erwin?"

"I don't like that you're going to record what I say."

"What's the difference if I record it or I take notes? Like I said, it's to your advantage: this way, you can't be misquoted. You want to make sure that every word is yours."

She reached over and turned the recorder on. When he reached for it, she pulled it back and rewound the tape. After a minute, she hit play and set the recorder in front of her.

"How many foster homes were you in, Lester Ray?" Regan's voice was clear on the tape.

"I don't honestly remember. There were so many . . ." Lester Ray's response was slightly muffled.

"Are there any in particular that stand out in your memory?" Regan again.

"Oh, sure. Not many of them so good . . ."

"That's that wimp Lester Ray," Capshaw sneered. "What, he thought he had it tough, being in foster care? Huh."

"Being in foster care, being shuffled from one home to another . . ." Regan began.

It was all she could do not to jump out of her chair when he pounded a fist on the desk. Behind him, Bliss sat up like a shot but wisely did not make a sound.

"You think foster care is the worst thing that can happen to a kid?" he growled. "Sometimes the place you came from is worse than any place you could go."

"Was that true for you?" The recorder had fallen on its side when he banged the desktop. She stood it back up and switched it from *play* to *record*. She prayed he couldn't see how his outburst had scared her.

"You a shrink?"

"No."

"The shrinks all think they understand everything, you know? But most of them don't understand jack."

He took a pack of cigarettes from his pocket and lit one. She looked around for something he could use for an ashtray—something he didn't seem concerned about, because he tossed the match onto the floor after he'd blown it out. On the windowsill behind her, she found a small flower pot she'd made at summer camp one year. She placed it on the desk in front of him. He looked at it, then at her, and smirked, but he flicked his ash into it all the same.

"What don't they understand?" she asked.

"My father was a real bastard. He beat my mother, he beat my brothers, he beat me so bad one time I pissed blood for weeks. Now, my sisters, he raped them, so they never got beat." His face hardened.

"Have you stayed in touch with any of them?"

"Nah." He shook his head. "What would be the point? We all left home as soon as we could. I never looked back. I bet none of them did, either."

"Don't you ever wonder what happened to—"

"I don't want to talk about them." His eyes went flinty again. "We're supposed to be talking about *me*."

"Talk away." She waved a hand.

"Where do we start?"

"Why not tell me about how you ended up in prison in the first place, and from there, we'll talk about how you were the first inmate to bring Eugene Potts to the attention of the authorities."

"Yeah, that's good. That's good." He nodded.

"And maybe you could tell me how you think the whole thing with Lester Ray played out. You know, how you think the killer got to him, how he fooled the cops into believing that Lester Ray had killed those women."

"Hey, sure." He smiled. "I could help the cops out with that. Sorta like that guy in that movie with that Foster girl, the one where she was in the FBI and needed help finding that serial killer."

"You mean *Silence of the Lambs*? Hannibal Lechter?"

"Yeah, that's the one."

Regan suppressed a shudder. *Thanks for putting that image in my head.*

"Okay, then, sure. Good idea," she said. "I guess when you were in prison, you met a lot of killers. I'll bet you picked up all kinds of insights from them that could help the police with this case."

"I got some ideas on that."

"It's interesting, don't you think, that Lester Ray could have been dead these past few weeks, yet the FBI lab has identified hairs found on the victims as having his DNA."

"Is that right?" He smirked.

"So they say."

"Well, then, maybe he wasn't dead when those girls were killed."

"The medical examiner in North Carolina thinks he was."

"He could be mistaken."

"Tough to make a mistake like that. They said the body had been out there long enough that it had pretty much decomposed."

"I read some place one time that bodies would rot faster if it's hot," he told her solemnly. "It's been hot in North Carolina. I saw it on the Weather Channel."

"Well, let's suppose the cops are right and it wasn't Lester Ray."

"Somebody must have somehow figured out how to make it look like he did it. Studied his MO, maybe."

"As far as I know, Lester Ray only killed one person. Carolyn Preston," she told him. "Not much to study there."

"Oh, hey, the newspapers down there in Florida were filled with the details of that around the time Lester Ray was getting all that publicity. Anyone could have figured out what he did and copied it."

"Anyone clever." She folded her arms over her chest.

"Oh, sure, he'd have had to have been clever."

"But if it wasn't Lester Ray, how could hair from his body end up on the victims?" She toyed with her pen and appeared to be perplexed.

Capshaw rubbed his chin as if in deep thought.

"Well, here's one way," he said as if it had just occurred to him. "If he did kill Lester Ray, he could have taken some hairs from his body and put them in something so he'd have them. Like a plastic bag, maybe."

"You mean, so that after he killed these other girls, he could plant the hairs and make everyone think Lester Ray was the killer?"

"Yeah, something like that."

"So the cops would keep looking for Lester Ray and wouldn't even bother looking for another suspect."

"Yeah. That would make sense for someone to do that, right?"

"Yes," she said slowly, playing along with him. "But what about his DNA, the killer's? Wouldn't there be some trace of him on the bodies?"

"There could be, but here's one thing you learn in prison." He leaned close enough across the desk that she could smell the tobacco on his breath. "There are a lot of lazy cops out there. They're not going to waste their time looking for something that's right under their nose."

"You mean, if there's something obvious found on the body, they won't look for trace from another source?"

"Most times, no. Now, once in a while, sure, you'll run into a smart cop, guy who wants to do the job, you know? But a lot of them will take the easy way out."

"And you think that's what this killer was betting on?"

"Could be." He leaned back in his chair and blew a smoke ring.

She tapped on the desk with the pen, wondering how much longer she could drag this out. Once his story was told, would he kill both her and Bliss?

All the while Regan questioned Capshaw, she was weighing her options. She had a black belt in tae kwon do and was a damned good shot. The martial arts training could only help her if she was sure she could get the gun from him, and without a gun in her hand, her marksmanship abilities were meaningless.

Capshaw started into a long, complicated story about how he was picked up as a peeping tom when he was nine. She looked behind him, through the window on the opposite side of the room, and searched the darkness for a sign of life. Nothing.

If the cavalry was coming, it was really late in getting here.

Twenty-eight

Mitch stood in the shadow of the trees that marked the back of the Landry farm and jammed his hands in his pockets, tension clogged in his chest solid as a tightly clenched fist. Behind him members of the Plainsville police department gathered, awaiting instructions.

"I'm thinking the best thing to do would be to approach the house from the back of the barn," Chief Muldare was saying. "That way, we could get all of our men right up there and station them around the house."

"That could be risky," Mitch replied, never taking his eyes off the lights in the farmhouse. "He's armed, and they're not."

"You're sure there are two women in there with him?" the chief asked.

"I'd put money on it. There was a lot of static on the call, and I was in a charter plane in the midst of some turbulence, but I'm pretty sure it was Regan's assistant on the line. It was definitely Regan's cell phone: the number came up on the screen. I think we should proceed on the assumption that Bliss and Regan are in there."

"I sent a patrol car as soon as you called me the first time." Muldare turned and looked around at the officers gathered in the clearing. "Art, you said you checked on the house earlier and only the assistant was there?"

"Yes, sir." The young officer who stepped forward looked to

Mitch as if he was barely out of high school. "She seemed normal enough, didn't seem like she was in any distress. She said Ms. Landry wasn't there yet and she was just getting ready to leave."

"And you didn't check the house?" Mitch's eyebrows raised almost to his hairline.

"There didn't seem any cause to. The lady said she was just going to set the alarms and—"

"I heard you the first time. But your department received a call from a clerk in a convenience store less than ten minutes from here, reporting that a man matching Capshaw's description had been in the store late this afternoon. It wouldn't have taken hours for Capshaw to find this place. Everyone in Plainsville knows where the Landry farm is. Hell, you can stop just about anyone on the street and they'll be more than happy to tell you where Josh Landry used to live."

"All I can tell you is the lady said no one was there and that she was setting the alarm and getting ready to leave." The young cop's jaw set defensively.

"All right, Art." The chief dismissed him. When he was out of hearing range, Muldare turned to Mitch and said, "He's young. You don't need to come down on him so hard."

"All well and good, Chief, but it isn't his girl in there."

"It shouldn't make any difference whose girl it is."

Because Muldare was right, and Mitch knew he was right, he turned and paced almost to the end of the tree line. From there, he could see that lights were on in the kitchen and in the study. He'd check the kitchen, but he'd bet money that they'd be in the study.

That would be his destination.

"Let's do this." Mitch walked back to the chief. "Your men take the barn, and stay there until you hear from me. The more people milling around the farmhouse, the more likely Capshaw is to notice. I know the property, I know how to get across the field with the least possibility of being seen."

"You know how to get into the house?"

"I'll get in."

"Are you sure you don't want backup?"

"Only as close as the barn, and you're going to have to go one by one across the field. There's a full moon tonight. I'm pretty sure he's in that middle room where you see the light. If he looks out that window and sees you or any of your men, those two women will be dead. If they aren't already. Give me the number for your cell. I'll program it in."

Mitch repeated the numbers back to the chief as he punched them into his phone for quick dial.

He slipped from the shelter of the trees, running the length of the tree line before cutting across the field toward the pond. There were tennis courts, unused for months, surrounded by a high fence, and he used this as a shield as he moved closer. Staying close to the shadows, he crept along the grape arbor to the back of the house. He took four steps and stumbled over something large and soft on the ground. Mitch didn't need daylight to know what he'd tripped over.

Oh, shit, he whispered as he knelt to find a pulse. The front of the man's shirt was sticky and cold. He took the small flashlight from his back pocket and shined it on the man's face. It wasn't Erwin Capshaw.

The man—whoever he was—was alive, but just barely.

It was clear they were going to need an ambulance. It was obvious to Mitch that the stranger had been down for some time, and there was no way of knowing just how much longer the badly injured man could hold on. Mitch called Chief Muldare to tell him what he'd found and to request medical help.

This was a complication Mitch hadn't anticipated. Somehow, he was going to have to get to Regan before the ambulance arrived.

"What was that?" Capshaw's head shot up.

"What was what?" Regan said calmly.

"That noise." He got up and went to the window and peered into the darkness.

"Could have been a raccoon." She shrugged. "Or a skunk. We

get all sorts of wildlife out here. Sometimes in late afternoon, the deer come right up to the backyard."

He scanned the night, his hands over his eyes.

"Who knows you were coming here?" He turned from the window. "Your boyfriend know you're here?"

"I haven't spoken to him in a couple of days. My cell phone conked out while I was in Chicago."

"Where is it now? The phone?"

"I left it in the hotel room on the desk." She pointed to the bag he'd already overturned. "If I had it with me, it would be in there. And you know it isn't because you already checked."

"Funny you didn't tell the boyfriend you were coming here." His eyes narrowed. "You looked pretty chummy down there in Corolla."

"How would you know—"

He snorted. "That's one fine place to stay, that Windham Inn, isn't it? Great food—hey, especially after what they used to give us in prison. And lots of nice people. I enjoyed my stay there. Hated to leave."

"You were at the Windham?" Her hands fell still on the desktop.

"Three rooms down from you on the left." Clearly pleased to have rattled her, and apparently convinced there was nothing more threatening outside than a nocturnal animal, he sat back down.

"How did you know . . ."

"That you were there?" He grinned. "I just happened to see you one day when I was there. I recognized you from the television."

Or you had Lester Ray's cell phone and listened to my message telling him where I was staying.

She opened her bottle of water to give her hands something to do besides shake, and took a few sips.

"Say, did you go on any of those tours they offer there? They take you right up through the wildlife refuge in one of those big SUVs, see the wild horses there on the beach. Dynamite."

"I must have missed that." She put the cap back on the bottle and gave it a good twist. It was all she could do to keep from striking out at him, if for no other reason than for spying on her and Mitch and making her feel like an idiot for not knowing that the killer was three rooms away.

"Well, here's something I didn't miss." He lowered his voice and leaned across the desktop into her face. "I didn't miss that that boyfriend of yours is law. Fed, right?"

They stared at each other, then she nodded.

"I thought so. He's got FBI written all over him." He eased back into his seat. "So it's making me wonder if you've been playing me all this time. You know, waiting for him to ride to the rescue."

"I haven't spoken with him in two days. That's the God's honest truth," she told him. "I suspect they might have sent him someplace on another job. After Lester Ray's body was found, they probably didn't need him down there in North Carolina. I've been in Georgia and Chicago since I left Corolla, and decided at the last minute to come here. If he's looking for me anywhere, I'd expect him to look in my house, in Maryland. It would be the logical place for me to go."

"Why'd you go to Georgia?"

"I wanted to find out about one of Lester Ray's foster mothers." She rolled the chair back slightly and tried hard to filter through the sounds outside the window. Now there was nothing to be heard except the faint rustle of a summer breeze through the lilacs. Maybe there'd been nothing there after all.

Just wishful thinking on my part, she told herself.

She was going to have to find that other gun.

"Lester Ray's foster mother? Huh." He grunted. "Let me tell you something about my mother."

"I think my tape is running low." She snapped off the recorder. "Give me a minute to get another one. I don't want to miss a word you're saying."

"Where are you going?" His hand caressed the gun, which lay across his lap.

"Just to the file cabinets right there. I think I have some new tapes in there."

Regan went to the first of the cabinets and pulled the drawer open. If her father had hidden a gun in here, it would most likely be in one of the top drawers. He was a tall man, and wouldn't have wanted to bend over and start shuffling through the lower drawers to find something he needed in a hurry.

She paused. Bliss had told her she'd gone through the first three filing cabinets. If there'd have been a gun in one of them, she'd have mentioned it, wouldn't she?

Regan went straight to the fourth cabinet.

"I wish I could remember where I put those damned things." From the corner of her eye, she saw movement near the barn. Lots of movement, and though the shapes were indistinct, she was pretty sure they were human. She could have wept with joy.

"Don't you just hate it when you can't find something?" she said, determined to keep him focused on her.

"Yeah."

"I just know I put that bag in one of these drawers."

He walked to the window, looking out at the night, and she held her breath.

She opened the fifth drawer.

Nothing.

On to drawer number six.

She was just about out of time.

Mitch worked as quickly and as quietly as he could on the window screen on the side of the house nearest the front door. The chief had agreed to meet the ambulance attendants on the road behind the woods at the back of the farm. From there, they would make their way across the field to the back of the farmhouse with a gurney for the injured man. There was danger involved no matter what they did, but no one had argued for bringing an ambulance up the main drive. Mitch would do his best to get inside the house as quickly as possible, but he wasn't willing to risk the lives of the two women to save the unknown man.

He'd slid around the side of the house and, standing flush to the wall, had listened at the study window. He'd heard Capshaw ask a question and could have shouted with relief when he heard Regan answer. He couldn't look through the window without being seen, but hearing her voice had been enough. There was still time.

He knew the layout of the house, and knew the best way in would be through a first floor window as far from the study as possible. Once inside, he'd have to find a way to make Capshaw come to him.

"Stay where you are," Capshaw snapped as he flew to the wall switch to turn off the overhead light.

"What?" Regan half turned toward him just as the room went black, her hand inside the cabinet drawer.

"What are you doing?" she asked. "Why did you turn off the light?"

"Someone's out there. Outside, someone's there. Cops, probably. I knew that boyfriend of yours would be along, he's out there, he's out there now. You, I want you here, now. Hurry."

His voice rose to a high pitch, his words shooting from his mouth in rapid fire.

Bliss bolted from the sofa and, panicking, fled for the door. He reached her in three steps and pulled her to him, positioning her body in front of his.

"Shut up!" he screamed in the ear of the sobbing woman. "Shut up, or I'll shoot you, hear? *SHUT UP!* I can't think."

His back was to the wall near the window, the gun pointed in Regan's general direction.

"You stay where you are." He clutched Bliss closer. "I don't need you. I have all the insurance I need right here."

"What are you doing, Erwin?" Regan tried to distract him.

"I saw them outside, don't think I didn't see them. You saw them, you know you did. He's there, the boyfriend, he's out there."

"I didn't see anyone," she said quietly. "Erwin, I don't think anyone is there."

"Liar." He fired a shot toward the cabinets but in the dark it went wide to the right.

She saw him move closer to the window, Bliss thrust before him like a human shield.

"Let her go, Erwin," Regan said, drawing her gun from the front of her waistband where she'd tucked it. She raised it slowly, wondering what kind of shot she was going to get from here, in the dark. She willed her hands steady. On the range, she'd been flawless, hitting her target every time. But it had been seven weeks since she'd gotten out to practice, and she'd never aimed at a human before.

And there was the matter of Bliss, so close to him.

"Please let her go," Regan pleaded.

He snickered dismissively and moved closer to the window. "Who's gonna make me?"

"I probably could." Mitch stepped behind him, his gun to Capshaw's head.

"I have the girl here." Capshaw stood stock still. "You back off and drop the gun, or I swear I will blow her brains out right now. You might shoot me, but three of us will still be dead. Me, her, and that baby."

"Do it, Mitch," Regan said from the opposite side of the darkened room. "Drop your gun and step away from him. He'll hurt Bliss. Just do what he says."

Mitch hesitated. The last thing any law enforcement officer wanted was to hand over his weapon to someone he knew wouldn't hesitate to use it. At the end of the room, he could just about make out Regan's silhouette.

"Please," she said again. "Please just do it."

With great reluctance, Mitch placed his gun on the desktop and backed away with his hands held in front of him. Capshaw moved closer still to the window, his back to the wall. From where Regan stood, a faint spot of moonlight fell on the left side of his head, inches above his ear.

The .38 Smith & Wesson had never been her favorite—she was much more comfortable with a slim-line Glock—but this time the weapon had chosen her.

Regan raised the gun with both hands and aimed for the tiny spot of light.

Don't move a hair, Bliss, she prayed. *Do not move . . .*

"This is what we're going to do," Capshaw was telling Mitch. "You're going to come to the window here and tell whoever it is out there that—"

The blast filled the room and for one long moment, time seemed to stop.

A dark spray of bone and blood and tissue spattered the short distance to the wall and covered the window.

Bliss covered her face with her hands and screamed. She fell to the floor, Capshaw falling with her and pinning her against the wall.

"I've got her," Mitch called to Regan as he hurried to extract Bliss from the tangle on the floor. "Hit the lights."

She snapped on the nearest lamp and nearly fell over herself to get to him.

"Oh, my God, Bliss . . ." Regan sobbed and dropped to her knees. With shaking fingers she brushed bits of tissue from her assistant's face.

"I think she just passed out when you fired that shot. Here, let me . . ." He lifted the pregnant woman in both arms and laid her gently on the sofa as Muldare's officers broke down the door and entered the house with their guns drawn.

Regan turned on the light and stepped aside as they filed into the room.

"Damn, but you are good with a thirty-eight." Mitch gave Regan's shoulder a squeeze.

"I'm lucky that I finally found the right drawer. I was starting to think maybe my dad had gotten rid of it."

"We're going to need the ME," one of Muldare's men said to no one in particular.

"Is the ambulance still here?" Mitch asked the chief who'd followed his officers into the house.

"It's on its way to the hospital with the guy you found in the yard," the chief said.

"It might be Robert McKinley, Bliss's husband," Regan told him.

"Bliss said that Capshaw had shot him, but she believed he was dead."

"He's damned close."

"This is his wife." Regan pointed to Bliss. "We need to get her to the hospital, too."

Muldare signaled for one of his officers to call for another ambulance. "You all right, Miss Landry?"

"I'm fine. I'm just worried about my assistant. She's pregnant and she's had a really scary time of it." Regan knelt next to the sofa where Bliss lay, her eyes just beginning to open.

"Agent Peyton, we're going to want your gun." The chief touched his arm.

"Not his, Chief Muldare." Regan stood and handed over the .38. "Mine . . ."

Twenty-nine

Mitch sat on the top step of the back porch, Regan cradled on his lap. The full moon was still visible, but the sun was beginning to color the horizon ever so slowly. All but the Bureau's lab crew had left the farm, and they would soon be on their way as well.

"I can't wait to be rid of this place," Regan told him. "Christ, my dad was murdered here, now this. I swear, if arson wasn't a crime, I'd burn the place to the ground."

"I think a for sale sign would serve your purposes just as well. Plus there'd be a lot less hassle from the cops."

"Good point. I think I'll just call the Realtors in town and have them take care of it for me. Sell the house and every damned thing in it. Just send me a check when they're done."

"You don't mean that."

She was agitated, more than he thought she might have been even considering the past twelve hours, and he sought to soothe her.

"You have all of your dad's work in there, his files. All the information he gathered, all the notes, the outlines for future books . . ."

"The library is welcome to it. The rest of it can be tossed."

"Hey, I know the past few weeks have been tough on you . . ."

"You don't know the half of it."

"Then clue me in."

"Where to start?" She shrugged as if too weary to make the effort. "Try the beginning."

"The beginning? Let's see, that would be around the very early 1950s. Fifty or fifty-one, I'm thinking." She settled back against his shoulder and chest.

"What happened then?"

"Eddie Kroll lured a classmate into a vacant lot where he and two of his so-called friends beat the kid to death."

"I've heard this story before."

"I know, but you said to start at the beginning. That's where the story begins."

"Ahhhh, I see. There's been a breakthrough in the quest for Eddie Kroll."

"I found him." She nodded slowly. "He was right under my nose, all these years."

"You lost me again."

"Eddie Kroll was my father," she said simply.

"Your . . . ?"

"Yeah. My *father*."

"You mean you were adopted by the Landrys?"

"No, I mean Eddie Kroll and Josh Landry were the same person."

"Holy shit."

"That sums it up nicely." She nodded.

"I'm assuming all this came from Dolly Brown." He paused. "Who, if I recall correctly, was Eddie's sister, so that would make her—"

"Right. My aunt."

"Well." He digested the news. "How does it feel to find out you have family?"

"I haven't gotten past the part about my father having lied to me all my life. About everything."

"Regan . . ." Mitch said cautiously.

"No, no 'Regan.' He lied to me about everything that mattered. Even his name." She sat up and turned to face him. "That's why my mother spent so much time away from home those last few years. Because he told her. She must have felt as betrayed then as I do now."

"I don't think it takes a genius to figure out why he changed his name, Regan," Mitch said softly. "The twenty-one-year-old man who came out after serving his sentence must have been a completely different person from the kid who went in at thirteen. You can understand why he might want to leave that kid behind."

"Dolly said he felt he'd disgraced the family and wasn't worthy to carry his father's name."

"I think you could probably understand that."

"I don't have a problem with that part. To be fair and objective, the Eddie Kroll who became Josh Landry accomplished a great deal. He got himself through college, he worked hard for many years, he became productive. I admire that he so totally turned his life around and made something of himself, in the truest sense of the words."

She shook her head slowly from side to side. "But I cannot understand why he never told me the truth."

"How difficult do you think it would have been for him to tell you that, that he'd killed a boy? Gone to prison?"

"How difficult do you think it's been for me to find out from someone else after all these years?" she snapped.

"I can appreciate that you're angry with him, but I don't think it's so hard to understand that, knowing the way your mother reacted, he'd have been afraid you'd abandon him, too."

"How could he think that of me? I never would have done that."

"I'll bet he never thought your mother would, either."

He thought for a moment that she was going to react with anger, but she fell silent.

"You know, all my life, he told me he had no one. He actually told me once that he'd only had one brother, and that he'd died in a car accident. That was all a lie. He had two brothers and two sisters. I never got to meet my uncle Harry or my aunt Catherine."

"What else did Dolly tell you?"

"That after my father disappeared, no one saw or heard from him for almost seventeen years. Then one time their brother Harry saw Dad's picture in the paper and showed it to them, and they all went to see him at a book signing in Chicago. She said after that they reconnected, and they all used to get together every time Dad went to

Chicago. She said it damn near killed him when Catherine died in that accident and he couldn't step forward at her funeral as her brother." She sighed heavily. "Even then, he couldn't bring himself to drop the façade."

"But all in all, he was a pretty good father, wasn't he?"

"He was a wonderful father," she admitted. "The best."

"Try not to judge him so harshly, babe. I'm sure he did what he thought was best for you."

"It wasn't best, that's the thing." She rested her head on his shoulder.

"He didn't know that." He rocked her slightly. "Parents sometimes make the wrong choices, just like kids do. Every decision isn't going to be the right one."

"Easy for you, having grown up with a slew of other Peytons. There was always someone there to catch you when you fell. I missed out on that, Mitch. I missed having that network, that security of knowing there was a whole bunch of people I was connected to."

"They're there now, aren't they? Cousins, aunts, uncles . . ."

"Uncles, no, they're all gone now. Cousins, though, yes. I met one of them. My aunts, Dolly and Stella, sure. They'd be there for me if I needed them," she admitted.

"You think it's too late to get to know them, too late to connect?"

"It just isn't the same. We have no history."

"No, but it's better than never. And history isn't confined to the past, right? Don't we make a little bit of history every day?"

"You're such a damned know-it-all," she grumbled and elbowed him in the chest.

"I don't know everything, but I do know families." He smiled. "And speaking of which, we're taking the next two weeks off and we're heading to Maine, you and I. We'll take a long, slow drive right up the coast, stop in every one of those pretty little towns along the way if we feel like it. Destination, Peytonville, and we'll sail and swim and lie in the sun and eat lobster till we burst."

"Until some whack job goes on a killing spree and John calls and—"

"Uh-uh." He shook his head. "No whack jobs this time, no calls from the office."

The back door opened and the three remaining members of the investigative team stepped onto the porch.

"We're done inside," the first one told him. "We've taped off most of the downstairs, but the body's gone and we've processed the scene as much as it's going to be. Not much mystery what happened here."

"Thanks," Mitch said. "Make sure I get copies of all the reports, would you?"

"No problem. And we'll get you the rundown on everything that was found in the car."

"What car?" Regan asked.

"The car Capshaw used to get here," the sole woman CSI replied. "We found it parked out there behind the barn. Lots of interesting stuff in there. Some rope, some tape, and a really nasty looking knife."

The three filed past and got into the Bureau-issued sedan.

The couple on the back steps watched the car disappear down the lane.

"At the risk of repeating myself, that was one damned fine shot you made in there," Mitch told her.

"I had some damned fine luck. If he'd been standing anywhere else, or if Bliss had moved, things would have turned out differently."

"I still can't believe you kept him talking all that time."

"I was afraid that once he stopped talking, he'd figure his story was told and there was no reason to keep us alive."

"Were you scared?"

"Shitless." She nodded. "But I knew I couldn't let him see it. If he'd known I was frightened out of my wits, he'd have played on that unmercifully. I couldn't let him have that kind of power over me. I had to convince him that without me, there'd be no bestselling book about Erwin Capshaw. He did think he was a fascinating subject."

"Looks like all those years studying serial killers came in handy."

"I guess I have my dad to thank for that. I remembered him

saying once that a lot of psychopaths are really self-centered, so I figured if I kept him talking about himself, and treated him seriously, maybe—just maybe—we'd have a chance of getting out of there alive."

"That was some legacy your dad left you. Saved your life."

"It did." She smiled slowly. "Saved yours, too."

"How's that?"

"He was the one who insisted that I learn how to shoot. Used to take me to the firing range every week." She laughed. "At first I thought it was crazy. Then as I got a little older, I thought it was pretty cool, you know?"

"You really spent a lot of time with him."

"Like I said, Mom preferred to be in England. Most of the time it was just me and my dad." Her eyes were wet.

"You had more of him than a lot of kids get of their fathers, babe."

"You're right." She sighed.

There was a splash from the pond and they looked up to see several Canada geese landing feetfirst in the water. Several ducks that had been lounging on the banks amidst the cattails rushed out to scold them. A hawk dove from a nearby tree and ducks and geese all took cover.

"Did Capshaw admit to killing those four women?" Mitch asked.

"Not in so many words, but I think it's pretty clear that he did. The tape was taken as evidence, but I'm sure you'll be able to get a transcript."

"How 'bout Lester Ray, did Capshaw admit killing him?"

"Again, not outright. But I'm sure he did. I'm sure they'll be able to retrieve that one shot he fired in the study. They can compare that to the shot that killed Lester Ray and see if they were fired from the same gun." She thought for a moment, then added, "I'm betting Capshaw killed Booth, too. He was so angry with him for getting Lester Ray in the news and keeping him there."

"What about Carolyn Preston?" Mitch asked.

"That was Lester Ray, I'm pretty sure. Capshaw made a reference to the killer studying Lester Ray's MO."

"What do you suppose there was about Preston that set Lester Ray off?" Mitch wondered aloud.

"Maybe there was something about her that reminded him of Rosemary, the foster mother he cared about."

"Well, that would fit. He must have been furious with Rosemary for having gotten sick and then dying on him. As a kid, one who'd been abandoned before, he must have taken that very personally."

"Think Carolyn was his first victim?"

Mitch gave it some thought. "Lederer believed there were others, he just wasn't able to get the evidence to tie them to Lester Ray."

"You think he would have killed again?"

"Eventually, yeah. After all the hoopla died down, I think sooner or later something would have set Lester Ray off again."

"I feel I should get in touch with the Preston family. I think they should hear from me that he's gone," she said. "I almost feel I owe them an apology."

"Your goal was to find the truth. You did that. That the truth turned out to be what they believed all along does not take away from the fact you pursued it honestly."

"Still, I keep thinking back to the scene at the courthouse, how angry and upset they were with me."

"It's up to you. Do what you think is best."

"I think I'll call the sister when I get home."

"Well, right now, let's get your things and head out. We're both dead on our feet and I don't think either of us would feel comfortable sleeping here. There's that really pretty inn out there on the road that runs along the river. Maybe we could check in there."

"It's almost seven in the morning. Odd time to check in. And it's June. There may not be a vacancy."

"Then we'll drive around until we find one. You can't go too far. Muldare is going to need to speak with you again." He stood up and pulled her with him. "Right now, I need a little down time with my girl."

"Your girl needs some down time with her guy." She held his face in her hands and kissed him, a long slow kiss that left her wanting more.

"Let me get my bag from inside."

They went in through the back door, down the hall, and were headed toward the study when they heard a beep.

"What was that?" Mitch asked.

"It sounded like the dead battery alert on my cell phone." She paused at the powder room door. "Bliss used my cell phone in here to call you. She must have hidden it someplace so Capshaw wouldn't know we had it."

She sorted through magazines in a basket. "It's not in there."

"There aren't that many places to look," he noted. "Try the potted plant."

"Ha." She pulled it out from among the long fronds. "Good thing it didn't start beeping a few hours ago. Capshaw would have known for sure that help was on the way. That would have gone very badly for us."

"How could it beep if the battery is dead?" Mitch watched her put the phone in her pocket.

She shrugged. "They must make it so that the last bit of juice is used to let you know it's just about gone."

She took his hand and they walked toward the study. "We need to check in on Bliss before we leave. I think we can just make a little detour to stop at the hospital first. Poor thing was scared to death. Scared for herself, for her baby . . . all that time thinking her husband was dead."

A length of yellow tape stretched across the study doorway.

"My bag's in there," she told him.

"They're done in here." He held the tape up so she could duck under it.

At some point during last night's scuffle with Capshaw, her bag had been knocked onto the floor and the contents spilled out. She scooped up everything and loaded it all back inside. When she finished, she glanced around the room.

"Maybe before the farm is sold, I should invite Stella and Dolly out. They never did see the house their brother lived in all those years. I think they'd love it."

"Nice," he agreed. "And since you're determined to rid yourself of the contents, maybe they'd like something, furniture or whatever, as mementos."

"Sure."

"I'll bet one of them will want the desk"—he walked into the room—"and this old chair of your dad's."

He sat in Josh's favorite chair and leaned back. "Actually, it's very comfortable."

"You're welcome to it," she told him, the fingers of her right hand running absently along the edge of her father's desk.

"I don't have room for it in my place." He got up and went to her. He folded her in his arms and said, "Maybe your den, though. Think you could find room for it?"

Regan smiled. "You are so damned transparent."

"Oh?"

"Don't think I can't figure out what you're doing." She pushed on his chest, not hard enough to push him away. "This is your way of telling me I should hold on to some of his things. Like maybe Dad's desk."

"Hey, once it's gone, it's gone." He rested his chin on the top of her head. "I just don't think you should get rid of things right now, while you're still working through your anger. Later, you'll wish you had kept the things that meant the most."

"Oh, you're right, of course you are. That desk, that chair. The old leather sofa, the wing chairs there. Even that ugly desk lamp with that goofy-looking duck on the base." She leaned into him. "They're all part of my dad. They're part of me."

It was his turn to smile. He knew her so well.

"Come on, babe. Let's check in on Bliss." He took her hand. "Then we'll go find that inn. Maybe with luck, they'll have a vacancy, room service, maybe even a Jacuzzi . . ."

MARIAH STEWART is the bestselling author of numerous novels and several novellas. She is a RITA finalist for romantic suspense and is the recipient of the Award of Excellence for contemporary romance, a RIO (Reviewers International Organization) Award honoring excellence in women's fiction, and a Reviewers' Choice Award from *Romantic Times* magazine. A native of Hightstown, New Jersey, she is a three-time recipient of the Golden Leaf Award and a Lifetime Achievement Award from the New Jersey Romance Writers, of whose Hall of Fame she is an honoree. Stewart is a member of the Valley Forge Romance Writers, the New Jersey Romance Writers, and the Romance Writers of America. She lives with her husband, two daughters, and two rambunctious golden retrievers amid the rolling hills of Chester County, Pennsylvania.

ABOUT THE TYPE

This book was set in Sabon, a typeface designed by the well-known German typographer Jan Tschichold (1902–74). Sabon's design is based upon the original letter forms of Claude Garamond and was created specifically to be used for three sources: foundry type for hand composition, Linotype, and Monotype. Tschichold named his typeface for the famous Frankfurt typefounder Jacques Sabon, who died in 1580.